Stories of the Seventies

81·68-970·72

Macmillan Short Stories

Girls' Talk, Boys' Talk   Bill Lucas and Brian Keaney
Family Matters   Bill Lucas and Brian Keaney
Class Rules   Bill Lucas and Brian Keaney
Taking Sides   Bill Lucas and Brian Keaney

Decades
The Sixties   Janet and Andrew Goodwyn
The Seventies   Janet and Andrew Goodwyn

MACMILLAN SHORT STORIES

DECADES

THE
SEVENTIES

Janet and Andrew Goodwyn

MACMILLAN

For our daughter Helena

First published 1991

Published by
MACMILLAN EDUCATION LTD
Houndmills, Basingstoke, Hampshire RG21 2XS
and London
Companies and representatives
throughout the world

Cover by Clive Spong

Printed in Hong Kong

British Library Cataloguing in Publication Data
Stories of the seventies. – (Macmillan short stories).
1. Short stories in English – Anthologies
I. Goodwyn, Janet   II. Goodwyn, Andrew
823'.01'08 [FS]
ISBN 0–333–51026–7

Contents

Contents

Preface

This collection of short stories draws on the work of major modern writers during a particular decade – the 1970s. These years saw many changes in British society, changes which are reflected in the subject matter and style of the writing. The stories combine to give a picture of life in Britain in this decade. The materials which support them – prose extracts, poems, essays and cartoons – assert a sense of continuity, both past and future, extending the range of the collection with other viewpoints, other voices and other times.

Most of the authors represented here are novelists or playwrights as well as brilliant practitioners of the art of short story writing. We hope that pupils will be stimulated by the stories and by the connections made with other types of writing and will want to read further in many of the authors' works. The extracts which make up the follow-on can be seen as models for writing in a particular style or genre and their thematic links with the stories show the variety of approaches to a subject which can be explored by reader and writer alike.

During the 1970s many of the issues which concern us as a society first became matters for widespread public debate: for example, the position of women and particularly women at work, questions of race and culture, the changing role and structure of the family and the extent to which the welfare state should support or even intervene in people's daily lives.

After each short story, there are follow-up activities. These provide a range of ideas for work related to each story. This anthology together with the activities was not assembled in order to fit into any narrow framework, but we believe that it provides the right material and the best kind of organisation for teachers working with their students in the true spirit of GCSE English and English Literature. We feel that both the stories themselves and the activities provide material that is ideally suited to fulfil the demands of English in the National Curriculum.

Following each story there are two sections of activities which focus on the story itself. First Response is short and informal to encourage pupils to respond creatively to the story. Looking Closely goes into the story more deeply using oral work in pairs or groups, role play and writing.

These sections are followed by a selection of poems and extracts from various kinds of writing coupled with further activities using the same pattern as those which follow Looking Closely. Each piece of writing has a Links with Story section as a starting point for comparative work.

We hope that all the activities and additional material will provide a valuable resource in themselves; many of the pieces included deserve individual study in their own right.

King's Cross

MAEVE BINCHY

Eve looked around the office with a practical eye. There was a shabby and rather hastily put together steel shelving system for books and brochures. There were boxes of paper still on the floor. There was a dead plant on the window, and another plant with a Good Luck in Your New Job label dying slowly beside it. The venetian blind was black – there was so much clutter on the window ledge it looked like a major undertaking to try and free the blind. One of the telephones was actually hidden under a pile of literature on the desk. In the corner was a small, cheap and rather nasty-looking table . . . which would be Eve's if she were to take the job.

And that's what she was doing now, as she sat in the unappealing room . . . deciding if she would take the job of secretary to Sara Gray. Sara had rushed off to find somebody who knew about holidays and luncheon vouchers and overtime. She had never had a secretary before and had never thought of enquiring about these details before she interviewed Eve. She had pushed the hair out of her eyes and gone galloping off to personnel, which would undoubtedly think her very foolish. Eve sat calmly in the room waiting and deliberating. By the time Sara had bounded back with the information, Eve had already decided to take on Sara Gray. She looked like being the most challenging so far.

Sara heaved a great sigh of relief when she heard that Eve would stay and work with her. She had big kind brown eyes, the kind of eyes you often see shown close up in a movie or a television play to illustrate that someone is a trusting, vulnerable character and therefore likely to be hurt. She looked vague and bewildered, and snowed-under. She sounded as if she needed a personal manager rather than a secretary – and this is where Sara Gray had hit very lucky because that's what Eve was.

From the outset she was extraordinarily respectful to Sara. She never referred to her as anything but Miss Gray, she called her Miss Gray to her face despite a dozen expostulations from Sara.

'This is a friendly office,' Sara cried. 'I can't stand you not calling me by my name. It makes me look so snooty. We're all friends here.'

Eve had replied firmly that it was not a friendly office. It was a very cut-throat company indeed. Eve had asked Sara how many of the women secretaries called their male bosses by their first names. Sara couldn't work it out. Eve could. None of them. Sara agreed reluctantly that this might be so. Eve pressed home her point. Even the managers and assistant managers on Sara's level were not going to escape, they all called Sara by her first name because she was a woman, but she felt the need to call many of them Mr. After two days Sara decided that Eve must be heavily into Women's Lib.

'There's no need to fight any battles on my behalf, Eve,' she said cheerfully. 'Look at how far I've got, and I'm a woman. Nobody held me back just because I'm a downtrodden put-upon female. Did they? I've done very well here, and I get recognition for all I do.'

'Oh, no, Miss Gray, you are quite wrong,' said Eve. 'You do not get recognition. You are the assistant promotions manager. Everyone knows that you are far better and brighter and work much harder than Mr Edwards. You should be the promotions manager not the assistant.'

Sara looked upset. 'I thought I could say I'd done rather well,' she said.

'Only what you deserve, Miss Gray,' said Eve who seemed to have acquired a thorough familiarity with the huge travel agency and its tour operations in two days. 'You should have Mr Edwards' job. We all know that. You *must* have it. It's only fair.'

Sara looked at her, embarrassed.

'Gosh Eve, it's awfully nice of you, and don't think I don't appreciate it. You're amazingly loyal. But you really don't know the score here.'

'With great respect, Miss Gray, I think it's you who doesn't know the score,' said Eve calmly. 'It is absolutely possible for you to have Mr Edwards' job this time next year, I'll be very glad to help you towards that if you like. I have a little experience in this sort of thing.'

Sara stared at her, not knowing what to say.

'Miss Gray, I'm going for my lunch now, but can I suggest you do something while I'm gone? Can you telephone one or two of the people on the list of references I gave you? You will notice they are all women; I've never worked for men. Ask any one of them whether she thinks it's a good idea to trust me to help. Then perhaps you might add that you will keep all this very much in confidence . . .'

'Eve,' interrupted Sara, her good-natured face looking puzzled, 'Eve, honestly, this sounds like the mafia or something. I'm not into power struggles, and office back-stabbing . . . I'm just delighted to have someone as bright and helpful as you in the office . . . I don't want to start a war.'

'Who said anything about a war, Miss Gray? It's very subtle, and very gradual and – honestly the best thing is to telephone anyone on that list, it's there in the file marked Personal.'

'But won't they think it rather odd. I mean, I can't ring up and ask them what do they think of Eve trying to knock Mr Edwards sideways so that I can get his job,' Sara sounded very distressed.

'Miss Gray, I have worked in five jobs, for five women, I chose them, they thought they chose me. At the very beginning I told them how a good assistant could help them get where they wanted. Not one of them believed me, I managed in a conversation like this to convince them to let me.'

'And . . . what happened?' asked Sara.

'Ask them, Miss Gray,' replied Eve, gathering her gloves and bag.

'They won't think I'm er. . .'

'No, all of them – except the first one, of course – rang someone else to check things out too.' Eve was gone.

Sara wondered.

You often heard of women becoming a bit strange, perhaps Eve was a bit odd. Far too young to be menopausal or anything, heavens Eve wasn't even thirty, but it did seem an odd sort of thing to suggest after two days.

Was there a wild possibility that she might have had a secret vendetta for years against Garry Edwards, the plausible head of promotions, who indeed did not deserve his job, his title, his salary or his influence, since all of these had been made possible only by Sara's devoted work?

Sara reached for the phone.

'Sure I know Eve,' said the pleasant American woman in the big banking group. 'You are so lucky, Sara, to have her. I offered her any money to stay but she wouldn't hear of it. She said her job was done. She acts a bit like Superman or the Lone Ranger, she comes in and solves a problem and then sort of zooms off. A really incredible woman.'

'Can I. . .er. . .ask you what problem she.'. . .er. . .' Sara felt very embarrassed.

'Sure. I wanted to be loans manager, they didn't take me seriously. Eve showed me how they would, and they did, and now I'm loans manager.'

'Heavens,' said Sara. 'It's a teeny bit like that here.'

'Well naturally it is, otherwise Eve wouldn't have picked you,' said the loans manager of a distant bank.

'And how did she. . .um. . .do it?' persisted Sara.

'Now this is where I become a little vague,' the pleasant voice said. 'It's simply impossible to explain. In my case there was a whole lot of stuff about my not getting to meet the right people in the bank. Eve noticed that, she got me to play golf.'

'*Golf?*' screamed Sara.

'I know, I know, I guess I shouldn't even have told you that much

. . . listen, the point is that Eve can see with uncanny vision where women hold themselves back, and work within the system without playing the system properly so – she kinda points out where the system could work for us, and honestly honey, it worked for me, and it sure as hell worked for the woman who Eve worked on before me, she's practically running industry in this country nowadays. In her case it had something to do with having dinner parties at home.'

'What?' said Sara.

'I know, it sounded crazy to me too, and I got real uneasy, but apparently she needed to show people that she could sort of impress foreign contacts by having them to a meal with grace and style and all pizzazz in her country home. Eve sort of set it up for her with outside caterers and it worked a dream. You see, it's different for everyone.'

Sara was puzzled. She walked down to the local snack bar and bought a salami sandwich. She ate it thoughtfully on the road coming back to the building. In the lift she heard that Garry Edwards was going to a conference in the Seychelles next week. It was a conference for people who brought out travel brochures, a significant part of promotions for any travel firm. Sara had done all the imaginative travel brochures, Garry Edwards had okayed them. Yet he was going to the Seychelles and she was eating a tired salami sandwich. When she opened her office door Eve was sitting there typing.

'I'll do it,' she said. 'Whatever it is, play golf, give foolish dinner parties . . . I'll do it. I want his job. It's utterly unjust that he's going to that conference, it's the most unjust thing I've ever known.'

'He won't be going to it next year,' said Eve. 'Right, Miss Gray, I have a few points ready to discuss with you, shall we put this sign on the door?'

'What is it?' Sara asked fearfully.

'It merely says, "Engaged in Conference", I made it last night.' Eve produced a neat card which she then fixed on the outside of the office door.

'Why are we doing that?' whispered Sara.

'Because it is absolutely intolerable the way that people think they can come barging in here, taking advantage of your good nature and picking your brains, interrupting us and disturbing you from whatever you are doing. We need a couple of hours to plan the office design, and it's no harm to let them see immediately that you are going to regard your job as important. It may only be half the job they should have given you, but don't worry, you'll have the right job very soon.'

'Suppose that the really big brass come along, or Mr Edwards or you know, someone important.' Sara was still unsure.

'We are having a conference, about the redesign of your office.'

'But there isn't any money to redesign it . . . even if they'd let me.'

'Yes there is, I've been up to the requisition department, in fact they looked you up on the book, and wondered why you hadn't applied. Whenever you're ready Miss Gray, we can start.'

Together they worked out how the office should look. It was a big room, but it was in no way impressive; apart from the inferior furniture, its design was all wrong. Eve explained that a separate cubicle should be built for her near the door. Eve should act as a kind of reception area for Sara, she could call through to announce visitors, even though it was only a distance of a few yards.

'They'll walk past and come straight on in,' said Sara.

'Not if I walk after them and ask can I help them. They won't do it twice, Miss Gray,' said Eve and Sara realised that most of them wouldn't even do it once.

The costing of the partition was not enormous, and it left a reasonable amount for the rest of the furnishings.

'We'll have the filing section in my part since you shouldn't really have to be looking things up yourself, Miss Gray, but it will of course be kept in a very meticulous way so you can always find anything.'

'What will I have in my part of the office then?' asked Sara humbly.

Eve stood up and walked around. 'I've been giving it a lot of thought, Miss Gray. You are really the ideas woman here. I'm sorry, I know it's jargon, but that's what you do for the promotions department. You thought up that whole idea about choosing a holiday from your stars in the zodiac and that worked, you thought of having a travel agents' conference in that railway station which suited them all since they had to come from all over the country and go back again by train. You thought up the scheme of having children write the section for children's holidays, so I think that this is what you should be doing really. Thinking. And let me handle the routine things, you know, the letters about "Can you trace what we did about Portugal two years ago?" If the filing system works properly then anyone will be able to do that for you. I'll set it up so that at least four-fifths of your incoming mail can be handled by any competent secretary. That should give you a great deal more time to do what you are really good at.'

Sara looked hopeful but not convinced.

'Me just sit in here with a chair?' She shook her head. 'I don't think it's on Eve, I really don't. You know they'd think I'd gone mad.'

'I wasn't suggesting a chair. I was going to suggest a long narrow conference table. Something in nice wood, we could look at auctions or in an antique shop. And about six chairs. Then, for you a small writing desk. Again something from an old house possibly, with your telephone and your own big diary and notebook, a few periodicals and trade magazines or directories you need, that's all.'

'Eve, in God's name, what is the long conference table for. Eve, I am the assistant promotions manager, not the chairman of the board. I don't give conferences, call meetings, ask my superiors to come in here with the hope of blinding them about policy.'

'You should,' said Eve simply. 'Listen,' she went on. 'Remember that children writing the brochure idea? It was marvellous. I've been looking through the files, you got not one word of credit, no letter, no mention, no thanks even. I would not be at all surprised if you, Mr Edwards and I are the only people who know you thought it up, and the only reason I know is that I see entries in your diary about going to schools and talking to children and spending a lot of your free time working on it. Edwards got the praise, the thanks and the job, for not only that but for everything you did. Because you didn't do it right.'

'It worked, though,' said Sara defensively.

'Miss Gray, of course the idea worked, it was brilliant, I remember seeing those brochures long before I ever knew you and I thought they were inspired. What I mean is that it didn't work for you, here within the company. Next time, I suggest you invite Mr Edwards and his boss and the marketing director and one or two others to drop in quite casually — don't dream of saying you are calling a meeting, just suggest that they might all like to come into your office one afternoon. And then, at a nice table where there is plenty of room and plenty of style, put forward your plans. That way they'll remember you.'

'Yes, I know, in theory you're right, Eve . . . but honestly, I'm not the type. I'm jolly old Sara Gray, with a nice, jolly, hopeless lover who comes and goes at home – and who is gone at the moment. And they all say to themselves, "poor Sara, not a bad old thing" – none of them would take me at a rosewood conference table for one minute Eve, they'd either corpse themselves laughing or else they'd think I was having a breakdown, they'd fire me. And you.'

Eve didn't look at all put out. 'I wasn't suggesting calling a conference tomorrow, I was suggesting having the furniture right. If you are someone who is valuable to the company for her ideas, you should have a space to think up these ideas, a platform to present them on, and the just recognition for them.'

'You're right,' Sara said suddenly. 'What else?'

'I think you should get into the habit of having Mr Edwards and others coming to this office, by appointment of course, rather than you rushing to theirs. It makes you more important. That's why we need the right furniture. Mr Edwards has an office like an aeroplane hangar, and very well laid out, I've inspected it. But yours could have a charm, it could become the place where ideas were discussed say on one particular evening a week, a Thursday, before people left. It would be relaxing, and pleasant, and *you* would be in control.'

As they talked on, it got darker outside, and they switched on the bright neon overhead light.

'That'll have to go for a start,' said Eve. 'It's far too harsh, there's no style, no warmth.'

A few times the door had been half-opened, but whenever people saw the two heads bent over the desk and lists, they muttered apologies and backed out.

'I never thought a notice would do that,' said Sara admiringly.

'Wait till we get things going properly, you'll be amazed,' said Eve.

Eve refused a drink, a girly chat and the offer of a share in a taxi. Instead she took out her notebook again.

'You should have an account with a taxi firm,' she said briskly. 'I'll set that up tomorrow, when I'm organising the flowers and your dress allowance.'

Sara stared at her in the windy, wet street as if Eve had gone completely mad.

'*What* are you organising. . .?' she began.

'Plants, flowers for the office, all the male senior executives have them, and they also get a special expense allowance for clothes because they have to travel, it being a travel company, and . . .'

'Eve, I'm not a senior executive, I can't have free flowers paid for by the office.'

'As assistant manager you are technically a senior executive. The other two assistant managers are elderly men who have been pushed upstairs, so if you equate your title with theirs then you can have flowers, nothing extravagant, about six nice flowering plants. I think we can choose them from a brochure, they'll arrive tomorrow.'

For the first time for a long time Sara sat back contentedly in her chair at home and didn't think about Geoff and wonder when his new obsession would end. Often she felt lonely and sad during his absences, so that she would hide from the feeling by having the television on or listening to music for long hours. But tonight she just sat calmly drinking her tea and looking into the fire. Eve's arrival meant that a lot of the tension in the office had been erased. It was like someone massaging your shoulders and taking away the stiffness – you didn't know how tense you had been until the massage was over – Eve was going to make things a lot better, and she was going to force Sara to take herself more seriously too. It was a bit exciting in a way.

Next morning was a Friday and Eve wanted to know whether Sara had any important plans and engagements for the weekend. Sara shrugged, 'I was going to sort out those figures for Mr Edwards, you know the ones he wanted on the breakdown of age groups on the coach holidays. We need to know where to direct some of the coach tour promotions this year.'

'Oh, that's done,' said Eve. 'I did it this morning, I saw his note. I've two copies here for you to sign, one for Mr Edwards and I thought you should send one to the head of marketing, just to let him know that you are alive and well and working harder than Mr Edwards.'

'Isn't that a bit sneaky?' asked Sara looking like a doubtful schoolgirl.

'No, it's standard office procedure. Mr Edwards is the sneaky party, by not acknowledging your part in all the work that is being done.'

With a weekend free Sara agreed happily to go to look at second-hand furniture and office fittings. Eve had already organised the office partition, and it began with great hammering and activity after lunch.

'I suggest you go and check out a few new outfits for yourself, Miss Gray,' said Eve. 'You can't possibly work here with all this noise.'

'Could you come with me, I'm not exactly sure what I. . .?'

'Certainly, Miss Gray, can you wait five minutes while I tell these gentlemen I shall be back in two hours to see how they are getting on?'

Eve managed to make three large men look as if they knew she was going to have them fired unless the partition was perfect. Then she went to the shop with Sara.

There was a brief objective discussion about what clothes Sara already possessed. Eve explained that she had only seen two tweed skirts and one black sweater in the three days she had been working there. Shamefacedly, Sara said she thought there were a couple of other sweaters and perhaps two more workable tweed skirts.

Eve seemed neither pleased nor put out; she was merely asking for information. In the store she suggested three outfits which could interchange and swap and make about a dozen between them. They cost so much that Sara had to sit down on the fitting-room chair.

'I took the liberty of getting you a credit card for your expenses, Miss Gray,' said Eve. 'I rushed it through, and what you are going to spend now is totally justifiable. You have to meet the public, you have to represent the company in places where the company may well be judged by the personal appearance of its representatives. What you are spending on these garments is half what Mr Edwards has spent in the last six months, and you have been entitled to expenses of this kind for over a year and never called on them.'

By Monday Sara could hardly recognise either herself or her new surroundings. On Eve's advice she had had an expensive hair-do; she wore the pink and grey wool outfit, put the pink cyclamens on her window sill, near the lovely old table with its matching half-dozen chairs which they had eventually found for half nothing since it was too big for most homes, and nobody except Eve would have thought of it as office furniture.

Eve was living in her purpose-built annexe surrounded with files and ledgers. She had just begun to compile a folio of Sara's work so far with the company, a kind of illustrated *curriculum vitae* which would show her worth and catalogue her achievements. Nobody was more surprised than Sara by all she seemed to have done during her years in the company.

'I'm really quite good, you know,' she said happily.

'Miss Gray, you are very good indeed, otherwise I wouldn't work with you,' said Eve solemnly, and Sara could detect no hint of humour or self-mockery in the tone.

Towards the end of the second week, Eve pronounced herself pleased with the office. She had bought an old coat-stand which ideally matched the table and chairs, and on this she urged Sara to hang her smart coat so that the whole place just looked as if it were an extension of her own creative personality. If anyone gasped with amazement at the changes in the room, Sara was to say that there was all this silly money up in requisitions for her to decorate the place, and she did hate modern ugly cubes of furniture so she had just chosen things she liked – which had in fact been cheaper. People were stunned, and jealous, and wondered why they hadn't thought of this too.

Remarks about her appearance Eve suggested should be parried slightly. No need to tell people that she now had regular twice weekly sessions with a beautician. Eve had booked her a course of twenty.

So on the second Friday of her employment Eve came into Sara's part of the office and said she thought that they were ready to begin.

'Begin?' cried Sara. 'I thought we'd finished.'

Eve gave one of her rare smiles. 'I meant begin your work, Miss Gray. I've been taking up a lot of your time with what I am sure you must have considered inessentials. Now I feel that you should concentrate totally on your work for promotions and let me look after everything else. I shall keep detailed records of all the routine work that I am doing. Each evening I'll leave you a progress report, too, of how I think we have been getting on in our various projects. These I think you should take home with you or else return to my personal file. We don't want them seen by anyone else.'

Sara nodded her thanks. Suddenly she felt overwhelmed with gratitude for this strange girl who was behaving not as a new secretary but as if she were an old family retainer blind with loyalty to the young Missie, or a kindergarten teacher filled with affection and hope for a young charge.

She felt almost unable to express any of this gratitude because Eve didn't seem to need it or even to like it.

'Are there any, er, major projects you see straight away?' she asked.

'I think you should look for an assistant, or a deputy, Miss Gray,' said Eve.

'*Eve*, you can't go, you can't leave me now!' cried Sara.

'Miss Gray, I am your secretary, not your assistant. I certainly shall not leave you for a year. I told you that. No, you need to train someone in to do your job when you are not here.'

'Not here?' Sara looked around her new office which she was beginning to love. 'Where will I be, why won't I be here?'

'Because you will be away on conferences, you will be travelling abroad to see the places the company is promoting, and of course, Miss Gray, you will be taking your own vacation, something you neglected to do last year I see.'

'Yes, but that'll only be a few weeks at most. Why do I need to have an assistant, a deputy? I mean it's like empire building.'

'You'll need to train an assistant to take over when you get Mr Edwards' job at the end of the year. One of the many reasons why women fail to get promotion is because management can say that there is nobody else to do their job on the present level of the ladder. I suggest you find a bright and very young, extremely young man.'

'But I can't do that. They'd know I was plotting to get Garry Edwards' job.'

Eve smiled. 'I'm glad you are calling Mr Edwards by his first name at last, Miss Gray. No, you need an assistant to do your work for you while you are away, of course. Otherwise, if this whole office is seen to tick along nicely without you in your absence, people will wonder why your presence is so essential. If on the other hand, it turns into total chaos, they will blame you *in absentia*. So you need a harmless, enthusiastic, personable young man to sign letters which I will write and to postpone anything major until your return.'

'Eve, why do you have to go away in a year?' Sara said suddenly. 'Why can't you stay and together we'll take over the whole place. Honestly, it's not impossible.'

'Oh, Miss Gray, there'd be no point in taking the place over. It's not what either of us want, is it?' asked Eve, accepting naturally that it would be perfectly feasible to take over the largest travel company in Britain if she put her mind to it.

'You never tell me what you want,' Sara said, impressed by her own daring.

'I like to see women getting their work recognised. There's so much sheer injustice in the business world – I mean really unjust things are done to women. I find that very strange. Men who can be so kind to stray dogs, lost strangers, their own children, contribute generously to charities and yet continue appalling unfairness towards women at work.'

She stopped suddenly.

Sara said, 'Go on.'

'Nothing more,' Eve said firmly. 'You asked me what I wanted. I want to see that injustice recognised for what it is, and to see people fight it.'

'You should write about it, or make speeches,' said Sara. 'I never even saw it in my own case until you came. I do agree now that I've been shabbily treated and now I've got a bit of confidence to demand more. And that's only after ten days with you. Think what success you'd have if you were to go on a lecture tour or on television or something.'

Eve looked sad.

'No. That's just the whole trouble. It doesn't work that way, damn it. That's why it's going to take so long.'

Politely she extricated herself from further explanations, from any more conversation, from having a drink at a nearby pub with Sara. She had to go home now.

'You never tell me about your home,' said Sara.

'You never tell me about yours, Miss Gray, either,' said Eve.

'I would if I got a chance,' Sara said.

'Ah yes, but you and I would not get on so well if I knew about your worries and problems!'

Sara took it as a very faint warning. It meant that Eve didn't want to hear about Sara's problems and worries either. She sighed. It would have been very helpful if Eve could apply her amazing skills to Sara's disastrous relationship with Geoff. He had been gone now three weeks. No, it couldn't be three weeks. It was. She could hardly believe it. The last ten days had passed so quickly she had scarcely missed him. She was so stunned by this that she hadn't heard what Eve said.

'I was only saying that I left your invitation for the supper party tomorrow night there on your desk,' Eve repeated as she gathered up her things. 'I hope you enjoy it. I heard that all senior executives were normally invited to meet the chairman and board members so I made sure your name was on the list. Nice chance to wear that black dress too, Miss Gray, I expect you're thinking.'

Sara's eyes were big with gratitude. As if by magic Eve seemed to have known that another lonely weekend was looming ahead. But she knew not to admit to any emotion.

'Great. I'll go in there and knock them dead. And on Monday we'll be ready to begin the campaign.'

'Excellent,' said Eve. 'I suggest you find out whether any of the board have young and hopefully stupid sons who might want to start in the business. As your assistant, you know. We need someone rather over-educated with no brains.'

'What are you going to do for the weekend?' asked Sara.

'This and that, Miss Gray. See you Monday,' said Eve.

Sara spent Saturday reading the company's reports which Eve had left thoughtfully on her desk. She took Eve's advice and wore the black dress to the party where Garry Edwards' surprise at seeing her was as exciting as any romantic flutter. 'I can see how people can become obsessed with all this infighting and competitiveness,' thought Sara.

She was charming to the chairman, she was respectful to Garry Edwards and risked calling him Garry once or twice: she caught him looking at her sideways several times. She was very pleasant to a middle-aged and lonely woman who was the wife of a noisy extrovert board member. The woman was so grateful that she positively unburdened her life story. Eve's face came like a quick flash across the conversation; Sara remembered how she had implied that people don't really want to be bogged down with personal life stories, particularly of a gloomy nature. She murmured her sympathy for the details and disclaimers of the woman's tale about neglect and being pushed into the background.

'All he cares about now is our son, he's coming down from Cambridge soon, with an Arts Degree: no plans, no interests.'

Eve would have been proud of her. She geared the conversation gently to her own office, to how she would be delighted to meet the boy – she even gave the woman her card with a little note scribbled on it. How amazing that she should suddenly find a need for those nice new cards which Eve had ordered for her and produced within days of her arrival. Garry Edwards came across at one stage to find out what she was up to; Sara steered the conversation away again.

'Where's that chap that you are seen with sometimes – and sometimes not?' asked Edwards, determined to wound.

'If he's not here, it must be one of the evenings I'm not seen with him,' said Sara cheerfully.

That night she went to sleep in her big double bed, hoping that Geoff would not come home. She had too much to think about.

The weeks went by, two more of them. She had already held three successful and supposedly impromptu gatherings in her office. Always she had included several people higher in the pecking order than Garry Edwards.

Everyone had thought it was a splendid idea to have the handsome young son of their important board member and his lonely wife in the department. He worked most of the time in the general promotions department and two afternoons a week he got what was described as a training from Sara. What it really was was an access to her files, permission to sit in her room as she worked out schemes with some of the other promotions executives, and he learned an almost overpowering respect for Miss Gray from Eve who stood up and expected him to do the same. Eve almost lowered her voice in awe when she spoke of anything Sara had done, and the well meaning, over-educated and not very bright Simon did the same.

Simply because Eve kept him under such an iron rule Simon did learn something. So much in fact that his parents were utterly delighted with him, and the head of marketing, who had opposed his appointment as the nepotism it undoubtedly was, had to admit that that young Miss Gray was able to do the most extraordinary things. He took to dropping in to her pleasant office occasionally, and once or twice that strange colourless secretary had told him very firmly that she couldn't be disturbed. When he implied that he was more important than whoever she could be talking to, the secretary had said very flatly that her instructions were to ask everyone to make appointments, or at least to telephone in advance if they intended to drop in. Since the head of marketing had been saying long and loud that too much socialising and twittering went on in his department in the name of work he could not be otherwise than pleased.

Geoff came back. His latest lady decided that she must go back to her husband and children. This she said was where her duty lay. She said it when all Geoff's money had run out. Geoff had shrugged and come back to Sara. Amazingly she wasn't at home. He let himself in one night with a bottle of champagne, a single rose and a long explanation, but there was nobody to receive any of these things so he just went to bed.

She wasn't there in the morning either. He checked her wardrobe, most of her sweaters and skirts seemed to be there. The place looked neater somehow, and there were no work files strewn about. She had a lot of much more expensive cosmetics in the bathroom too. He wondered what had been happening. He couldn't have been gone more than a month. She hadn't run out, surely? She couldn't have decided to end with him, surely? After all she hadn't changed the lock or anything. His key still opened her hall door.

He called her next morning, and a very cool voice that was not Sara's answered him. 'Miss Gray's office.'

'Oh we have gone up in the world,' giggled Geoff. Loyalty to Sara and building her up to her colleagues was never his strong suit.

'I beg your pardon?' said the voice.

'Listen, it's Geoff here, can I talk to Sara?'

'Can I know who wants to speak to Miss Gray please?' asked Eve.

'Hell, I've just told you. It's Geoff. Sara's chap, Geoff. Put me onto her will you, sweetheart.'

Eve answered very pleasantly. 'I'm afraid you must have the wrong number.'

Geoff sounded annoyed, 'Sara Gray's office, right?'

'Yes this is Miss Sara Gray's office, now will you kindly tell me who this is speaking?'

'Geoff. Geoff White, for Christ's sake, who is that?'

'I am Miss Gray's secretary. Mr White, can you please tell me your business. You're taking up a lot of time.'

She didn't actually lie when Sara asked had Geoff phoned. She said that a totally inarticulate man had called but it could hardly have been Geoff. Sara had only paused momentarily to wonder. She had spent five days at a sales conference in Paris, and had told Eve excitedly how she had been asked to address the meeting twice about new brochure ideas. Mr Edwards – or that buffoon Garry as she was now calling him – looked positively yellow with rage. He had tried to make a pass at her which she had rejected with amazement and something akin to distaste. Eve was full of praise.

Next day Sara said: 'The inarticulate man must have been Geoff. His things were in the flat, but I couldn't bear to be woken at three a.m. with champagne and tears and all, so I bolted my door and didn't hear whether he called or not.'

Eve nodded in her cool way. She wanted to hear no more, not one word of Sara's private life. Yet she looked pleased. Things were going as hoped for. Sara was now too busy to worry about Geoff, and soon she would be too confident to accept his amazing behaviour which was already a legend in office gossip. The new Sara would either throw him out or make him behave in a civilised way. Very satisfactory.

The weeks passed again. By now it was already office gossip that Sara would shortly take over from Garry Edwards. People who hadn't rated her much before, were saying now that she had been holding back. Others said that she was always brilliant and that it was only a matter of time before it was recognised.

Garry Edwards blew it. He tried to drop Sara into great trouble for one of his own mistakes. Unlucky Garry Edwards that he had joined battle with Eve's filing system, the relevant documents were produced in a matter of minutes; quite obviously Sara had dealt with the problem, had recommended a correct course of action.

It was shortly after this that Eve asked Sara to come into her small cubicle and go over the filing system with her.

'Let's do a test,' Eve said. 'Suppose you had to find Press Comment on Senior Citizen Campaign, where would you look?' Sara checked first under 'publicity' then under 'Senior Citizens'. It took her five minutes.

'It's too long,' said Eve firmly. 'Perhaps you should have a look for something every day for the next month or so. Just to familiarise yourself.'

'You're going to leave me, aren't you?' asked Sara.

'I think so,' said Eve.

'It's not the year, it's not even half a year,' Sara complained.

'But there's nothing left to do, Miss Gray. We get you a new efficient typist, we both explain to her and to Simon what the routine is, you'll be leaving shortly anyway for Mr Edwards' job, we'll just make sure that any changeover here goes smoothly.'

'Can't you come with me, upstairs?' Sara nodded in the direction of the promotions manager's office. 'Please.'

'No, you can do it better on your own really. And it's better for you.' She was like a swimming instructor encouraging a bright but apprehensive pupil.

'The office, Eve, how will I do up the office so that it's like this . . . I mean I hate his furniture, I hate his style.'

'You choose, Miss Gray. A few months ago you wouldn't have even noticed his office or his style.'

'Eve, a few months ago you know very well nobody would have noticed me.'

'You underestimate yourself, Miss Gray. Shall I advertise for a secretary, I'd be happy to advise you on any points during any interview.'

'God, yes Eve,' Sara looked at her. 'I won't keep asking you but you know there's no problem about salary.'

Eve shook her head.

Sara put her face into a bright smile. 'In a few months I suppose I'll get a telephone call from some bewildered woman asking me do I know Eve and can I possibly recommend her insane notions.'

Eve looked solemn. 'Well, yes, if you don't mind. I should like your name as a reference.'

'And I'll say Miss whoever you are. . . Eve is not from this planet.

Let her have her way with you and you'll be running your company in months.'

Eve stood up briskly. 'Yes, if you think it was all worth it.'

Sara put out her hand and held Eve's arm.

'I know you hate people prying but why, just why? You're far brighter than I am, than the woman in the bank, than the other woman – the one you told to have dinner parties. I mean, why don't *you* do it. Why don't you do it for *you*. You know better than any of us how to get on. It's like a kind of crusade for you but you stay in the background all the time. I don't know what you're at. What you want.'

Eve shrugged politely. 'I like to see you do well, Miss Gray, that's enough reward for me. You deserve it. You were being passed over. That wasn't just.'

Sara nodded. 'Now I promise, all the rest of the time you are here, I'll never ask again. Never. Just tell me. Why this way? If you feel there's discrimination against women there must be better ways to fight it.'

Eve leaned against the beautiful table and stroked it. 'If there are I can't find them. I simply know of no better way to fight it than from within. You have to use the system. I hate it but it's true.'

Sara didn't interrupt. She knew that if Eve was ever going to say anything it would be now. She let the pause last.

'How do you think I, as a feminist, like asking intelligent, sensitive women like you and like Bonnie Bernstein in the bank, and Marrion Smith in the ministry to dress properly? As if it mattered one goddamn whether you wore woad to the office . . . all three of you are worth more than any man I ever met in any kind of business. And I could say that for seven or eight other women, too. But women don't have a chance, they don't bloody know . . .'

Sara sat breathless.

'It's so *unjust*.' Eve stressed that word heavily. 'So totally unjust. A married man has a woman to look after his appearance and his clothes and his meals and his house, a woman does not. A single man has a fleet of secretaries, assistants, manicurists, lovers to look after him. A single woman is meant to cope. A man is admired for sleeping with people on his way up, a woman is considered a tramp if she does. A man. . .' She paused and pulled herself together, almost physically. 'Miss Gray, you must excuse me. I really don't think I should be taking up your time with all this. I do apologise. I feel ashamed of myself.'

The moment was gone, the spell was broken.

'I don't suppose you'll tell me why you feel like this? I mean was there some experience in your life, Eve, you are so young, too young to be bitter about things.'

Eve looked at her. 'No, of course I'm not bitter, I'm very constructive. I just try to get some justice for strong, good women who deserve it. When I've got it I move on. It's very satisfying. Slow but satisfying. Now, about this advertisement. I don't think we should phrase it "travel business," it will attract the kind of woman who thinks in terms of cheap flights and free holidays.'

Sara played along. She owed Eve that much.

'Oh yes, of course. Let's word it now, and put it in whenever you want to. The later the better of course. You know I don't want you to leave here ever.'

'Thank you very much, Miss Gray. But I think really if you agreed I'll get it into tomorrow's papers.'   Sara looked up.

'So soon?'

'There's a lot to be done,' said Eve.

First response

- Why do you think that Eve is leaving Sara so soon? What has she got left to do elsewhere?

- Do you think Sara deserves Eve's special help?

- How do you feel towards Garry Edwards?

- What sort of relationship do Sara and Eve have, would you say there were friends?

- Do you find Eve a likeable character? Do you admire the way she works?

Looking closely

Talk

Pair work

Would you say that this story has a message? Look closely at the last two pages; what do you think Eve feels so strongly about? Is that the main idea of the story? Discuss this together and see if you can agree on a statement about the message of the story.

Eve says she is a "feminist". What does this word mean, can you agree on a definition? Are either of you feminists?

Group work

Now working in groups, think about the way in which Eve spends a great deal of time on changing Sara's appearance and that of her office. Go through the story together and make some notes on what she actually changes. Then agree on what the difference is between Sara at the beginning and the end of the story. How is it that after all this effort Eve can say "As if it mattered one goddamn whether you wore woad to the office. . ."?

Look at these two pictures carefully. What do you think each woman does? How did you decide – was it the clothes?

Do you think that it matters what people wear? Do you all support the wearing of school uniform? Should it be exactly the same for boys and girls?

Role play Choose one of the following situations and improvise the conversation which takes place.

Imagine that Garry Edwards comes down to Sara's office and tries to persuade her not to take his job.

It is several months later and someone 'phones Sara to ask her to give a reference to Eve.

Imagine that a reporter from a women's magazine comes to interview Sara about the secret of her success.

Write Write about the two main characters and their relationship. What are they like as individuals, how much does each one change during the course of the story? What particular things do they say that reveal their feelings and ideas? Find some useful quotations to support your opinions of the two characters.

Is this a good, "feminist" story?

Imagine that Sara had kept a diary during the course of the story; write some extracts from it that reveal how she changes and develops through Eve's influence.

Poem For My Sister

My little sister likes to try my shoes,
to strut in them,
admire her spindle-thin twelve-year-old legs
in this season's styles.
She says they fit her perfectly,
but wobbles
on their high heels, they're
hard to balance.

I like to watch my little sister
playing hopscotch, admire the neat hops-and-skips of her,
their quick peck,
never missing their mark, not
over-stepping the line.
She is competent at peever.

I try to warn my little sister
about unsuitable shoes,
point out my own distorted feet, the callouses,
odd patches of hard skin.
I should not like to see her
in my shoes.
I wish she would stay
sure footed,
        sensibly shod.

LIZ LOCHHEAD
FROM DREAMING FRANKENSTEIN AND COLLECTED POEMS

Talk

Pair work

Go through the poem carefully and then work out an argument to persuade the little sister why she should not wear high heels; use the ideas in the poem itself as the basis for your argument.

Group work

Why is the poet so concerned about her little sister wearing her shoes? She obviously used to wear them, so why is she unhappy about them now? Do you think girls in general wear things that are not very sensible? Are there pressures on girls to wear clothes, shoes and so on just to please boys? Does it matter to you whether girls wear high heels?

Write

1. In some ways this is a very simple poem but the words have been chosen and placed with great care. Look at the following list of words from the poem and write your own comments on why you think the poet chose them and placed them where she did: strut, admire (used twice), spindle-thin, wobbles, peck, never-missing, over-stepping, distorted, sure footed, sensibly shod. Think about other possible words that the poet might have chosen to help describe her subject.

2. Would you like to protect a child from some of the things that you have already been through? Write your own poem for someone which expresses a warning that you feel is important. Try to think about the words you choose.

Read this essay by D. H. Lawrence. You may not understand all the references at first, but don't let this put you off. Try to respond to the ideas and opinions expressed.

Give Her a Pattern

The real trouble about women is that they must always go on trying to adapt themselves to men's theories of women, as they always have done. When a woman is thoroughly herself, she is being what her type of man wants her to be. When a woman is hysterical it's because she doesn't quite know what to be, which pattern to follow, which man's picture of woman to live up to.

For, of course, just as there are many men in the world, there are many masculine theories of what women should be. But men run to type, and it is the type, not the individual, that produces the theory, or 'ideal' of woman. Those very grasping gentry, the Romans, produced a theory or ideal of the matron, which fitted in very nicely with the Roman property lust. 'Caesar's wife should be above suspicion.' – So Caesar's wife kindly proceeded to be above it, no matter how far below it the Caesar fell. Later gentlemen like Nero produced the 'fast' theory of woman, and later ladies were fast enough for everybody. Dante arrived with a chaste and untouched Beatrice, and chaste and untouched Beatrices began to march self-importantly through the centuries. The Renaissance discovered the learned woman, and learned women buzzed mildly into verse and prose. Dickens invented the child-wife, so child-wives have swarmed ever since. He also fished out his version of the chaste Beatrice, a chaste but marriageable Agnes. George Eliot imitated this pattern, and it became confirmed. The noble woman, the pure spouse, the devoted mother took the field, and

was simply worked to death. Our own poor mothers were this sort. So
we younger men, having been a bit frightened of our noble mothers,
tended to revert to the child-wife. We weren't very inventive. Only the
child-wife must be a boyish little thing – that was the new touch we added.
Because young men are definitely frightened of the real female. She's too
risky a quantity. She is too untidy, like David's Dora. No, let her be a
boyish little thing, it's safer. So a boyish little thing she is.

There are, of course, other types. Capable men produce the capable
woman ideal. Doctors produce the capable nurse. Business men produce
the capable secretary. And so you get all sorts. You can produce the
masculine sense of honour (whatever that highly mysterious quantity may
be) in women, if you want to.

There is, also, the eternal secret ideal of men – the prostitute. Lots of
women live up to this idea: just because men want them to.

And so, poor woman, destiny makes away with her. It isn't that she
hasn't got a mind – she has. She's got everything that man has. The only
difference is that she asks for a pattern. Give me a pattern to follow! That
will always be woman's cry. Unless of course she has already chosen her
pattern quite young, then she will declare she is herself absolutely, and no
man's idea of women has any influence over her.

Now the real tragedy is not that women ask and must ask for a pattern
of womanhood. The tragedy is not, even, that men give them such
abominable patterns, child-wives, little-boy-baby-face girls, perfect secretaries, noble spouses, self-sacrificing mothers, pure women who bring forth
children in virgin coldness, prostitutes who just make themselves low, to
please men; all the atrocious patterns of womanhood that men have
supplied to woman; patterns all perverted from any real natural fulness of
a human being. Man is willing to accept woman as an equal, as a man in
skirts, as an angel, a devil, a baby-face, a machine, an instrument, a bosom,
a womb, a pair of legs, a servant, an encyclopedia, an ideal, or an obscenity;
the one thing he won't accept her as, is a human being, a real human
being of the feminine sex.

And, of course, women love living up to strange patterns, weird patterns
– the more uncanny the better. What could be more uncanny than the
present pattern of the Eton-boy girl with flower-like artificial complexion?
It is just weird. And for its very weirdness women like living up to it.
What can be more gruesome than the little-boy-baby-face pattern? Yet the
girls take it on with avidity.

But even that isn't the real root of the tragedy. The absurdity, and often,
as in the Dante-Beatrice business, the inhuman nastiness of the pattern –
for Beatrice had to go on being chaste and untouched all her life, according
to Dante's pattern, while Dante had a cosy wife and kids at home – even
that isn't the worst of it. The worst of it is, as soon as a woman has really
lived up to the man's pattern the man dislikes her for it. There is intense
secret dislike for the Eton-young-man girl, among the boys, now that she

is actually produced. Of course, she's very nice to show in public, absolutely the thing. But the very young men who have brought about her production detest her in private and in their private hearts are appalled by her.

When it comes to marrying, the pattern goes all to pieces. The boy marries the Eton-boy girl, and instantly he hates the *type*. Instantly his mind begins to play hysterically with all the other types, noble Agneses, chaste Beatrices, clinging Doras and lurid *filles de joie*. He is in a wild welter of confusion. Whatever the pattern the poor woman tries to live up to, he'll want another. And that's the condition of modern marriage.

Modern woman isn't really a fool. But modern man is. That seems to me the only plain way of putting it. The modern man is a fool, and the modern young man a prize fool. He makes a greater mess of his women than men have ever made. Because he absolutely doesn't know *what* he wants her to be. We shall see the changes in the woman-pattern follow one another fast and furious now, because the young men hysterically don't know what they want. Two years hence women may be in crinolines – there was a pattern for you! – or a bead flap, like naked negresses in mid-Africa – or they may be wearing brass armour, or the uniform of the Horse Guards. They may be anything. Because the young men are off their heads, and don't know what they want.

The women aren't fools, but they *must* live up to some pattern or other. They *know* the men are fools. They don't really respect the pattern. Yet a pattern they must have, or they can't exist.

Women are not fools. They have their own logic, even if it's not the masculine sort. Women have the logic of emotion, men have the logic of reason. The two are complementary and mostly in opposition. But the woman's logic of emotion is no less real and inexorable than the man's logic of reason. It only works differently.

And the woman never really loses it. She may spend years living up to a masculine pattern. But in the end, the strange and terrible logic of emotion will work out the smashing of that pattern, if it has not been emotionally satisfactory. This is the partial explanation of the astonishing changes in women. For years they go on being chaste Beatrices or child-wives. Then on a sudden – bash! The chaste Beatrice becomes a roaring lioness! The pattern didn't suffice, emotionally.

Whereas men are fools. They are based on a logic of reason, or are supposed to be. And then they go and behave, especially with regard to women, in a more-than-feminine unreasonableness. They spend years training up the little-boy-baby-face type, till they've got her perfect. Then the moment they marry her, they want something else. Oh, beware, young women, of the young men who adore you! The moment they've got you they'll want something utterly different. The moment they marry the little-boy-baby-face, instantly they begin to pine for the noble Agnes, pure and majestic, or the infinite mother with deep bosom of consolation, or the perfect business woman, or the lurid prostitute on black silk sheets; or, most idiotic of all, a combination of the lot of them at once. And that is the logic of reason! When it comes to women, modern men are idiots. They don't know what they want, and so they never want, permanently, what they get. They want a cream cake that is at the same time ham and eggs and at the same time porridge. They are fools. If only women weren't bound by fate to play up to them!

For the fact of life is that women *must* play up to man's pattern. And she only gives her best to a man when he gives her a satisfactory pattern to play up to. But today, with a stock of ready-made, worn-out idiotic patterns to live up to, what can women give to men but the trashy side of their emotions? What could a woman possibly give to a man who wanted her to be a boy-baby-face? What could she possibly give him but the dribblings of an idiot? – And, because women aren't fools, and aren't fooled even for very long at a time, she gives him some nasty cruel digs with her claws, and makes him cry for mother dear! – abruptly changing his pattern.

Bah! men are fools. If they want anything from women, let them give women a decent, satisfying idea of womanhood – not these trick patterns of washed-out idiots.

D. H. LAWRENCE
FROM SELECTED ESSAYS

Talk

In groups, work through the essay together and sum up what you feel are its main arguments; make a note of any references or words with which you would like assistance. These questions may help:

- What is the real trouble with women?
- What is it that women ask for?
- What do men really dislike women for?
- Why is modern man a fool?
- What kinds of logic do men and women have?
- What is wrong with modern patterns?

Now consider the fact that this essay was written 60 years ago:

- Could it have been written today?
- Are there many people who share its ideas?
- Look at these pictures from magazines. Do you think that women are still conforming to patterns?

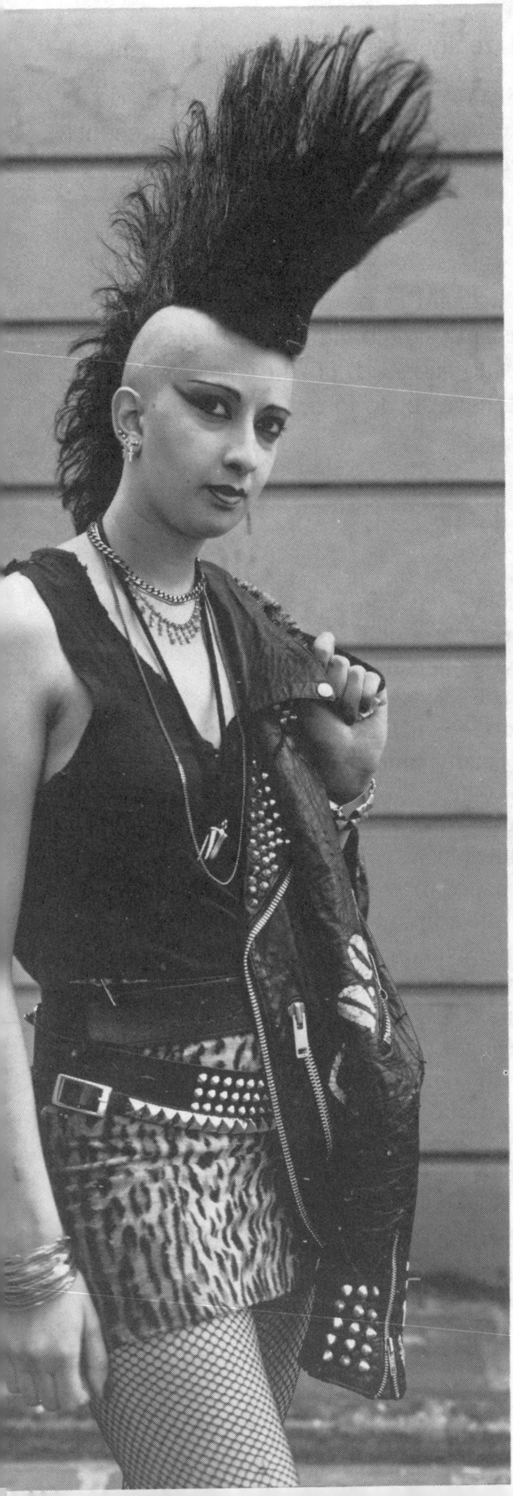

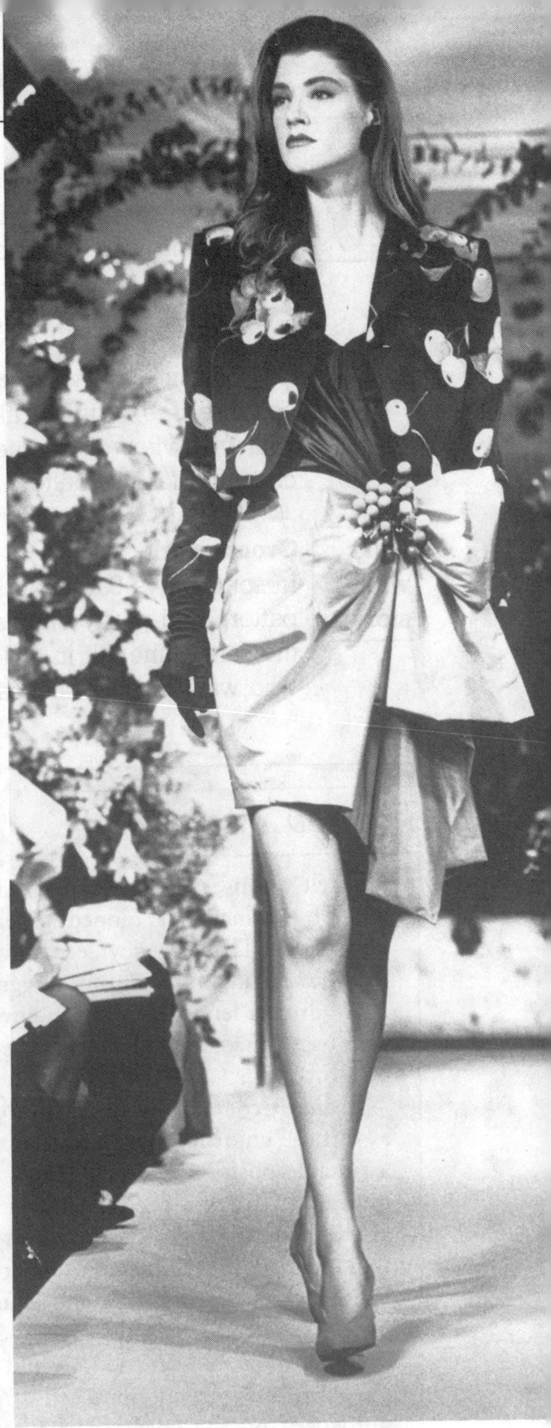

<table>
<tr><td>Write</td><td>

1. Imagine that this essay appeared in a magazine and readers were asked to send in their replies agreeing or disagreeing with it and explaining their own views; write your reply.

2. "Modern woman isn't really a fool. But modern man is."

Do you think that there is some truth in this statement or do you disagree with it? Take it as your starting point to present your own view of whether modern men and women are changing for the better.

</td></tr>
</table>

Links with story

Group work

In some ways Sara could be said to be partly adopting a male pattern and partly emphasising her femininity to please men at the same time, all in order to succeed. Is that what women who want to be a success have to do to compete with men?

The job or no job

I've felt a sense of urgency ever since I left school last month, scouring the job vacancy ads pinned to career noticeboards and in every daily newspaper. That urgency seems now to be substituted by fear.

I chewed anxiously on my fingernails. I glanced at my watch: 8.35 a.m. I withdrew a letter from a torn envelope which had been folded inside my handbag. I had re-read the letter so many times I could recall the words by heart.

It didn't contain the usual sympathy on the lines of: 'Your application as Office Junior has been unsuccessful, but we wish you success in finding a suitable position' etc . . . Just a chance of an interview glowed deep in my mind. I caught my reflection in the window of the bus. I stared back at the daunting face, covered in a mask of make-up as if trying to hide the identity of the person underneath it – ME. I rubbed the excess eyeshadow from my eyes and squinted a little at the window. I pressed my face against the cold glass, feeling its chill against my skin as the crowds of people scurried to and fro. They started to fade against the images forming in my mind as I drifted into a light sleep. My mind became unfocused on the images as I filtered through daydreams; I daydream a lot, too much according to my parents.

As the bus rolled down into the Leicestershire countryside, Madonna's raunchy effort, 'Like a Virgin', penetrated across the bus from a boy's Walkman. He was sitting opposite me. He looked up and smirked at me through the blond fringe that covered his left eye. I smiled back, not in recognition of him but of the presence of Madonna and her music. Though like many other girls I detested her image, you really couldn't but feel a little proud of her originality of dress and her attitude towards life in general; her domination of the music scene in a still male-governed world proved that we women could make it to the top. But, of course, her looks, her figure and voice were her advantage, in comparison to my small, plump frame and appalling 'singing' vocals.

I picked up my magazine and flicked through the pages. The slender, tall models glazing the pages did nothing to ease my mind. But smiling red-headed Sarah Ferguson, whose curvy figure graced the back cover spontaneously brought a grin to my face as I reached for my Mars bar.

I had thought of nothing but my job interview since last Friday. It's a shock to think that I am now sixteen years old and will probably work until I'm twenty. I'll marry and by the time I'm thirty be blessed with two or three children, which will finalise our stereotyped family in Britain today. Not all women want that, do they? Maybe we don't have a choice, unless it means searching for that far-off dream. Yes, I know women are treated more independently now, but where I live, as soon as you leave school, girls are supposed to fit into a category of jobs: hosiery, clerical or hairdressing – though even those jobs are becoming few and far between now. Unemployment is still high in my area and there's still a lot of advice for school-leavers regarding their skills. But you can hardly answer your careers teacher: 'I want to be an author and a song writer.' They would probably look at me in complete amazement and push a careers leaflet into my hands either to do with college courses or starting up your own business! Even if I sent endless numbers of scripts to publishers, I would have to get a job to support me. It's unfair maybe, but perhaps it's a challenge to those who want to be successful in their own minds rather than those unwilling to make the effort.

I glanced back to the bus window. The hour I had spent perfecting my hairstyle now seemed like one minute; I watched in despair as my spikes started to waver, then fall gently to flatten themselves upon my head. I poked furiously at my hair, trying to achieve the impossible with its untamed waves. I wished now that I had brought my can of hairspray. I chuckled quietly to myself as I recalled the other uses my can of hairspray had found over the last few weeks. With my bedroom curtains closed, my bedside lamp as a spotlight and dressed in scanty clothing (clothes which I wouldn't dare wear in old, wary Barwell) and with either a can of hairspray or bottle of Impulse as a microphone, I could turn my bedroom into a stage from 'Top of the Pops' or 'The Tube'. I recalled imaginary interviews I had conducted on the edge of my bed, smiling and nodding my answers to questions posed by Jools Holland, Paula Yates or newspaper reporters and journalists from *Smash Hits* and *Just Seventeen*. Singing a duet in my bedroom mirror with Morten Harket from A-Ha to the twelve inch of 'Hunting High and Low' now seemed like a distant dream.

'Just practising becoming famous,' I would answer my mum, when she protested against my off-key singing which drowned out the sensual quality of Morten Harket's voice. Kissing A-Ha's poster, each member in turn, before I snuggled deep into my bed as I drifted into another dream. Maybe I thought, just maybe. It's not just the glamour and the money which attracts me to the career of songwriter and ever-hopeful singer. Being a household name enables you to do things which are impossible to do as an ordinary young girl.

Smoke hung in the air, causing me to cough. I turned round to watch a girl a little older than myself puff absent-mindedly on a cigarette, its ash sparking red at the end as a sign of danger. As it dangled between two fingers of her right hand, I turned away in disgust. I felt her eyes glaring deep into my back; my spine tingled and shuddered in anticipation as she noticed my expression. I could hear her whistling to herself, her notes flowing against the noise of the bus engine. Oh yes, I had seen her type so many times, at my own school in fact. They would sit in groups on the walls outside the school gates, cross-legged in their school uniform, trying to look so sophisticated and adult.

I recalled back to last year when I read in our local newspaper that small, quiet Barwell, the village where I live, was in fact a central point for drugs dealing in the Midlands. Somehow Barwell villagers' attitudes changed towards the young people of the area. The media still continued to claim that fifteen- to sixteen-year-olds were at the most vulnerable age for smoking, drug-taking and that the number of teenage girls becoming pregnant was rising. Even as my friends and I walked along the streets of Barwell, you could feel the eyes of the villagers roaming your body from head to toe, trying to catch and notice the symptoms of addiction and pregnancy for local gossip.

I can't help but feel the sense of being watched in some shops, though. Shop assistants move closer towards you to watch your every move. It's ironic, but I was in Barwell's Co-op only last week and an elderly man was caught shoplifting. Tins of soup, packets of meat and biscuits were found hidden in the inside pockets of his overcoat. I couldn't help but allow a sarcastic smirk to light my face in triumph as he was questioned intently. I held my head high and walked out the shop with pride and my mum's shopping. . .

I felt a few raindrops wet upon my hand. Water was starting to form on my watch's face. Through its misty pane it read 9.05 a.m. The clouds were starting to disperse now, leaving the sky clearer as the bus entered Leicester. Just outside Leicester there is a tall white sign which features the words: 'You are now entering Leicester: a Nuclear Free Zone.' It stands proudly, half hidden by a nearby cluster of trees. After staring at it for a few minutes, I laughed quietly to myself. 'A Nuclear Free Zone,' I thought. Well that's a joke for a start, especially as there's a number of bombs directed for Leicester, Coventry and Birmingham – the three major cities of the Midlands; everyone within those cities would either be dead or badly injured. Though, after watching 'Threads' I was as frightened as everyone else; if there was a nuclear war, I thought, I would rather be killed outright instead of surviving in a lost world, or suffering from the fallout of radiation poisoning where you die a painful death. I recalled a quote that I once read, which had stuck in my mind ever since: 'Neither America nor Russia will start a Nuclear War, because neither knows what they're actually starting.'

The bus was now nearing my stop. My watch read 9.20 a.m. I gathered my bag and coat together and strolled with the other passengers towards the door. As I stepped out onto the pavement, I felt as hopeful and as panic-stricken as any other teenager, from whatever walk of life, facing their job interview . . . taking the next step up onto the next rung of the ladder of my life.

ANN-MARIE JEBBETT
FROM BITTER-SWEET DREAMS

Talk

Pair work
In pairs, talk about what you have learned about the writer from her essay. Try to jot down some ideas about what she seems to be like and also what she hopes for and what she expects to get from life.

Group work
The writer makes several points about the way women and girls are treated in society. Go through the essay in groups, collecting these points, and then see whether you agree with her ideas.

Do you feel that she is a typical representative of teenagers' views about starting work and also starting 'adult' life?

Write

1.   The essay is written as if the events are happening as we read about them, and the thoughts and feelings of Ann-Marie are put forward spontaneously. Her main topics seem to be getting a job, men and women in society, her ambitions, the way teenagers are viewed by others and the threat of nuclear war; quite a list. Try writing your own piece based on a real or imagined journey in which you are thinking about some of the most important concerns in your life.

2.   "as hopeful and as panic-stricken as any other teenager

... taking the next step up ..." What will be the next step in your life or what would you like it to be? You could, if you prefer, write a short story about a teenager taking this vital step.

Links with story

Are the writer of this essay and Sara facing the same kinds of problems in a male-dominated society? Do you think that men and women have exactly the same opportunities to succeed in all careers?

Reverie for a Secretary

Feeling fragile and incredibly bored I listen to my boss
saying he takes five newspapers to get other viewpoints
from which he makes up his mind on world events.
I give him my look of awe thinking,
well bully for you, with a brain like that
you are paid nine times more than me?

Over his head and through the window
the sky is blue and beckoning. I wish I had wings.
'The return on capital investment is up two per cent'
Dear God, who really cares?
Wouldn't we be happier making daisy chains?
How disgustingly fat he is.
His hair parting would just fit an axe.
I am not brave. I can't walk out
leaving a question mark in the air.
I am your natural serving maid
dropping curtseys to the gentry.
Those figures are not correct?
How would you know?
You can only just crayon picture books.
He must know these figures came from the computer
and he supplied the original figures.
I could walk up and wack him over the head
with that dictaphone he can't use,
then drag him and push him out of the window.
From seventeen storeys he would splash.
Suicide while the balance of his pea brain was disturbed.
Mercy killer breaks down in dock.
Blonde in penthouse drama.

He is looking at my legs and breathing through his nose.
Now he will ask about my boyfriend.
Here it comes right on cue.
'Yes, we went dancing last night.'
Stark naked and I gave myself to fifteen rugger players.
Should I tear off my clothes and scream rape?
They wouldn't believe me. They say he is one of those.
And now he wants a cup of coffee.
That's his seventh and he hasn't been to the loo.
My cool lily white hands deftly serve him
and my beautiful body glides round his desk.
My cool lily white hands want to pour it in his ear
and my beautiful body wants to dance as he screams.
He has hairs growing out of his nose.
I never noticed them before, and he reeks
of that lousy after shave lotion, yecch,
he doesn't even smell like a man.
Now he is going to lunch. Listen to him wheeze and puff.
'You will be back at three Mr Chatterton?'
Smile you bitch smile. He is bound to have a coronary
carrying all that blubber about.
Oh mummy, for this you made me do my homework?

STELLA COULSON
FROM STANDPOINTS

Read

Read through Stella Coulson's poem and think about why, if she hates her boss so much, does the secretary go on working for him?

What do you make of her last remark about doing her homework?

Talk

Pair work

Work out a joint reading of the poem with different voices and tones for the boss and for the secretary.

Group work

What is a reverie? Do you all think that she would really like to do what she is thinking about? How do you feel towards the boss in the poem? Is he truly horrible or just ordinary? Or are most ordinary bosses truly horrible to their secretaries?

Write	*Either*

Write 'Reverie for a Boss'; what is going through his mind?

or

Continue the poem for the rest of the day; what happens when he gets back from lunch?

Links with story	• Is the position of women working in offices really as awful as the story and the poem suggest?

• What do you know about life in an office?

• Is it an environment that you expect to work in?

• What will your attitudes and behaviour be like?

Hardly Ever

WILLIAM BOYD

'Think of it,' Holland said. 'The sex.'

'Sex,' Panton repeated. 'God . . . Sex.'

Niles shook his head. 'Are you sure?' he asked. 'I mean, can you guarantee it? The sex, that is. I don't want to waste time farting around singing.'

'Waste bloody time? Are you mad?' Holland said. 'It only happens every two years. You can't afford to miss the opportunity. Unless you're suffering from second thoughts.'

'What, *me*?' Niles tried to laugh. He looked at Holland's blue eyes. They always seemed to know. 'You must be bloody kidding, mate. Jesus, if you think . . . God!' he snorted.

'All right, all right,' Holland said. 'We agreed, remember? It's got to be all of us.'

Niles had never asked for this last fact to be explained. Why – if, as Holland attested – the sex was freely available, on a plate so to speak, why did they all have to participate at the feast? Holland made out it was part of his naturally generous personality. It was more fun if you all had a go.

'Let's get on with it,' Panton said.

They walked over to the noticeboard. Holland pushed some juniors out of the way. Prothero, the music master, had written on the top of a sheet of paper: GILBERT AND SULLIVAN OPERA – HMS PINAFORE – CHORUS: BASSES AND TENORS WANTED, SIGN BELOW. Half a dozen names had been scrawled down.

'Cretins,' Holland said. 'No competition.' He wrote his name down. Panton followed suit.

Niles took a biro from his blazer pocket. He paused.

'But how can you be so sure? That's what I want to know. How can you tell that the girls just won't be – well – music-lovers?'

'Because I know,' Holland said patiently. 'Every Gilbert and Sullivan it's the same. Borthwick told me. He was in the last one. He said the girls only come for one thing. I mean, it stands to reason. What sort of girl's going to want to be in some pissing bloody operetta. Ask yourself. Shitty orchestra, home-made costumes, people who can't sing to save their life. I tell you, Nilo, they're doing it for the same reason as us.

They're fed up with the local yobs. They want a nice public school boy. Christ, you must have heard. It's a cert. Leave it to Pete.'

Niles screwed up his eyes. What the hell, he thought, it's time I tried. He signed his name. Q. Niles.

'Good old Quentin,' Panton roared. 'Wor! Think of it waiting.' He forced his features into a semblance of noble suffering, wrapped his arms around himself as if riven with acute internal pain and lurched drunkenly about, groaning in simulated ecstasy.

Holland grabbed Niles by the arm. 'The shafting, Nilo my man,' he said intensely. 'The royal bloody shafting we're going to do.'

Niles felt his chest expand with sudden exhilaration. Holland's fierce enthusiasm always affected him more than Panton's most baroque histrionics.

'Bloody right, Pete,' he said. 'Too bloody right. I'm getting desperate already.'

Niles sat in his small box-like study and stared out at the relentless rain falling on the gentle Scottish hills. From his study window he could see a corner of the dormitory wing of his own house, an expanse of gravel with the housemaster's car parked on it and fifty yards of the drive leading down to the main school house a mile or so away. On the desk in front of him lay a half-completed team list for the inter-house rugby leagues and an open notepad. On the notepad he had written: *The Rape of the Lock*, and below that '*The Rape of the Lock* is a mock heroic poem. What do you understand by this term? Illustrate with examples.' It was an essay which he was due to hand in tomorrow. He had no idea what to say. He gazed dully out at the rain, idly noting some boys coming out of the woods. They must be desperate, he thought, if they have to go out for a smoke in this weather. He returned to his more immediate problem. Who was going to play scrum-half now that Damianos had a sick-chit? He considered the pool of players he could draw on: asthmatics, fatsos, spastics everyone. To hell with it. He wrote down Grover's name. They had no chance of winning anyway. He opened his desk cupboard and removed a packet of Jaffa cakes and a large bottle of Coca-Cola. He gulped thirstily from the bottle and ate a few biscuits. *The Rape of the Lock*. What could he say about it? He didn't mind the poem. He thought of Belinda:

'On her white breast a sparkling cross she wore,'. . . He found her far and away the most alluring of the fictional heroines he had yet encountered in his brief acquaintance with English Literature. He read the opening of the poem again. He saw her lying in a huge rumpled bed, a lace peignoir barely covering two breasts as firm and symmetrical as halved grapefruits. He had had a bonk-on all the English lesson. It hadn't happened to him since they'd read *Great Expectations*. What was her name? Estella. God, yes. She was almost as good as Belinda. He thought about his essay again. He liked English Literature. He wondered if he would be able to do it at university – if he could get to university at all. His father had not been at all pleased when he had announced that he wanted to do English A-level. 'What's the use of that?' he had shouted. 'How's English Literature going to help you sell machine tools?' Niles sighed. There was an opening for him in Gerald Niles (Engineering) Ltd. His father knew nothing of his plans for university.

Niles ran his hands through his thick wiry hair and rubbed his eyes. He picked up his pen. 'Alexander Pope,' he wrote, 'was a major poet of the Augustan period. *The Rape of the Lock* was his most celebrated poem.' He sensed it was a bad beginning – uninspired, boring – but sometimes if you started by writing down what you knew, you occasionally got a few ideas. He scanned Canto One. 'Soft bosoms', he saw. Then 'Belinda still her downy pillow prest'. He felt himself quicken. Pope knew what he was doing, all right. The associations: bosom and pillow, prest and breast. Niles shut his eyes. He was weighing Belinda's perfect breasts in his hands, massaging her awake as she lay in her tousled noonday bed. He imagined her hair spread over her face, full lips, heavy sleep-bruised eyes. He imagined a slim forearm raised to ward off Sol's tim'rous ray, Belinda turning on to her back, stretching. Jesus. Would she have hairy armpits? he wondered, swallowing. Did they shave their armpits in the eighteenth century? Would it be like that French woman he'd seen on a campsite near Limoges last summer? In the camp supermarket, wearing only a bikini, reaching up for a tin on a high shelf and exposing a great hank of armpit hair. Niles groaned. He leant forward and rested his head on his open book. 'Belinda,' he whispered, 'Belinda.'

'Everything okay, Quentin?'

He sat up abruptly, banging his knees sharply on the bottom of his desk. It was Bowler, his housemaster, his round bespectacled face peering at him concernedly, his body canted into the study, pipe clenched between his brown teeth. Why couldn't the bastard knock? Niles swore.

'Trying to write an essay, sir,' he said.

'Not that difficult, is it?' Bowler laughed. 'Got the team for the league?'

Niles handed it over. Bowler studied it, puffing on his pipe, frowning. Niles looked at the sour blue smoke gathering on the ceiling. Typical bloody Bowler.

'This the best we can do? Are you sure about Grover at scrum-half? Crucial position, I would have thought.'

'I think he needs to be pressured a bit, sir.'

'Right-ho. You're the boss. See you're down for *Pinafore*.'

'Sorry, sir?'

'*Pinafore*. HMS. The opera. Didn't know you sang, Quentin? Shouldn't have thought it was your line really.'

'Thought I'd give it a go, sir.'

Bowler left and Niles thought about the opera. Holland had said it was a sure thing with the girls: they only came because they wanted to get off with boys. Niles wondered what they'd be like. Scottish girls from the local grammar school. He'd seen them in town often. Dark blue uniforms, felt hats, long hair, mini-skirts. They all looked older than him – more mature. He experienced a sudden moment of panic. What in God's name would he do? Holland and Panton would be there, everyone would see him. He felt his heart beat with unreasonable speed. It was a kind of proof. There was no chance of lying or evading the issue. It would be all too public.

They gathered in the music room behind the new chapel for the first mixed rehearsal. There had been three weeks of tedious afternoon practices during which some semblance of singing ability had been forcibly extracted from them by the efforts of Prothero, the music master. Now Prothero watched the boys enter with a tired and cynical smile. This was his seventh Gilbert and Sullivan since coming to the school, his third *HMS Pinafore*. Two sets of forms faced each other at one end of the long room. The boys sat down on one set staring at the empty seats opposite as if they were already occupied.

'Now, gentlemen,' Prothero began. 'The ladies will be here soon. I don't propose to lecture you any more on the subject. I count on your innate good manners and sense of decorum.'

Niles, Holland and Panton sat together. Whispered conversations were going on all around. Niles felt his lungs press against his rib cage. The tension was acute, he felt faint with unfamiliar stress. What if not one of them spoke to him? This was dreadful, he thought, and the girls weren't even here. He looked at the fellow members of the chorus. There were some authentic tenors and basses from the school choir but the rest of them were made up of self-appointed lads, frustrates and sexual braggarts. He could sense their crude desire thrumming through the group as if the forms they were sitting on were charged with a low electric current. He looked at the bright-eyed, snouty expectant faces, heard whispered obscenities and saw the international language of sexual gesticulation being covertly practised as if they were a gathering of randy deaf-mutes. He felt vaguely soiled to be counted among them. Beside him Holland leaned forward and tapped the shoulder of a boy in front.

'Bloody Mobo,' he said quietly and venomously. 'Didn't you get the message? No queers allowed. What are you bloody doing here? It's girls we're singing with. Not lushmen, Mobo, no little lushmen.'

'Frig off, Holland,' the boy said tonelessly. 'I'm in the choir, aren't I?'

'Bloody choir,' Holland repeated, his face ugly with illogical aggression. 'Bloody frigging choir.'

Then the girls came in.

No one had heard the bus from town arriving and the room, to Niles' startled eyes, seemed suddenly to be filled with chattering uniformed females. He heard laughter and giggles, caught flashing glimpses of cheeks and red mouths, hair and knees as the other half of the chorus sat itself down opposite. The boys fired nervous exploratory glances across the two yards of floor between them. Niles studied his score with commendable intensity. He noticed Holland brazenly scrutinizing the girls. Cautiously, Niles raised his eyes and looked over. They seemed very ordinary, was his first reflection. Dark blue blazers, short skirts some black tights. There was one tall girl with a severe, rather thin face. Her hair was tied up in an elaborate twisted bun and at first he thought she was a mistress, but then he saw her uniform. He scanned the features of the others but their faces refused to register any individuality – he might have been staring at a Chinese football team.

Holland bowed his head.

'Mm-mm. I've seen mine,' he said in a low voice. 'The blonde in front.' He gave a whimper of suppressed desire. Some boys looked round and smiled, complicity springing up instantly, like recognition.

'Right, everybody,' Prothero shouted, banging out a chord on the piano. 'Page twenty-three please.'

'And I'm never ever sick at sea,' Prothero sang.

'What never?' boomed the chorus of sailors.

'No never,' replied Prothero.

'What *never*?' the chorus sceptically inquired again.

'Hardly ever,' Prothero admitted.

'He's hardly ever sick at sea . . .'

'Fine,' Prothero called. 'Good, that'll do for today. Thank you, ladies. Your bus should be outside. Scores on the end of the piano as you go out, please.'

The bus was late and the girls had to wait for five minutes outside the chapel. Niles took his time finding his coat in the vestibule and when he went outside Holland and Panton were already talking to four girls.

'Niles, Niles,' they shouted as he emerged into the watery sunlight of a February afternoon. 'Over here.' He walked over, the blood pounding in his ears like surf. Holland stood behind a slim blonde girl with moles on her face, Panton by a cheery-looking redhead. Niles approached. One of the two remaining girls was the tall sharp-faced one he'd seen earlier. The other was small with wispy fair hair and spectacles.

'This is Quentin,' Holland said. 'Hero of the rugby field, captain of the squash team. Master flogger extraordinaire.'

'Shut up!' Niles exclaimed, appalled at this slander. 'You bastard.'

'What's a flogger?' Holland's girl asked. Panton was doubled up with mirth. The tall girl looked on expressionlessly.

'Never mind,' Holland said. 'Sorry, Quent. Little joke. Now, this is Joyce,' he indicated Panton's girl. 'This is Helen,' pointing to his own. 'And,' he looked at the tall girl, 'Alison? Yes, Alison. And, um . . .'

'Frances,' said the small girl.

Niles had moved round to stand beside Alison. Frances was clearly on her own. She stood undecidedly for a moment before wandering off without a further word.

Holland and Panton had instinctively sensed out the kind of girl they were after. Innuendoes were already being exchanged with a wanton suggestiveness. Niles looked at Alison. She was tall. In her high heels slightly taller than him. She appeared older, in her twenties almost, but the severity of her face was partly an illusion caused by her schoolmarmy bun. Her skirt was not as short as Helen's or Joyce's; it stopped two inches above her knees. Her legs were long and shapely. On the lapel of her blazer were numerous badges: three Robertson's gollies, a small Canadian maple leaf, a yellow square, and a blue rectangular one with 'monitor' written on it in plain silver letters. She wore a white shirt, and a tie with the smallest knot in it Niles had ever seen.

He had to say something. He cleared his throat. 'Campaign medals?' he said, pointing to the badges. He realized his finger was two inches from her right breast and he snatched his hand away. He thought she gave the thinnest of smiles in response but he couldn't be sure.

'Cold though,' he said, huffing and puffing into his cupped hands.

She rummaged in her blazer pockets. 'Cigarette?' she asked taking out a packet and offering it to him.

Niles was taken aback by this unselfconsciously adult gesture. 'Christ no,' he said hurriedly. 'I mean, we're not allowed.'

But she was already offering them to Joyce and Helen. Alison took out a box of matches and lit the others' cigarettes. For some reason Niles was impressed by the capable way she did this – she obviously smoked a lot. Meanwhile Holland and Panton aped nicotine starvation. When

Joyce and Helen exhaled they chased the clouds of smoke about, beating it into their gaping mouths with their hands as if it were vital oxygen. The girls laughed delightedly.

'What I'd give for a fag,' said Holland through gritted teeth.

'Oh yeah?' said lissom Helen.

'Now see what you've done,' Niles said to Alison with more accusation in his voice than he'd meant.

Alison laughed briefly.

Niles brushed his teeth, alone at the row of basins. He rinsed his mouth out and went to stand in front of the large mirror by the urinals. He looked at his square face. He rubbed his jaw. He'd need to shave tomorrow. He had to shave every two days now. Somebody shouted 'virile!' through the washroom door. Niles whirled round but he didn't see who it was. When he turned back to the mirror his face was red.

He thought about Alison. Everything about her was maddeningly indistinct and ambiguous. All he'd heard her say was 'cigarette?' and 'bye'. It wasn't much to build a relationship on. He had an image of the back of her long legs in their tan tights as she'd climbed on to the bus. He wondered what her breasts were like. Her 'soft bosoms'.

He sighed and belted his dressing gown tighter around him. He walked through the quiet empty house towards his dormitory. A junior came padding down the corridor in pyjamas.

'Where are you going, Payne?' Niles said tiredly.

'For a slash, Niles.'

'Where's your bloody slippers and dressing gown then?'

'Oh Niles,' Payne moaned.

'Get back and bloody put them on.'

'Oh God, Niles, *please*, I just want a pee. I'll only be a second.'

'Go on, you little shit,' Niles raised his hand menacingly. Payne turned and ran back up the corridor.

Niles walked on towards his dormitory. It was a small one, only eight beds. He opened the door quietly. It was well past lights out. The long room was quite dark. He closed the door softly behind him.

'Okay, folks,' came a voice. 'Stop flogging, here's Niles.'

'Shut up, Fillery,' Niles said. Fillery was fat and wicked. His mother was an actress who lived in Cannes.

'What's she like then, Niles?' Fillery said.

'Who?'

'Who? The bloody bird of course, that's who. *Pinafore*. What's your one like?'

'Yeah, go on, Niles,' said another voice. 'Tell us, what's she like?'

'Shut up. I'm warning you lot.'

'Come on, Niles,' Fillery said wheedlingly. 'I bet she's all right. I bet you got a good one.'

Niles got into bed. He lay down and put his hands behind his neck. 'She's okay,' he said grudgingly. 'I'm not complaining.' There were soft groans of envy at this. 'Not bad, I suppose,' he went on. 'She's got nice long legs.'

'What's her name?'

'Alison.'

'Oh Alison, Alison.' People tried out the name on their tongues as if it were a foreign word.

'Tits?' Fillery asked.

'You filthy bugger,' Niles said. 'Trust bloody Fillery.' But Niles felt the lie rise unprompted in his throat. 'They're nice if you must know,' he said. 'Average size. Sort of pointy, if you know what I mean.' There was a chorus of groans at this, deep and despairing. Someone jiggled furiously up and down on his bed causing the springs to creak and complain.

'Shut up,' Niles hissed angrily. 'That's your lot. Now get to sleep.'

He saw Alison at the next rehearsal a week later. Already people had paired off, Helen and Joyce making straight for Holland and Panton at the first break.

'Fifteen minutes, ladies and gentlemen,' Prothero called.

Niles wandered over to Alison. Again he was impressed by her mature looks.

'Hi there,' he said, as casually as he could.

'Oh . . . hello.' She smiled. 'It's, um, Quentin, isn't it?'

Niles hated his name. ''Fraid so,' he said.

'Phew,' she said. 'Any chance of us having a quiet smoke somewhere?'

They picked their way through the small wood at the back of the chapel. It had rained heavily that morning and the stark trunks of the beech and ash trees were wet and shiny. Alison puffed aggressively at her cigarette. Niles had declined again. He turned up the collar of his blazer and remarked on the inclemency of the season. Alison looked suspiciously at him, as if he were making a joke. Her hair was mid-brown and her skin was very white. She had a thin mouth but her lips were well formed, there was a deep and pronounced dip to her cupid's bow. Niles found this detail endearing, as if somehow this validated his choice of her. His heart seemed to swell with emotion. Their elbows touched as the path narrowed. Niles checked his watch.

'Better not go too far,' he said, then paused before adding, 'they might get suspicious . . .'

'Sure,' Alison said, flicking her cigarette away. 'Smoking like a chimney. I've got Highers in a few months.'

'Mmmm,' Niles sympathized. 'I've got my A's,' he said. 'Then Oxbridge.'

'Are you going to Oxford?' Alison asked. She had a mild Scottish accent, she pronounced the 'r' in Oxford.

'Yes,' he said. 'Well, that's the general idea.' He wondered why he'd lied.

'I'm going to Aberdeen,' she said.

'Ah.'

They walked slowly back to the music room. They were the last to arrive. Holland and Panton looked up admiringly at him as he regained his seat.

'Quent,' Holland whispered. 'You bloody sex-maniac.'

'Shagger,' Panton accused. 'Bloody old shagger, Quent.'

'Quiet please,' Prothero called. 'If you're quite ready, Niles. Now can we have the ensemble? Jolly tars, female relatives and Josephine: "oh joy oh rapture unforeseen, for now the sky is all serene," right? Two, three.'

'What happened next?' Fillery prompted.

Niles lay in bed. He could sense the entire dormitory waiting in quiet expectancy. Hands on their cocks, he thought.

'We went round the back of the chapel,' he continued. 'Walked into the wood a bit. We sat down on a log. Chatted a bit . . . I could feel the atmosphere between us just building up. We were talking about work, but not talking about it, if you know what I mean. It was more just something to say.'

'Who made the first move?' Fillery asked.

'I did of course. I was talking. Then I stopped, and looked up. She was looking at me . . . in that sort of way.'

'Oh God.'

'She was looking at me, as if to say . . . and we just sort of moved close together and kissed.'

There was a pause.

'Get your tongue down?'

'*Jesus*, Fillery. One track bloody mind . . . Yeah, yeah, if you must know every detail. Not at first – the third or fourth kiss. But it got pretty passionate. Frenching just about all the time.'

'Stop it! Stop it!' somebody called. 'I can't stand it any more.'

'What else happened,' Fillery implored. 'Did you . . . you know?'

'We kissed mainly. Hell, we didn't have much time. She was just sort of running her hand through my hair. I got a bit of a feel but not much. I'll have to wait until next week.'

Fillery was quiet. 'God you bastard, Niles,' he said. 'You lucky bastard.'

On Saturday, after lunch, Holland and Panton bicycled the three miles to the coast. Helen's family kept a caravan on the caravan site by the beach. Helen and Joyce had arranged to meet the boys there. Niles was playing in a first XV rugby match. He heard all about their exploits later in the afternoon. He was in his study changing out of his rugby kit – the school had lost and he thought he'd pulled a muscle in his thigh – when Holland and Panton burst in.

'Oh my God, Quent,' Holland crowed. 'I don't believe it. It was incredible. They had booze too. I'm pissed.' He held up his middle finger. 'Sticky finger, Quent. First time.'

Niles plucked at his laces. An irrational hatred and resentment for Holland and Panton festered inside him. Holland he didn't mind. Pete was screwing all the time by all accounts. But Panton? He was short-arsed and had spots. Why should he have any luck?

'Get your rocks off then?' he asked without looking up.

'Not this time. They wouldn't let us. But, my God, Nilo, we could, you know, we could. We've got to fix something up.'

Niles felt a vast relief. Just feel-ups then. Big bloody deal.

'Here,' Holland said. 'Almost forgot. A message from Alison. Wey-hey!' With a flourish he handed over a lilac envelope. Niles felt his throat contract. He opened it carefully.

'Any clippings?' Holland asked with a snigger.

'Hardly,' Niles said. Holland had a French girlfriend who used to send him cuttings of her pubic hair. They were cherished and passed round like sacred relics. This fact had single-handedly boosted Holland's reputation to near-legendary heights.

'Dear Quentin,' Niles read. 'I was wondering if by any chance you would like to come and have tea tomorrow (Sunday). I realize this is short notice but if I don't hear from you I'll expect you at four. I hope you can make it. Sincerely, Alison.'

Niles felt his pulled muscle twitch spasmodically in his thigh. 'I hope you can make it.' That was good. But 'sincerely'? really!

'What is it, for Christ's sake?' Panton asked.

'Tea,' Niles said. 'Tomorrow afternoon.'

Holland shook his head admiringly. 'You got it made, Quent boy. You are home and dry . . . We must get something fixed up though.

For all of us. After the last performance maybe. Jesus, the bloody show's over in a couple of weeks.'

Alison's house was a grey sandstone bungalow at the better end of the small Scottish county town near the school. Niles cycled the six miles there through a fine rainy mist and arrived damp and chilled. He met Alison's parents – Mr and Mrs McCullen – and her fourteen-year-old sister Diane. They sat in a warm immaculate sitting room and ate scones and pancakes. The family were kind and genial and Niles relaxed almost immediately and made them laugh with anecdotes of school life. He was a great success with Diane. Alison sat quietly for most of the time, occasionally passing round plates or pouring out more tea. She was wearing jeans and a tight pale blue sweater that gave her a firm breasty look. It was the first time he'd seen her out of uniform and the first time he'd seen her with her hair down. It was long and wavy, dull and thick. It made her look less severe. He felt buoyant with lust and desire, as if he were over-inflated, as if his lungs were crammed with extra capacity of air. He had a sherry before remounting his bike for the long ride back. He reached the school in time for supper.

'I undressed her very slowly,' he told the dormitory. 'As if she was, sort of fragile, or very weak. I unfastened her bra and I kissed her breasts gently. Then . . . then I pulled down her pants and I told her to stand there while I looked at her. She was very slim. Her breasts were firm with almost perfectly round nipples . . .' He swallowed, gazing up unblinkingly at the ceiling as he elaborated his fiction. Even Fillery was silent. 'Then I undressed and we got into bed. I ran my hands all over her body. I wanted to make love but, well, we couldn't because I . . . I didn't have a johnny.'

'I've got dozens,' Fillery said. 'If you'd only asked me.'

'How was I meant to know it would happen?' Niles protested. 'That her parents weren't going to be in? I thought it was just an invitation for tea, God's sake.'

Niles, Holland and Panton stood at the back of the assembly hall. They were wearing cadet force naval bell-bottoms rolled up to mid calf, singlets and red-spotted neckerchiefs. In front of the stage Prothero was trying to get the school orchestra into tune. On stage Mr Mulcaster, the art teacher, was applying final touches to his backdrop depicting the poop deck of HMS *Pinafore*. Mulcaster's initials were T. A. M., Thomas Anthony Mulcaster. He was known as Tampax Tony.

'Christ almighty, look at Tampax,' Panton said scornfully. 'It's pathetic. I think he's actually painting in a seagull.'

'Ah, now that's an original touch,' Holland confessed. 'Almost as good as rigging and halliards.'

'A seagull,' Niles said. 'What's it supposed to be doing? Hovering in one spot for the entire course of the play?'

'Oh no. He's painting in a ship on the horizon. A three master me hearties, ar.'

'We've got to work something out,' Holland said seriously. 'We must have something arranged for after the cast party. Think of something for Christ's sake.'

'I've already told you,' Panton said. 'It's got to be the squash courts. They're ideal.'

'Not a chance, mate,' Niles said. 'Do you know what would happen to me if we got caught?'

'Yes. You'd lose your squash colours.' Panton said with heavy sarcasm.

'Jesus, Nilo,' Holland pleaded. 'You're captain of squash. You've got the keys. We can lock the doors behind us. No one'll know.'

'It's all very well for you. I'll get the bloody boot.'

'Come on, Quentin. Think of the orgy we can have. I've got blankets, booze. Look, I promised the girls we'd have a party. They're expecting one. We haven't got much time. It'll all be over after Saturday night. Gone. Finished.'

Niles was pondering Holland's use of the word 'orgy'.

'Okay,' he said. 'I'll think about it. But I'm not promising anything, mind.'

Alison wore a long flouncy dress, that looked as if it were made out of mattress ticking, and a bonnet. Niles stood beside her in the wings. He could hear the audience taking their seats.

'Like the costume,' he said. 'Nervous?'

Alison cocked her head. 'No, I don't think I am actually.' Niles looked more closely at her. She grew daily more inscrutable. They had seen more of each other during the final run-up to the play but he felt that the bizarre intimacy of their first encounter had never been approached. The prospect of inviting her to the party seemed an awesome task.

'Listen,' he began. 'Some of us are having a little "do" after the cast party on Saturday night. Wondered if you'd fancy coming. You know, select little gathering.'

'Saturday night? After the cast party? Yes, okay.'

'And I want you lot to think about me this time tomorrow night,' Niles told his cowed and quiescent dormitory, 'because,' he paused, exultation setting up a tremor in his voice, 'because this time tomorrow night I shall be making love. Got that? Making love to a real girl.'

Niles gazed transfixed across the stage at Alison. The final performance of *HMS Pinafore* was almost over. Mr Booth, the physics master, as Captain Corcoran sang to Buttercup – a pre-pubescent boy called Martin – that wherever she might go he would never be untrue to her.

'What, never?' Niles and Alison and the company wanted to know.

'No, never,' asserted Captain Corcoran.

'What . . . *never?*' the cast repeated.

'Well . . .' ad-libbed the Captain. 'Hardly ever.'

'Hardly ever be untrue to thee-ee-ee. . .' the cast echoed at full volume.

'I mean, be honest,' Holland said to assorted members of the cast. 'It's pretty bloody really. I mean, how these people turn up year in year out and pay good money to see that crap I'll never know.' He ate some more of his cream bun and put his arm round Helen. 'Ah. Quentin old son,' he said as Niles came into the dressing room with a paper cup of Coke for Alison. 'A word in your ear.' Niles came over. 'I think we can make our move now. Discreetly though. See you outside the squash courts in five minutes.'

'Be careful,' Niles said to Alison. He held her arm supportively. 'Watch out for these paving stones.' Alison's high heels seemed to ring out with unpropitious clarity as they walked across the courtyard to the squash courts. It was cold and dark and their breath hung in the air long enough for them to walk through the thin clouds before they dispersed. Alison's hair was down and Niles thought she had never looked so beautiful. Her proximity to him and the thought of what was waiting suddenly seemed to make the simple act of walking hideously complicated. He felt as if a sob were lodged in the back of his throat ready to spring from his mouth at any moment.

'I'm okay,' Alison said, and he released her arm.

Holland and Panton were already there with Helen and Joyce.

'At last,' Holland said. 'What've you two been up to? Couldn't wait, eh?' Everyone giggled. Niles bent his head more than he needed to unlock the door into the squash courts.

Inside number three court they spread rugs on the boards and sat in a circle round a solitary candle placed in a jam jar. Holland unpacked the picnic. There was some Gouda and Ryvita, a piece of Stilton, slices of salami, gherkins and two long, knobbled Polish sausages. From his coat pockets Panton produced a bottle of South African sherry and half a bottle of gin. Paper cups were distributed and the drinks passed around.

Niles drank some neat gin. 'To Gilbert and Sullivan,' he toasted the company.

'Ssh,' Holland said. 'Keep it down, Quentin. Your voice I mean.' There were sniggers at this. Niles didn't dare look at Alison's shadowy face.

They ate their meal with a certain urgent decorum, conscious of the fact that it had to be got out of the way – but in no unseemly rush – before the night's real business could commence. Eventually, after a pre-arranged nod from Holland, Panton said, 'Quiet. I think I can hear someone outside.' Then he leant forward and blew out the candle. This act was followed by a muffled squeal from Joyce and a flurry of whispered instructions, scuffles and collisions as Holland and Panton, Joyce and Helen, gathered up rugs and paper cups and groped their way out of the door to their respective squash courts, leaving number three to Alison and Niles.

Niles sat in a darkness so total it seemed solid and shifting, like deep water. He realized he was holding his breath and let it out slowly. He peered intensely in front of him, a screen of blasting mental supernova and arcing tracer bullets exploding before his eyes, brightening the absence of vision. Only the unyielding firmness of the court floor beneath his buttocks anchored him to the dimensional world.

He heard Alison move. How close was she?

'Are you all right?' he whispered. He stretched out his hand, encountering nothing.

'Yes,' she said. 'Is there anyone?'

'I don't think so. False alarm. Just Panton panicking.' His hand touched her shoulder. 'Sorry. Can't see a thing.'

'I'm here.'

'Oh.' The darkness began to retreat. He sensed rather than saw Alison. He moved across the rug, closer to her.

'Bloody dark.'

'Yes.'

He moved his head towards hers, gently, almost blindly, like two docking space craft. After some soft bumps and readjustments, their lips connected tenuously, then sealed. Niles felt his heart swell to inflate his chest as he felt her thin cool lips beneath his. This was the fifth girl he had kissed properly. It remained as thrilling and exciting as the first time. He wondered if he would always feel this way. With little grunts and discreet pressures he managed to lie Alison down on the rug. Her long hair caught across his face, strands filling his mouth which he had to pull free with his fingers. They kissed again. Niles felt enormously humble and reverential. The accumulated sensations of triumph and release in a kiss were almost enough for him really, but he promptly banished such heretical thoughts from his mind. He managed to get both his arms round Alison and he felt her hands move on his back. His head was resting comfortably on his own left shoulder, Alison's head nestled in the crook of his left elbow. Their knees were touching, her face was perhaps three inches away from his. Some faint source of light picked out a curve on a cheekbone, a glimmer in an eye. The warm breath of her exhalations grazed his cheek. What should he do now, he wondered? Had he much time? What would she like him to do? What was she expecting? Perhaps she wanted to make love too? The novelty of this last idea came to him as rather a shock. He felt suddenly vulnerable and insecure: he sensed the alien presence of her feminity descend on and enfold him. He became immediately aware of his vast ignorance about Alison – the person, the girl – separating him ineluctably from her. Despite the fact that they were lying in each other's arms they might have been facing each other across some great river estuary. The figure on the far bank was a girl's, yes, but that was all he knew.

He felt a gentle shaking. He woke up with a start. His eyes were open but he saw nothing. He sat up. His left arm was dead. It flopped lifelessly at his side.

'You've been asleep,' Alison said. 'I've got to go.'

'What?'

'It's just gone eleven. I've got to get the last bus.'

'Jesus. Asleep? You mean I . . . How long was . . .?'

'You just drifted off. You've been sleeping about half an hour. I didn't want to wake you.'

Niles felt shame and disgrace cause tears to prickle at the corner of his eyes. He picked up his left hand and started to massage it. In the darkness it was like holding an amputated limb. To his right hand his nerveless left felt rough and calloused, like a stranger's.

'Can you find the door?'

They went outside. Alison wondered about the remains of the picnic. Niles told her he'd clean up in the morning before anyone came.

He was about to lock the door. 'What about the others?' he asked, fighting to keep the bitterness from his voice.

'They left about ten minutes ago. I heard them going.'

Niles locked the squash court door. He gazed bleakly around him. Alison stood patiently, knotting her scarf at her throat. It was a sharp. frosty night. The school buildings loomed on either side, dark and unpeopled.

'I'd better go, Quentin,' Alison said.

'I'll come with you to the bus stop.'

They set out together, Niles looking nervously back over his shoulder. He was taking a calculated risk. The bus stop lay half a mile beyond the school gates. If he was caught out of bounds with a girl at this time of night he would be in serious trouble. But equally he felt that whatever happened nothing should prevent him from being with Alison at this moment. They walked on in silence. Niles' mind was a tangle of conflicting emotions. Sentences formed in his head only to split into whirling separate words like some modish animated film. He felt he should say something, explain that he hadn't meant to fall asleep, allude to his romantic plans, but his tongue and his mind refused to co-ordinate. His brain seemed to lock into an imbecilic stupidity. He couldn't do anything right.

At the school gates he let Alison stride confidently through and go a little way down the road before he snaked beneath the lodge windows, squirmed through the side gate and made a sequence of zig-zag dashes from bush to tree trunk, like a commando behind enemy lines, before he caught up with her.

Alison stood in the middle of the road waiting for him. 'That's a bit dramatic, isn't it?'

'I'm out of bounds, you see. If I get caught. . .'

'I don't want you to get into trouble, Quentin.'

'Forget it, really. I don't care.' He took her hand. There was a small shelter by the bus stop . . . 'Come on, let's go.' They walked briskly down the road.

The shelter was empty. A nearby street light threw the graffiti carved on its green wooden bench into high relief. Small drifts of cigarette packs, soft drink cans and wrappers were banked beneath it.

'Alison,' Niles began. 'Listen. I have to say this, I don't want you to think that . . .'

'Here it comes,' cried Alison, as the bus appeared round the corner. 'That was lucky.'

The bus stopped. She gave him a swift kiss on the cheek, so swift it was almost a clash of heads, and got on. Niles looked at the single decker bus. Inside it was soft yellow and smoky. A couple of old women looked curiously back at him. On the rear seats some louts drank beer from cans. Alison stood at the top of the steps, her back to him, buying her ticket from the driver. Her long legs seemed twin symbols of rebuke.

'I'll phone,' he shouted, louder than he meant. It sounded like a grievance, a threat. She turned, smiled, and walked down the bus to take her seat. Niles saw her thick dark hair on her blazer, saw her head toss as she sat down. She waved. The bus drove off. He didn't wave back.

Niles walked morosely up the drive. He walked on the verge, ready to duck behind one of the beech trees that lined the road should a car come by. He stumbled over a root, stopped, turned and kicked savagely at it. In a sombre mood of reassessment he cursed his school, the closed society he was compelled to live in, his demanding, predatory, so-called friends. 'Women,' his father had once patronizingly told him, 'are a lifetime's study.' He was off to a late start then, he observed grimly, and wondered if he would ever catch up. He felt suddenly exhausted by the daily, monotonous absorption with sex, disgusted by the lonely idolatry of masturbation. He felt that his sexual nature, whatever it might be, was irretrievably corrupted.

He paused and took a few deep breaths, trying to shake the mood from him. At this point the drive curved gently to the right, back towards main school. On his left and ahead of him lay a wide flat expanse of playing fields, fixed and still under a faint starlight. His house lay in that direction. It would be quicker, but he wondered if he dared expose himself on the open space. He made up his mind. He set off, breaking into a steady jog, feeling the frost cracking under his feet, puffing his condensed breath ahead of him like a steam engine. He loped silently and strongly across the pitches. He felt that he could run for ever. He would be back in the dorm before twelve. They would all be waiting for him. Fillery had said they'd stay up specially. They wanted to know everything, Fillery had said, every little detail. The bastards, Niles said to himself, smiling. His mind began to work. He'd give them a good story tonight, all right. They wouldn't forget this one in a long time. He ran on, a strange jubilation lengthening his stride.

First Response

- Why is Niles determined to give them "a good story tonight"?

- Is he a different sort of character from the other two boys?

- What made Alison invite him to her home while the other two girls were arranging their caravan meeting?

- Why did Alison let him stay asleep?

- Do you think they will meet again?

- Has Niles learnt anything from this experience?

Looking Closely

Talk

Pair work

Look over the story together and jot down the kind of language used by the boys to describe girls. What do you notice about it? Compare your notes with another pair.

Group work

What impression have you gained of the kind of school that Niles attends? Go over the story together in groups and try to agree on a few phrases that sum up the school. Is your own school similar in any way? Would any of you wish to go to such a school?

Role play

1.   Working in threes choose either the three male or the three female main characters and improvise their conversation the next time they meet. Think about what really may have happened and what they would be likely to say happened.

2.   Imagine that one of the teachers has some idea of what has been going on and that he has definitely heard about the squash courts being used. Work out the scene in his office when he calls the three boys in to see him.

Write

1.   Continue the story for the rest of that night; what sort of tale does Niles tell? Then you might go on to write more scenes e.g. when Niles meets Holland and Panton, when Niles next sees Alison and so on.

2.   Choose a section of the story and rewrite it from Alison's point of view. As we do not know very much about her thoughts and feelings, you will have to take a close look at the story to find out what is revealed about her. Think about how she seems different from the other two girls, her confident way of smoking, how she behaves at home and so on.

3.   Imagine that Niles kept a secret diary about his life. Then write some pages for his diary during the time he was involved with Alison. You could include his thoughts and feelings about the boys at his school and the worries that he has about his own future as well as his comments on Alison.

Trying to impress

"I SENSED THAT BRENDA WAS TRYING TO IMPRESS ME....."

Talk

Much of the story is about impressing people; the boys trying to impress the girls, Niles making up stories about Alison and so on. This cartoon looks at showing off from a light-hearted point of view. How does it work? Look at the picture itself and then the caption; which one uses understatement?

Schoolboy

Before playtime let us consider the possibilities
of getting stoned on milk.

    In his dreams,
scribbling overcharged on woodbines,
mumbling obscure sentences into his desk
'No way of getting out,
no way out. . .'
           Poet dying of
too much education, schoolfriends, examinations,
canes that walk the nurseries of his wet dreams;

satchels full of chewing gum, bad jokes, pencils;
crude drawings performed in the name of art. Soon will
come the Joyful Realisation in Mary's back kitchen
          while mother's out.
All this during chemistry.

(The headmaster's crying in his study.
His old pinstripe pants rolled up to his knees
in a vain attempt to recapture youth; emotions
skid along his slippery age; Love, smeared across his face,
like a road accident.)

The schoolyard's full of people to hate.
Full of tick and prefects and a fat schoolmaster
and whistles and older and younger boys, but
he's growing
    sadly
      growing
          up.

Girls,
    becoming mysterious, are now more important
than arriving at school late or receiving trivial awards.
Postcards of those huge women
                seem a little more believable now.

(Secretly, the pale, unmarried headmaster telling him
Death is the only grammatically correct full-

                                    stop.)
Girls,
    still mysterious;
arithmetic thighed, breasts measured in thumbprints,
not inches.
Literature's just another way out.
History's full of absurd mistakes.
King Arthur if he ever existed
would only have farted and excused himself
from the Round Table in a hurry.

(The headmaster, staring through the study window
into the playground, composes evil poems about
the lyrical boy in class four)
                    'He invited us up sir,
                but not for the cane,
                    said the algebra of life
                        was too difficult to explain
                        and that all equations
                            mounted to nothing. . . .'

Growing up's wonderful if
                you keep your eyes
                        closed tightly, and
if you manage to grow
            take your soul with you,
                nobody wants it.
So,
playtime's finished with;
it's time to pull the last sad chain
                on his last
                    sadschoolgirlcrush.

It is time to fathom out too many things.
To learn he's no longer got somebody watching over him;
he's going to know strange things, learn
how to lie correctly, how to lay correctly,
how to cheat and steal in the nicest possible manner.
He will learn amongst other things, how to enjoy
his enemies, and how to avoid friendships. If he's unlucky
he will learn how to love and give everything away
and how eventually, he'll end up with nothing.

        He won't understand many things.
He'll just accept them. He'll experiment with hardboiled
        eggs all his life
and die a stranger in a race attempting Humanity.

        And finally,
the playground full of dust,
        crates of sour milk lining the corridors;
            the headmaster, weeping quietly among the saws and
                                                    chisels
            in the damp woodwork room;

        The ghosts of Tim and Maureen and Pat
        and Nancy and so many others,
        all holding sexless hands, all
                doomed to living, and
one pale boy
in a steamy room
looking outside across the roofs and chimneys
where it seems, the clouds are crying,
the daylight's gone blind
and his teachers, all dead.

BRIAN PATTEN
FROM LITTLE JOHNNY'S CONFESSION

Does the poem feel familiar to your experience of school and growing up? Are there any particular lines or ideas that you especially admire or enjoy?

<table>
<tr><td>Talk</td><td>Prepare the poem to be read aloud in a group. Look closely at the way that it is organised and divided up and work out how you can use your various voices to gain the most effect? Think about the different kinds of feeling in the poem; for example, some sections are jokey, others have a much more melancholy air. How will you create such differences?</td></tr>
</table>

Is the poem just about being at school, or is it also about what growing up means? How does the poet feel about the way we grow up? Look through the poem together and pick out the lines that deal with growing up. How do they contrast with the lines that describe life at school?

Write	1. Try writing a new version of the poem to be called 'Schoolgirl'.

2. 'School days are the ------'. Complete the sentence and then use it as the title for a poem of your own about school life.

Links with story	**Group work**

• Are there any similarities between the boys in the story and the schoolboy in the poem?

• Do they share any common attitudes and interests?

• Do you think the two writers have similar views of boys at school?

Read this poem by Eileen McAuley.

The Seduction
(A clumsy poem of teenage angst!!!)

After the party, early Sunday morning,
He led her to the quiet bricks of Birkenhead docks.
Far past the silver stream of traffic through the city,
Far from the blind windows of the tower blocks.

He sat down in the darkness, leather jacket creaking madly,
He spat into the river, fumbled in a bag.

He handed her the vodka, and she knocked it back like water,
She giggled, drunk and nervous, and he muttered 'little slag'.

She had met him at the party, and he'd danced with her all
night.

He'd told her about football; Sammy Lee and Ian Rush.
She had nodded, quite enchanted, and her eyes were wide and
bright

As he enthused about the Milk Cup, and the next McGuigan
fight.

As he brought her more drinks, so she fell in love
With his eyes as blue as iodine,
With the fingers that stroked her neck and thighs
And the kisses that tasted of nicotine.

Then: 'I'll take you to the river where I spend the afternoons,
When I should be at school, or eating me dinner.
Where I go, by meself, with me dad's magazines
And a bag filled with shimmering, sweet paint thinner.'

So she followed him there, all high white shoes,
All wide blue eyes, and bottles of vodka.
And sat in the dark, her head rolling forward
Towards the frightening scum on the water.

And talked about school, in a disjointed way:
About O levels she'd be sitting in June
She chattered on, and stared at the water,
The Mersey, green as a septic wound.

Then, when he swiftly contrived to kiss her
His kiss was scented by Listerine
And she stifled a giggle, reminded of numerous
Stories from teenage magazines. . .

When she discovered she was three months gone
She sobbed in the cool, locked darkness of her room
And she ripped up all her *My Guy* and her *Jackie* photo-comics
Until they were just bright paper, like confetti, strewn
On the carpet. And on that day, she broke the heels
Of her high white shoes (as she flung them at the wall).
And realized, for once, that she was truly truly frightened
But more than that, cheated by the promise of it all.

For where, now, was the summer of her sixteenth year?
Full of glitzy fashion features, and stories of romance?
Where a stranger could lead you to bright new worlds,
And how would you know, if you never took a chance?

Full of glossy horoscopes, and glamour with a stammer;
Full of fresh fruit diets – how did she feel betrayed?
Now, with a softly rounded belly, she was sickened every
                                                    morning

By stupid stupid promises, only tacitly made.

Where were the glossy photographs of summer,
Day trips to Blackpool, jumping all the rides?
And where, now, were the pink smiling faces in the picture:
Three girls paddling in the grey and frothy tide?

So she cried that she had missed all the innocence around her
And all the parties where you meet the boy next door,
Where you walk hand in hand, in an acne'd wonderland,
With a glass of lager-shandy, on a carpeted floor.

But, then again, better to be smoking scented drugs
Or festering, invisibly, unemployed.
Better to destroy your life in modern, man-made ways
Than to fall into this despicable, feminine void.

Better to starve yourself, like a sick, precocious child
Than to walk through town with a belly huge and ripe.
And better, now, to turn away, move away, fade away,
Than to have the neighbours whisper that 'you always looked
                                                    the type'.

EILEEN MCAULEY
FROM THE CAMBRIDGE POETRY WORKSHOP

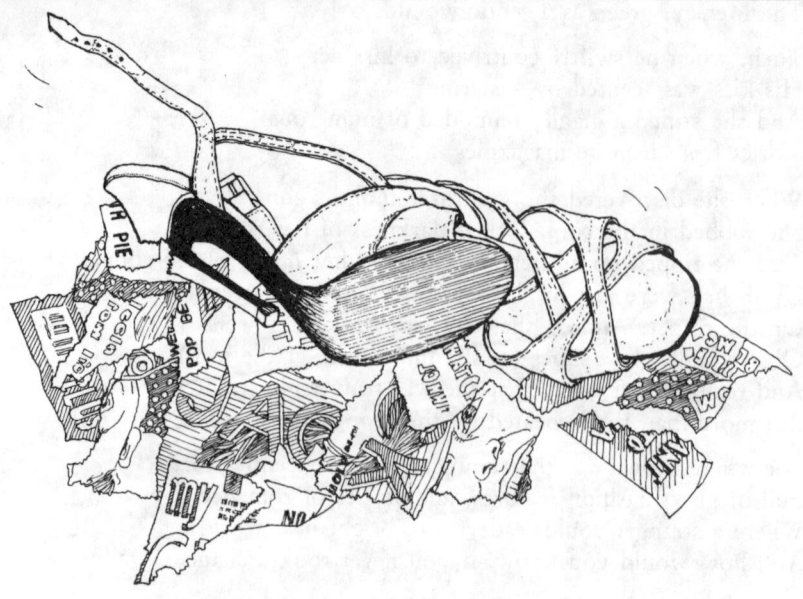

- How do you feel towards the girl?

- If she asked you for help, what would your advice to her be?

- Do you think this is a clumsy poem?

Talk

Pair work

The poem tells a particular story and has two characters. Go through it carefully in pairs and jot down what you feel you know about what happens and what kind of people the two characters are. What do you think of the boy; is he entirely to blame for what happens?

Group work

Now work in larger groups. Does the poem deal with a subject that you think is important to most young people?

Would you say that it acts as a kind of warning? If it does, who is it warning? If you were illustrating this poem, what pictures would you choose?

What makes the girl tear up her magazines and break her high heels? Do they represent anything special or important?

Do you think the title seems right?

Write

1. Rewrite the poem either as a story or as a script. Keep to the events and feelings of the poem but use your imagination too.

2. Continue the poem, either as a poem or as a story, into the summer. Concentrate on how the girl copes with her situation.

Links with story

Is there anything similar between the attitude of Holland and Panton to girls and that of the boy in the poem?

This novel is about four women who meet on a training course for salespeople. It goes on to tell their different stories, in particular how their personal lives have affected their professional lives.

Closing

'I'm so jealous,' said Oliver, 'that I want to spit.'

'Why?'

'Going back to school and socking it to them.'

'I'm not going to sock anything to anybody. I'm just going to tell them that industry is fun and their country needs them. Never mind darling – ' she had started calling him darling. 'Your day will come.'

'Me? My school hated me. My face didn't fit. It was a tradition that everyone in the sixth form was made a prefect. It didn't mean much but it looked good on the UCCA forms. My year they made an exception. "This particular poacher cannot be trusted to turn gamekeeper." They actually said that.'

'Why is it,' Gina wondered aloud, 'that men always boast about how bad they were at school?'

'And women always boast about how good they were? Different schools, in our case. Very different.'

'All right, so I went to a good school. Doesn't mean I liked it.'

'Don't give me that. I bet your name's up there in gold.'

It would be. It would be fun to see it.

She spent a long time deciding what to wear for the careers evening. The girls would be watchful and critical. She had a dim memory of hats and gloves . . . but that must have been speech day, surely . . . for a careers evening a speaker must look businesslike. She decided to splash out, buy the outfit that she would eventually wear for her interview at Stalton's, and break it in at the careers evening. She bought a smart purple-and-black patterned skirt with a co-ordinated jacket and a silky blouse with a tie neck. In for a penny, she finished herself off with a printed leather bag and new shoes.

'Now you're not to say anything awful,' she warned Oliver.

'Any suggestions?'

What she meant was that she did not want him to say anything that would lead the nuns to realize that she was having sex before marriage. She wondered if they knew that their old girls did.

'You look wonderful,' he said. 'They'll all get crushes on you, like me, and besiege the labs. Hey, you're nervous. Why are you nervous?'

'I want to be – ' she hunted for the word ' – dignified.'

'You will be dignified. You're the most dignified person I know.'

'I just think – when I get there – I won't be grown-up any more.'

They reached the school half an hour early and were shown, by an unknown and deferential nun, into a reception parlour which Gina had never seen before. The carpet was thick and soft, and on the wall there was an Old Master with a religious theme. Gina could hear nuns moving around outside the room, the soft, familiar swish of their robes and the rattling of beads.

Oliver was eyeing the furniture. 'This must be worth a few quid. I thought they took a vow of poverty.'

Gina said irritably, 'People say such obvious things about nuns.'

'No one asked them to be nuns. But what's the point in being a nun if you're going to live in the lap of luxury?'

'You'll be saying next, what's the point in sending people to prison if you let them have tobacco and televisions? You sound like a Tory lady –'

'You would know,' said Oliver.

'They can't leave,' said Gina. 'Well, not without a great fuss.'

'What's stopping them?'

'Something in themselves. They've made a promise. It's nothing to laugh at. Listen, that's Sister Brede.'

'I can't hear anyone.'

Sister Brede's approach had a unique sound, for she always carried the keys to the science labs, bashing against her crucifix as she walked. She looked just the same, she had not aged. She embraced Gina and kissed both her cheeks, which Gina found very moving. She shook Oliver by the hand.

'Your fiancé, Gina! I didn't know.'

'I only asked her recently, Sister,' said Oliver. Gina wanted to hug him. She had instructed him in etiquette. Always say *Sister* at the end of sentences, and if you say *Jesus* bow your head. *Why should I say Jesus?* he had replied. 'I've just been admiring your furniture, Sister.'

'Thank you. This cabinet is particularly beautiful, isn't it?'

Quite right, thought Gina. *Don't justify it by saying it was a bequest, or it's just for visitors.* Sister Brede must be magnificent in confession. *Here I am, Father,* she would say: *and here is what I've done.*

A tray was brought in with a decanter and seven glasses. The other two speakers – a local government official whom Gina recognized but hardly knew, being three years her junior, and a publisher friend of the school – arrived with their partners and they all stood about drinking sherry. *Sociologists*, thought Gina mischievously.

The publisher's wife lit a cigarette, and Sister Brede fetched an ashtray without comment, so Gina and Oliver lit up too. Sister Brede explained between sips at her sherry that each speaker would have ten minutes and then there would be time for questions from the audience of fifth and sixth formers and their parents. When the little party left the parlour, Gina felt completely grown-up.

She was not ready, though, for what met her eyes when she entered the school hall: the impossibility of telling which of the women in front of her were really girls and which their mothers. The mothers looked so young, but they must have been at least ten years older than Gina to have daughters of this maturity. Gina wished the daughters had been told to wear their uniforms.

The mood of the evening was subdued, even depressed. The two speakers who went before Gina had little for the comfort of their audience. What they said was, in essence, the same. If anyone had an ambition to go into local government or publishing, she could shorten the odds against herself by starting to prepare now (taking an interest in politics; reading widely outside her exam subjects) but her best plan was to consider alternatives, because she would probably not get in, all vacancies being, in the experience of the speakers, heavily oversubscribed.

Understanding now why Sister Brede had kept her for last, Gina rose to her feet. 'Industry is crying out,' she said, 'for scientifically qualified people. With a degree in science, computer studies, technology or engineering – or even with A levels – you will find a wide range of jobs open to you. You may find that you don't have to apply for them. They will apply for you!'

She saw Oliver smiling encouragement from the front row. No one else was smiling, though, and her heart failed her: had that remark been too boastful? She moved on hastily to talk about road surfacing, a subject upon which she had been working to make herself an authority. 'However we came here this evening – by car, by public transport or on foot – we took it for granted, didn't we, that the road we used would bear our weight and the weight of our vehicle. And so we should – and so it did – but it didn't happen by chance. The purpose of scientific advance is to make life easier for all of us, including those who think they aren't interested in science.

'I'm here to offer you the challenge of getting interested; the challenge of contributing to the industries that give you your cars, your clothes, your cold-cures . . . and the skid-resistant surfaces on your roads.'

As Gina spoke, she wished she had three eyes: one for her notes, one for her watch (the other speakers had not overrun, so she must not either) and one for her audience. She had read somewhere that the secret of public speaking was to forget about speaking to a roomful of people, to single out one person and speak to them. Gina was looking for two people. She was looking for a girl who, like her younger self, was already awed and fascinated by her growing knowledge of what could be done with the earth's gifts, oil and gas and minerals; and another who, until this moment, had been a sociologist, but who, fired by Gina's enthusiasm, would go tomorrow to Sister Brede and ask to change subjects.

Time was getting on and she did not want to be remembered solely as the person who had told her audience everything they ever wanted to know about bitumen binders, so she moved her eyes to her next key word which, underlined in fluorescent yellow, was 'UNFEMININE?' If girls had anxieties on that score, there was no point in ignoring or despising them; far better to meet them head on, to instance herself and the happy state of both her personal life and her professional life as proof that girls today could have everything they wanted, if they just wanted it enough. But something made her hesitate. To have her speak so personally might embarrass Oliver. It might embarrass everybody, herself included. The local government officer had explained briefly about working part-time for a while to accommodate the needs of her children; the publisher had not mentioned personal or domestic matters at all. Gina decided to follow his example.

'Modern industry employs the best man or woman for the job. It cannot afford to do otherwise.' Let these girls form their own conclusions from her appearance and manner, the diamond on her finger, the glow in her eyes.

There were no questions. Sister Brede, from the chair, seemed embarrassed about this and Gina guessed that the girls would be in for a contemptuous scolding in the morning, for their spinelessness. But when Gina and Oliver were getting ready to leave a rather truculent man came over. 'I've got a question.'

A girl called from the door. 'Come on, Dad. We're going.'

'That's Felicity, my eldest. We've got twins at home. Sylvia and Stanley, they're seven. We've always treated them exactly the same, my wife's like you, she's very hot on that. Whatever one's had, the other's had. They're seven now –'

Annoyed at the man's aggressive attitude, Oliver said, 'You mentioned that.'

'Seven, they are, and Sylvia's interested in dolls and helping her mother and Stan likes machines. If an aeroplane goes over, he looks up and wants to know all about it, she couldn't care less. What does that say to you?'

Gina said, 'I don't know.'

'Don't think about it, do you? None of you do.' He stumped off triumphantly.

Gina was bewildered. 'What was all that about? I'm not interested in making girls do science if they don't want to.'

'If we have children,' said Oliver, 'they'll do exactly what they want.'

'Right. What do you mean, if? Don't you want to have children?'

'Not yet.'

'Of course not yet,' she said. 'But –'

'In about five years,' he said.

'You've got it all worked out, then?'

'You'll be thirty. Lots of women have their first pregnancy when they're thirty.' Sister Brede was coming over to say goodbye and thank you. Gina trod on Oliver's toe. 'Change the subject,' she whispered.

ZOE FAIRBAIRNS
FROM CLOSING

- What point do you think Gina wants to make to her audience during the careers evening?

- Why does she take such care over her appearance?

- Did she look forward to going back to her old school?

- Why do you think the parent of the twins came to speak to Gina before he left?

Talk

Group work

Gina gives her talk at her old, all girls' school. Obviously she is a success in her job and has been invited to impress her audience. In groups, discuss whether you think that girls and boys could do better if taught separately, either at single sex schools or in single sex classes? Do boys try to dominate some subjects and girls others? Is working in the presence of the opposite sex a bad thing which distracts you from learning or is it a good thing which prepares you for adult life?

The group could present its conclusions as a short speech in support of single or mixed education.

Role play

What would Gina and Oliver say to each other on the way home? Improvise their conversation.

Write

1.   Imagine that in ten years' time you are asked to go back to your present school because you have been successful in your job. Describe the evening and the speech you would give.

2.   Does your school offer equal opportunities to everyone regardless of sex, colour and so on? Either write an essay about your school and its efforts in this area or prepare a speech to make to the school governors in which you suggest what they might do to improve things.

Links with story

Do you think Niles will look back on his school with affection as Gina does? Is he the sort of pupil that they might want to ask back in the future?

The China Set

FARRUKH DHONDY

My nan is much wiser than my dad. He says she's so smart she can imagine a stick with only one end. Not that my dad's stupid, he must be quite smart 'to make up a thing like that, but he doesn't take time to think as he's always telling us to do. He's a postman. Sometimes he says he should have stayed in India and become a goldsmith like his father and his grandfather. It makes you feel rich playing with other people's gold, he says, but the gold ran out or something and he had to leave Bombay and come to England and send money back to keep his brothers and sisters.

He's lovely, my dad, though I think I love my nan best. She only came to live with us last year and she still doesn't speak a word of English. She gets along though, goes down to the shops by herself, a little old Indian lady in a *sari*, not even the sort Mum wears, but black or brown because her husband's dead, and tied round in the old fashioned way with the loose flap coming over her shoulder from back to front. She travels by bus and tube all over London, and my brother and I teach her to say 'I'm a senior citizen' instead of 'No English, no speaking' like she does, and to say 'Sorry, I don't speak English so please speak to me in Gujerati or Hindi'. My brother taught her that, though I think it's silly because if she really did go around saying that, they'd think she was daft.

She's only been in London for a year, and she never complains about the cold or anything like that. She says, 'Where my grandchildren are, there I want to be, their faces make the sun shine,' and funny rot like that. She's always telling us stories about when she was a girl in India. We've given her a room on her own, the back room on the first floor of our house in Ealing, just near where the BBC studios are.

Anyway, this story really starts with a song. No, it starts with this boy in school – I might as well be frank since I'm writing this down, and I don't care if Dad or Mum gets to see it. The boy's name is Ralph and his dad's an actor. If you've seen the play *Canterbury Tales* in the West End, or on telly, then you've seen his dad, because he's in it. Ralph's very sweet. I'm the only Indian girl in our class at school, and even though all of them are very friendly, Ralph is the only boy who ever talks to me seriously. He once asked me if I was going to get married to an Indian boy, somebody my dad chose for me. I said maybe I will, but that the ideas in my family are changing, that we are really not superstitious or anything like that.

'Why does your dad get so jumpy every time I come round? He puts on a face like I was going to rape you or something.'

Until two weeks ago he used to be going with this girl called Andre. She's also in our class at Goldhawk Comprehensive. (The boys always call it Colditz Comprehensive.) Andre was his girl, but he used to still sit next to me in class and make her jealous and behave as though he didn't notice that she was staring. If the teachers don't have enough texts and we're sharing books, he always gets one between us and touches my hand when he turns the pages. She's always watching, Andre, but pretending that she's not. He calls me Minihaha because he says I'm small, Indian and funny.

Ralph's going to be an actor. He always gets the highest marks in English and takes over the drama class whenever he's feeling like it. He's clever. He can play the guitar and I think he tries to look like a pop star, with shaded glasses and a sort of smart haircut, long at the back and short on top. He brings the best records to school, not all that reggae rubbish and Donny Osmond and Slade. He listens to David Bowie and the Rolling Stones and all sorts of new groups that no one's ever heard of. He says he's learning to play the sitar from the lead guitarist of a group he's going to join.

One day, about a week ago, he said he wanted to listen to some Hindi pop and I said my dad's only got film songs and he gets them straight from India so he won't let them out of his sight. 'In that case I'll have to listen to them up your house, won't I?' he said.

To tell you the truth, I was very glad he said that, and I told him I'd tell him when he could come because my dad had to be got in the right mood. If Ralph came too often he'd start getting ideas and making a fuss.

I talk to my nan about my friends, so I told her about Ralph and she asked if he was from a good family and whether I liked him. I said that I did like him a little, and there weren't any good or bad families in Britain, they were all the same. She said that that could never be, there was always a difference between gold and lead and the older you get the better you could tell.

My dad has the same sort of ideas. You can't blame him because he must have got them from her. He lectures us on and on about such things. When we went to pick up Nan from the airport, he was saying he hadn't lost respect for his own dad, even though he was dead. My brother's quite cheeky and he said, 'Neither did Hamlet,' but my dad doesn't understand about Shakespeare so the joke was no good on him.

Dad always says that English people put their parents in old people's homes because they have no shame, but we Indians know how to look after our own. Sometimes when he talks that way I like it, it makes me feel different and also better than the rest, because it's true I suppose, they don't have any old folk's homes in India. But there are beggars and hungry people all about the streets and when I point that out my dad says it's true, but what can one do, there are rich and poor everywhere and poor people may be starving but they have good hearts.

'Can't pay the rent with good hearts,' my brother says.

When Dad speaks like this it frightens me too, because I don't really know anything about India. Since I was four I've lived in London and now that I'm fifteen I often think of going to India. My mother always says we're going next year, but Dad says there's not enough money saved and next year never comes. If I start earning my own money I'll save up and go, just for a visit.

The day Ralph came Dad was on the evening shift. Ralph turned up, as always with books and LPs in his hand. We sat in the front room where the record player was and where Mum could have kept an eye on us while she cooked next door in the kitchen. Ralph had been there a few times and he always sat politely, not like at school where he sprawls out on the desks and sits with his trousers pulled to his shins, cross-legged on the cement flower pots in the school playground.

Nan was in the house when he arrived, and Mum had just nipped out to the launderette with two loads. Nan came and sat in the front room with us while we played the discs and talked in English. I kept watching the door for Dad, knowing it wouldn't really matter, if Nan was in the same room. She wanted to know why Ralph wore a necklace – he had a chain and pendant, the sort you buy for a few bob in Shepherds Bush Market. She wanted to know if he was a prince of some sort, or whether he was a dancer. I translated for her and Ralph said that he was the Prince of Darkness, but Nan didn't get the joke and said he was so white, he shouldn't say that about himself.

After we played through some of Dad's LPs, Ralph wanted to put on his own and asked if it was all right. 'There are Indian bells on this one, remind you of the cows tinkling home in the sunset, listen,' he said.

Now I don't listen much to pop, but I was relieved that Dad wouldn't come home to find us playing with his records. So Ralph put on the Stones and we listened. We sat through it and talked. Then he said, 'What about all the old Indian hospitality then, you haven't even offered me a bleeding cup of tea?'

I wished he hadn't said that, because I didn't want to ask Nan to make it and if Mum had been there it would have been all right, but according to Hindu custom you only serve up tea to a young man when your dad has brought him home to look you over as a marriage proposition. I said to Nan that there were cokes in the fridge and she got the hint and perhaps she understood that it was awkward for me so she went and got them herself, and she did a very sweet thing, she brought them on a tray with a can-opener. Ralph said it was a good idea and began to open the can with the can-opener and I split myself laughing because Nan didn't understand what she'd done wrong. She began talking to Ralph in Gujerati as though he understood every word and he just smiled at her.

'Hey, listen to this one,' Ralph said as one song came to an end and another started. 'Are you sure your nan doesn't understand English?'

I didn't know it was going to be a rude song. Personally, I don't think there's anything rude about that song or any other. It's about this girl who likes going out with pop stars and film stars, and I think girls dream about that, at least lots of them in our school do, but this song puts it in a slightly different way. I might as well be frank and say what the song actually says. The words are something about 'star-fucker, star-fucker, star-fucker, star . . .' and about missing her two-tongued kisses and wrapping his legs round her thigh, and making her scream all night. We listen to that sort of thing every day in school and there are much worse songs on the radio which have two meanings, like the one about 'my ding-a-ling', which is not really about a bell at all. Even so, I knew that my dad would feel that this was his house and no filth should be brought into it.

I was going to say that to Ralph. I could see from his face that he wanted to see how far he could go with me, he had that sort of defiance, pretending that he was listening to just some old love song. But it was too late. Dad came in taking his grey jacket off, and Ralph said,

'Hello, Mr Desai.'

Dad grunted and he went into the kitchen, asking Nan for the house keys which she kept tied to her *sari*, in a big bunch on her waist. When she first came from India, Dad made a big thing about it and handed them all over to her, saying that she was the boss of the house. He was just going upstairs when he stopped in the doorway and turned round with lines on his brow, crumpled like crushed paper. It was as though someone had said, 'stick 'em up' from behind and he didn't quite understand. He was standing in the door, his body half going out and half coming back, listening to the words that came out of the loudspeakers. I knew he was too shy to say anything in front of Ralph. Still, there was a silence and Nan pushed her way into it, speaking to him about the letters she had to write to India and saying that Mum had the one from her youngest son, Dad's brother, and he could see it when she came back from the launderette. The record was saying something about 'giving it to Steve McQueen' when Dad decided to leave it and went upstairs.

'Can we put something else on?' I asked Ralph. He changed the record and as he looked round at me he grinned slyly, as though he knew that he'd done some mischief and that the thunder behind Dad's frown would soon come crashing down. He finished his can of coke and said he was going straight to his evening job.

'I'll leave the records for you, you can bring them to school tomorrow,' he said.

'Why don't you take them with you? I might forget,' I said. I wanted him to get them out of the house, but I also wanted him to leave them so I could show the others in class that Ralph had been at my house when I took them back. I felt that he wanted to show them, and Andre, that too.

'No, bring 'em in tomorrow. I can't take them to work, they'll most likely get nicked.'

When Ralph had left I wanted to know what sort of a mood Dad was in so I went up to his room and he was sitting on the bed, still looking angry.

'I'm going to help Mum down the launderette,' I said.

'What kind of boys do you bring into my house?' he asked.

'Oh Dad, don't be so sticky, there aren't any other kind of boys, at least not at our school, and Ralph is best at work, he gets top marks all the time, and you're always telling me to make friends with the top ten.'

Dad didn't reply, he just made a face.

When I came back with loads of washing, the records were still on the player, so I picked them up, intending to take them to the room I shared with Lekha, my sister. I went through the records and found that the Rolling Stones one was missing. I shouted all round the house, but nobody could tell me where it was. I knew that Dad had taken it, so I crawled all round the front room and pretended to be looking for it under the table and behind the couches and under the newspaper. Dad just put on his glasses and began to read the letters my mum gave him, taking not the least bit of notice of me.

I didn't want to start an argument, because I knew he was waiting for me to ask him to give it back and then he'd start on about how English people were different from us, and some words should never pass a girl's lips or ears. I was fed up of telling him that I was Indian but also English, because where you live matters, even more than the blood you have in you, and that my mind was English in a way because I had two sets of ideas, one for the English people I knew and one for the Indians.

When Dad settled down to eat, with Mum fetching him his food, because he ate before all of us, I went up to his bedroom and looked all round. The record wasn't anywhere, but his cupboard was locked. And this is where my nan comes in, and her story, the one she told me.

I saw Ralph in school the next day and told him that I was still listening to his wretched records and my brother wanted to tape them and so I'd bring them back later.

'Your old man looked like Geronimo yesterday,' he said. 'I thought hang on, he's gone to the kitchen for his tomahawk.'

'He's funny sometimes,' I said, but I couldn't tell him about the record. It was the same for two days. Ralph would make silly jokes, he'd say I was making record curry and all that. He knew I felt rotten about it.

I went up to Nan's room and sat talking to her that evening. She didn't ask me what was on my mind. I think she knew. So she began telling me her story.

She said that when she was my age in Bombay, which must have been long before the First World War (I can't even *think* that far back except in history lessons), they used to live all together in a big house, nineteen brothers and sisters and cousins and four sets of parents, her own and her uncles and aunts, and her grandad. He must have been my great-great-grandad, and they were all scared of him because he was the chief of the household. He was a kind of tyrant, but he earned the first pay packet in the house, and that made him lord and master. He always wore a turban, and he worked as a goldsmith and she said he was a very good artist and made the most fabulous ear-rings and bangles and things.

One day when the men were all out at work and the boys had gone to school with their slates and chalks (they didn't send girls in those days) the women and girls trooped out of the house to their local market. It was called Grant Road and was spread out under a huge railway bridge near their house. The women had heard that there were all sorts of new things at the market, just off the ship from England and they'd better go fast. Like the sales in Oxford Street, I suppose. She went along with the rest, because she said one thing that girls were taught to do by their mothers and aunts was to bargain with tradesmen and bring the prices down and pretend you weren't going to buy and walk away and come back and keep your face straight to show you didn't really like what they had to sell.

Only the wives of the house, that's Nan's mum and her sisters-in-law, had any money. When they got to the market, there was a huge crowd gathered round a particular street stall. You know what they were selling there? China – English tea-sets and dinner-sets and vases. My nan laughed when she told it. She was remembering the delight with which they looked at these things, because they hadn't seen crockery for home use before. They looked at the coloured patterns and the salesman let them handle the cups and plates. Well, she said, they had seen them before but this was the first time they'd got so close. There was a dinner-set there with a Chinese pattern on it, with bamboo branches and beautiful birds, all red and blue and yellow, in the branches, the same pattern on each plate and dish. They asked the price. They could manage it, they decided, if they pooled their money. Her mum made the decision. Yes, they'd buy them, they'd use all their own money and not touch the housekeeping. When the man wrapped them up in tissue paper and put them in a box, they carried them home like they'd won a trophy in the World Cup or something.

That evening, without telling any of the menfolk, they laid the dinner-set out as a surprise.

'You wouldn't get any like it nowadays,' she said. 'It was all little patterns, carefully done like a silversmith had been working on it.'

They sat down to dinner a little uncertain and very excited. Then the storm broke. Her grandad came in from work and hung up his turban and took off his work shoes and put on his slippers and walked into the dining room, where the women were supposed to serve the meal to the sitting menfolk. His daughters and daughters-in-law watched his face as he saw the china set instead of the silver and brass trays that they normally ate off. They were proud of their display and had even put a table cloth down, 'like the memsahib's house', Nan said.

Her grandad took one look at the Chinese bird crockery and his eyes went blazing mad. He grabbed the table cloth and before their eyes, as they held their breaths, he picked up the lot, took it to the window, and flung it crashing downstairs, two floors down to the courtyard. The crash brought the neighbours to their windows and they caught the last act of the play.

'We are Indians, high caste Indians,' he shouted. 'I won't have this foreign mud in my house, shiny mud that's all it is. Trust women to be fooled by pictures of parrots. I won't eat off shiny mud plates and nobody from my house is going to waste my money on heathen inventions.'

That was the end of that. The women folded their arms before them, and not one of them dared go out to pick up the pieces till he gave the order. The table was set as usual with metal trays in a matter of seconds. Nan said they were always scared of a beating in those days.

'That was sixty years ago, or something,' I said, 'and our dad he still thinks the same. He's thrown away my friend's record, just because he doesn't understand the songs.'

'Sshh, he hasn't thrown it away,' she said, and she giggled like a little girl. 'He was listening to your record when you went to school yesterday, and he locked it up in his cupboard, but I've got the key, so I stole it.'

She pulled the LP out from under her bed.

'What about Dad?' I asked, worried that he'd blame me for going through his cupboards.

'Thieves can't complain about stealing,' she said.

'What happened about the crockery?' I asked her a few days after that. 'Did you ever get to eat off china?'

'Not when my grandad was alive,' she replied. 'It was really different in those days. Men were gods.'

First response

- Why did Nan take the record and give it back to her grand-daughter?

- What was the connection between Nan's story and what happened to the record?

- Do you think Ralph was right to play the record?

- Do you feel sympathetic towards Mr Desai; what do you think were his reasons for taking the record?

- What do you expect him to do once he realises that the record has gone?

Looking closely

Talk

Pair work

In pairs, look closely at the story and pick out the sections which tell us about Nan. How do we know that she is ignorant of some aspects of English life and yet wise about life in general?

Group work

The girl in the story has to live in both an Indian and an English world. How well do you think she is coping? In groups make two lists of her customs and manners, one for each of the two worlds she 'lives' in.

Role play

1.   Imagine that it is the next day at school and the girl brings the record back to give to Ralph who is talking to Andre. Taking one part each, improvise their conversation.

2.   What will Mr Desai and his mother say to each other when they are alone? Improvise their conversation about Ralph and the records.

Write

1.   Imagine that Nan writes a letter to a relative in India and that the main part of this is her version of the story of the record. Use the story to look for clues to the way she feels and then write the letter.

2.   If the girl in the story was asked to write an essay entitled 'My Home and Family', what would it be like? How would she explain some aspects of her home life to her English teacher?

3.   Imagine that she and Ralph start to go out together. Do you think that they will have any problems with her family and perhaps his? Look carefully at the details of the story and then use your own imagination to describe the events of the next few weeks. You could write it as a story or in diary form. Write it from the point of view of the girl in the story or Ralph.

4.   What does Farrukh Dhondy want to make us think about in this story? First make notes on the various characters, what they are like, how they get on with each other and so on, and then concentrate on what you think is the theme of the story. How do you feel towards the different characters, and particularly the girl who is caught between being Indian and English? Write up your answer so as to explain what you think Farrukh Dhondy is trying to say.

A Country Full of Huts

Britain is a multicultural country. People from all over the world live in Britain and follow their customs in this country. I am an Indian and I get on well with girls at my school from other cultures. But I have noticed that people can be very rude about other people's races. We have three Indian teachers in our school and nearly all the girls make fun of them and their accents.

One way of dealing with a multicultural society is to teach the people about each other's culture. When I was in India I never heard of racial prejudice. We all respected each other's culture. There are many cultures in India, for instance the Hindus and Muslims. In school we were taught about their culture and they were taught about ours. So we grew up to respect them knowing that they were not practising anything sinister or unnatural. We were brought up to respect their religion just as they respected ours. We celebrated their feasts and they celebrated ours.

I don't think people in this country have respect for others, their culture or religion. This may be because they don't know about other people's way of life and cannot accept that it's different from theirs. I've noticed that as soon as someone's opinion on something important differs there is a build-up of tension. Either it's because one person is too proud to admit he's wrong or because someone can't accept that another person doesn't agree with her.

If people are being taught about other cultures they should just be taught the basic facts and left to form their own opinions. They should be taught the good and the bad points of a culture or a society. I'll never forget when I first came to Britain being asked if I lived in a hut. I was not hurt or insulted by this; only surprised. I thought, not for the first time, what an ignorant bunch of girls. This was a surprise because in India we'd been brought up to respect the British and other foreigners and had given them credit for having a little bit of common sense.

I later found out that it was not the children's fault. As I sat through lesson after lesson I realised that India was a country full of huts with people dying all the time and being basically a country with no proper facilities for anything. I completely agree that there are some areas, particularly the remote villages, which are like this. But to this day, after two years, I haven't heard anyone saying that there are buildings in the city; there's a good water supply, stores and shops, proper sanitation etc. The place I used to live at had a free school financed by the government.

So, from what I've heard, the children have an impression that India is a country with no buildings where all the people live in huts. People are dying and starving everywhere. Because of this the people of the more developed countries look down on people from less developed countries and treat them with disrespect.

Another way of making a multicultural society work is by making people of authority like bosses and specially teachers set an example. Bosses should try not to be prejudiced and I think action should be taken against them if they promote a white person who has worked in the office for a few months instead of a coloured person who has worked equally well for a longer period of time.

Teachers should also try to teach children of all cultures equally and not to be very strict with the coloured children and excuse the behaviour of the white children, particularly when they are young. This should also be the case with black teachers. They should not teach the children of their colour with leniency and children of other colours strictly.

My essay so far has been prejudiced. I've written about whites treating blacks badly. This is just habitual as I'm coloured. I never said that blacks are prejudiced against whites. I sometimes go around with some black girls during lunch break and I realise that some of them are as bad as the white girls. They criticize every little mistake a white person makes for the simple reason that the person is white. I was surprised when I saw them do this because they accuse whites of being racially prejudiced but they don't realise that they themselves are being prejudiced.

The best way, I think, to make a multicultural society work is to make each culture respect the others. This may be done by the children being taught about the way of life of other people and other cultures and being told of the contribution those cultures have made to the world.

JOVITA PEREIRA
FROM SAY WHAT YOU THINK

Talk

Pair work
Look over the passage carefully and see if you can either agree on what you think is the most important sentence in the essay or sum up its message in a sentence of your own. Compare your sentence with another pair's.

Group work
How far do you agree with the writer of this essay? She was a pupil at school when she wrote her piece – just as you are now – so hers is an ordinary view. Think carefully about what your view is and then look again at the points she is making. Jot down the ones that you agree with and make notes of those you feel unhappy about.

Look at these pictures of India. Which one is most like the way you imagine India to be?

Write

Write an essay about your own view of our society. What would you like to see happen in the future? Think of some of the areas Farrukh Dhondy covered e.g. schools, pupils, teachers, bosses, respect, prejudice, knowledge about other cultures and so on.

The writer makes it clear that she does not blame the children she met for their prejudiced comments. She realises that they have a distorted picture of life in her original country. What is your view about the origins of racism and prejudice?

Read this extract from Sumitra's Story by Rukshana Smith. Sumitra's family came to England when she was a young girl. Now she is sixteen and is trying to establish an identity of her own. In this section she feels caught between what seem like two different worlds.

Sumitra's Story

The hall was hushed. Sumitra lifted the guitar, pushed her long hair behind her back, strummed an introduction and began to sing. Her voice rang out clear and sweet, the audience hung on every word. In the front row a woman sobbed with emotion.

As the song ended the audience rose with one accord, cheering and applauding wildly. Sumitra bowed, turned to walk off the stage, but they would not let her go. 'Sing it again!' they yelled. 'More, more!' She smiled and began to play another tune.

'Belt up, Sumitra,' shouted Sandya from the next room, banging crossly on the wall. 'I'm trying to do my homework!' Mai was calling up the stairs, 'Come and help me, stop playing that guitar. I wish Martin had never given it to you!' Sumitra closed her eyes as the anger spluttered like a fire-cracker inside her. The vision of headlines reading: 'Sue Patel Takes New York by Storm! Beautiful Girl Singer from London, England an Overnight Success!' faded, and she strummed three angry chords before throwing the guitar on her bed. She went downstairs to exchange the sweet smell of success for the acrid fumes of boiling *ghee*.

As she fried the rounds her mother rolled out, a huge wave of misery engulfed her. Hilary and Lynne had gone to a local college dance, while Cinderella Patel remained at home, reeking of oil and dry flour. She turned suddenly and looked at Mai. 'Do you like cooking?' she asked, wondering how her mother could bear this life, day after day. Mai was bewildered. 'What questions you ask!' she replied. 'I don't know. Women cook for their families. You must help me and learn to cook for your own family. You are sixteen. Soon we must start thinking about looking for a husband. It is good you have passed your exams. You will marry well!'

Sumitra's tongue stuck to her mouth like an uncooked lump of dough. She turned the *poori* deftly as her mind screamed, 'Never, never, never!' in the kitchen of her brain. The words of a pop song sizzled in the fat:

'And all the songs I was going to sing, I'll never sing them now.
And all the bells I was going to ring, I'll never ring them now.
And all the lives I was going to live
And all the loves I was going to give
I'll never live them now
I'll never give them now.'

Mai patted her arm, leaving a floury impression like a palm print decorating a temple. 'It's all right,' she said with unusual gentleness. 'It is the custom. You'll get used to the idea, there's no need to be shy. We all get used to it.'

It had never occurred to Mai that her daughters might be questioning their way of life. Despite their smart clothes and the fact that at the week-ends they wore sweaters and jeans like any other teenager, she was sure that their attitudes and conventions were Indian. She had never sat down and thought about it; she never thought about her children as separate entities. When she told Bap that she was worried about them, she meant that she was concerned that they would take suitable jobs, choose the right friends, marry decent partners. The criterion in each case was whether or not she would approve of their choice. So Mai was part of the Banquo line, carefully bequeathing to her children the ideas and philosophies that had been bequeathed to her. The fact that these conventions had evolved in different ages and in different countries was immaterial.

Mai never doubted that the girls would lead their lives in the same way as she lived hers, marrying someone carefully chosen by the parents, bearing children who would, of course, speak Gujarati and Hindi. She had no reason to doubt it when all around her she saw other cultures passing on their various truths to their own children and carefully isolating them from the British tradition in which they lived. She had seen synagogues, mosques, Greek and Russian orthodox churches, and behind each of these institutions was a sub-culture energetically devoted to keeping a particular tradition alive.

Mai, like thousands of other mothers of minority groups, had many ways of perpetuating tradition. There was emotional, social and financial pressure. Thus the little dictatorships of family life flourished in the British democracy. Children were unhappy, rejected their parents' demands temporarily, made their heroic gestures, but were usually defeated by the sanctions imposed. Mothers wept, fathers talked of sacrifices, grandparents disapproved, and the son or daughter conceded and was sucked back into the family group.

Life continued as it had always done. The shrine was cleaned and polished, sandalwood paste prepared. Offerings were left for the gods and roses decorated the ceremonial place. The girls plaited Gopal and Jayant braids at Rakshabandan in order to ensure their health and happiness. They all went to the temple and, occasionally, to Indian films and dances.

As long as the outside culture remained beyond her house, Mai was content. The letters and notes from the alien society were ignored as if they had no right to be there. Requests to attend school functions or parents' evenings were left unanswered. What could she or Bap do at school? She trusted the teachers to do their job and, besides, she couldn't speak English. So she lived in her comfortable cocoon, only venturing out to go to work and surrounding herself with the friends she had known in Uganda.

Sumitra and some of her Indian friends, however, were beginning to resent the tight community laws. They objected to being relegated to the Bottom Division at the back of the temple. As sexual objects women distracted the men from their prayers, so the men prayed while the women sat behind the barrier and gossiped. Then the women went to the communal kitchen to prepare food for the men. This division of labour annoyed the girls, who at school were encouraged to be independent, thoughtful, integrated, and at home to be docile, submissive and dutiful. Sumitra had to listen to the adults decrying the British way of life, while being educated into it herself.

Sumitra and her parents lived under the same roof without speaking to each other. Of course they talked; they spoke about things that did not matter, but about the serious business of the meaning of life they were silent. There was no point of contact, and any questioning was called disobedience and would cause a scene. So Sumitra acted one part at home and another at school, and was never sure which role was really hers.

Sometimes events on the news reached out and touched them. Incidents of growing racial tension in Notting Hill, Birmingham, Southall. The places were different but the causes were the same: a lack of Government awareness and initiative and an unfriendly host population causing the immigrants to turn in on themselves. One side felt threatened, the other rebuffed.

Sumitra felt all these pressures. One part of her wanted to live as an Indian girl, carrying on the great traditions and culture, while another part of her wanted to participate in Western freedom. On the one hand they read of incidents in Southall, of young Asians being attacked and even murdered. This made them fearful, retreating into the group. These racial incidents defined certain boundaries between the immigrants and host society, and caused Bap to give his weekly lecture on the superiority of their own way of life.

On the other hand there were occasionally reports in the paper about young Asian girls killing themselves because they had not wanted to go through with an arranged marriage, or because the strain of living two lives was overwhelming. As she watched yet another *poori* puff up and turn brown, Sumitra wondered if that was the only way out. She had often wished lately that she was dead.

RUKSHANA SMITH

- How would you describe Sumitra's feelings?

- If she asked you for advice what would you say to her?

- Do you think schools are doing enough to make us into members of a tolerant and multicultural society?

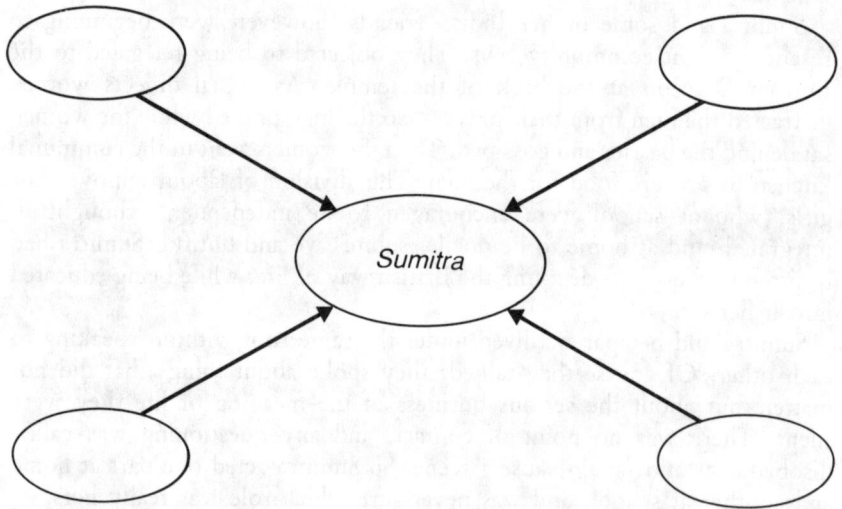

Sumitra

| Talk | **Group work** |

Draw a diagram with Sumitra at the centre and place around her the various pressures that she is feeling. Try to make the strongest pressures stand out by giving them larger letters and larger circles.

Do you think that her thoughts of suicide are easy for other young people to understand?

| Role play | Imagine that Sumitra tries to explain some of her feelings to her father and mother and improvise this conversation. |

Write	1. What does Rukshana Smith mean by "the little dictatorships of family life"? Does every young person suffer from them? Either write down your views, trying to give an example to back up each point you are making, or write a story with this idea as its main theme.

2. Imagine that you have been asked to produce a documentary about some of the themes explored by Rukshana Smith in this extract. Discuss in groups how you might go about this and then write down your ideas for various scenes and some examples from your script. You might want to conduct some interviews or organise a survey to collect people's views. Work out who you might talk to and what you might ask them. Jot down a list of ideas as you talk.

3. Is there someone you know who you feel could tell you something about another culture? Ask if you can interview her/him and then use the notes you make of the interview as a part of your documentary script.

Links with story	How similar are the two girls as individuals and how comparable are their situations?

Inglan is a bitch

we'en mi jus' come to Landan toun
mi use to work pan di andahgroun
but workin' pan di andahgroun
y'u don't get fi know your way aroun'

Inglan is a bitch
dere's no escapin' it
Inglan is a bitch
dere's no runnin' whey fram it

mi get a lickle jab in a big 'otell
an' awftah a while, mi woz doin' quite well
dem staat mi aaf as a dish – washah
but w'en mi tek a stack, mi noh tun clack – watchah!

Inglan is a bitch
dere's no escapin' it
Inglan is a bitch
noh baddah try fi hide fram it

w'en dem gi' you di lickle wage packit
fus dem rab it wid dem big tax rackit
y'u haffi struggle fi mek en's meet
an' w'en y'u goh a y'u bed y'u jus' cant sleep

Inglan is a bitch
dere's no escapin' it
Inglan is a bitch fi true
a noh lie mi a tell, a true

mi use to work dig ditch w'en it cowl noh bitch
mi did strang like a mule, but, bwoy, mi did fool
den awftah a while mi jus' stap dhu ovahtime
den awftah a while mi jus' phy dung mi tool

Inglan is a bitch
dere's no escapin' it
Inglan is a bitch
y'u haffi know how fi suvvive in it

well mi dhu day wok an' mi dhu nite wok
mi dhu clean wok an' mi dhu dutty wok
dem seh dat black man is very lazy
but if y'u si how mi wok y'u woulda sey mi crazy

Inglan is a bitch
dere's no escapin' it
Inglan is a bitch
y'u bettah face up to it

dem have a lickle facktri up inna Brackly
inna disya facktri all dem dhu is pack crackry
fi di laas fifteen years dem get mi laybah
now awftah fifteen years mi fall out a fayvah

Inglan is a bitch
dere's no escapin' it
Inglan is a bitch
dere's no runnin' whey fram it

mi know dem have work, work in abundant
yet still, dem mek mi redundant
now, at fifty – five mi gettin' quite ol'
yet still, dem sen' mi fi goh draw dole

Inglan is a bitch
dere's no escapin' it
Inglan is a bitch fi true
is whey wi a goh dhu 'bout it?

LINTON KWESI JOHNSON
FROM RACE TODAY

- What difference does it make to your reading that this poem is in a dialect?

- Is it more, or less, effective as a poem because of its sound?

| Talk |

Pair work

Go carefully through the poem and make sure you agree what its main ideas are; try reading it out loud.

If this was a song what sort of music would you consider most suitable for it and why?

How many jobs has the narrator had and why has he had so many?

Group work

Create a rhythm to use with the poem and then try reading it with this rhythm. You might use a backing tape or something simpler like a drum or tambourine, even clapping. When you organise your reading think about the way the chorus comes in and how each last line is different.

The poem represents one point of view and finishes with the question, what are we going to do about England? Can you suggest why someone might feel this way about England? Jot down any things that occur to the group and then agree on one thing that you all feel could be changed. Decide how this could be achieved and prepare a short speech to support your choice.

| Write |

The poem shows how powerful language can be when it is not so-called standard English. Where you live do most people have an accent or even a dialect? Write a poem about your area in which you use the sound of its voices. The poem might be a description of the area and the people who live there but it could be about you or an entirely imaginary story.

| Read |

Read this extract which comes from Edmund Gosse's autobiographical study of his relationship with his father who was a devoutly religious and puritanical man. Edmund was still a little boy when this incident happened. Miss Marks was his governess.

Father and Son

On Christmas Day of this year 1857 our villa saw a very unusual sight. My Father had given strictest charge that no difference whatever was to be made in our meals on that day; the dinner was to be neither more copious than usual nor less so. He was obeyed, but the servants, secretly rebellious, made a small plum-pudding for themselves. (I discovered afterwards, with pain, that Miss Marks received a slice of it in her boudoir.) Early in the afternoon, the maids, – of whom we were now advanced to keeping two, – kindly remarked that 'the poor dear child ought to have a bit, anyhow', and wheedled me into the kitchen, where I ate a slice of plum-pudding. Shortly I began to feel that pain inside which in my frail state was inevitable, and my conscience smote me violently. At length I could bear my spiritual anguish no longer, and bursting into the study I called out: 'Oh! Papa, Papa, I have eaten of flesh offered to idols!' It took some time, between my sobs, to explain what had happened. Then my Father sternly said: 'Where is the accursed thing?' I explained that as much as was left of it was still on the kitchen table. He took me by the hand, and ran with me into the midst of the startled servants, seized what remained of the pudding, and with the plate in one hand and me still tight in the other, ran till we reached the dust-heap, when he flung the idolatrous confectionery on to the middle of the ashes, and then raked it deep down into the mass. The suddenness, the violence, the velocity of this extraordinary act made an impression on my memory which nothing will ever efface.

EDMUND GOSSE

- What made his father react so violently?

- Why do you think that the boy felt a pain after eating Christmas pudding?

- Would you ever react in a similar way to someone eating something or bringing a particular object into your house?

Talk | **Pair work**
- Why do you think the little boy remembers this incident so clearly?

- Do you think his father was justified given that he had banned any attention to Christmas from the house?

- Would you call Mr Gosse a fanatic because of his behaviour?

Group work

To what extent do you think parents should control what you bring into the house? Can you think of any examples of times when you have disagreed about using something at home? Write down five rules of the house that you all agree would be a fair way for parents and their children to live together.

| Write |

Imagine that the year is 2057. Write a story or description of an event based on the same kind of incident. What will parents be reacting about in the twenty-first century? Do you think it will be similar to the things parents react to now?

Think of an incident in your own life about which you have fallen out with your parents or other members of your family. Write about what happened and see if you can explain it now with the advantage of hindsight. Do you feel differently now about who was to blame? If you had the chance would you change what happened?

| Links with story |

What similarities can you see between the behaviour of Nan's grandfather and that of Mr Gosse? Do you think that all parents and grandparents could behave like this?

The Voice of God in Adelaide Terrace

PENELOPE LIVELY

Miss Avril Pemberton, in her fifty-seventh year, suffered from insomnia. She did not consider this an insupportable affliction; she would lie with her eyes open in the protective darkness of her bedroom, think her thoughts, and listen to the nocturnal London sounds. These were not many, for Adelaide Terrace was a quiet and respectable neighbourhood, its inhabitants given to early nights and not inclined to car ownership.

It was on such a night, in that static tract of time between three and five in the morning so familiar to insomniacs, that Avril first heard the voice.

She was a devout woman and a regular churchgoer. Even so, she did not regard herself as blameless; merely as a reasonably proficient Christian, given to occasional error rather than deliberate transgression. She had certainly never expected to be singled out in this way.

The voice said, 'Avril?'

She sat up, and stared into the dusky cavern beside the wardrobe from which it seemed to come; later, she recalled its curious sexlessness, the voice of neither man nor woman.

'Avril,' it said, 'are you listening carefully? There is something I want you to do.'

Avril, wide awake, more interested than awed, said, 'What would You like me to do?'

'I shall explain,' said the voice. 'Pay attention. I wish you to make a start with the attic room . . .'

Avril listened, with mounting astonishment.

It should be explained at this point that Avril Pemberton let rooms. She let rooms because her mother had done so before, ever since, indeed, Mr Pemberton had died in 1951, because the house was too large for her own needs and because the money came in very handy. Without it, she would have found it difficult to manage on her salary from the part-time secretarial work for a local firm of accountants. She let the first-floor front and back (single, with washbasins) and the large attic room (own bathroom). Cooking facilities for the tenants were provided in the small scullery on the first floor. Avril herself occupied the ground floor, using the second-floor front as her bedroom. The two small back rooms on the second floor remained empty, in use as boxrooms. Her mother had not liked the house to become overcrowded.

Mrs Pemberton had died four years before, irascible in extreme old age. To the bitter end, she had exercised her powers of discrimination over would-be tenants, vetting them, finally, from her bed. Avril had found it all extremely embarrassing; so, presumably, had the tenants. Two of the present three, Mr Harris, the bank clerk in the first-floor front, and the nursing sister in the attic had been her mother's choices. Sandra Lee, the student from the teacher training college around the corner, Avril had admitted a year or so ago, irritably aware that the pasty girl, with her total absence of personality, opinion or discernible tastes, was exactly the kind of person of whom her mother would have approved as a tenant.

There had never been any shortage of people wanting rooms. Adelaide Terrace was conveniently near bus routes and a tube station, not too far from central London, but quiet. The area was something of a buffer state; to the east, middle-class 'reclamation' had sent prices rocketing and let loose a tide of primrose and terracotta front doors, bay trees in tubs and petunia-crammed window-boxes; to the west, quite other things had been going on. There, Indian take-aways alternated with Chinese, the market stalls were piled high with garish and glittery stuffs, peculiar vegetables and cut-price carpets and pop records. The streets ran with black school children and the pubs blared forth unfamiliar music. The inhabitants of Adelaide Terrace kept their eyes turned resolutely to the east, and hoped for the best.

And, where possible, played a part. Many of the tall terrace houses, like the Pembertons', belonged to elderly people and diminished families who let out rooms; others were divided, rather inefficiently, into flats. The long-term inhabitants, such as Mrs Pemberton and her immediate neighbour, Mrs Fletcher, knew one another well and were resolute as to certain matters, though divided about methods of exercising that resolution.

Mrs Fletcher sported, for many years, a small notice stuck to the inside of a glass panel in the front door. It said 'No Coloureds' and had been nicely lettered, with stencils, by her niece who had done a year at art college.

Mrs Pemberton thought this silly and unnecessary. It was a simple matter, she said, to make one's position perfectly clear without that. Occasional small unpleasantnesses might arise, but could be quickly dealt with: front doors open, but they also close again. It was with a certain satisfaction that she had pointed out to Mrs Fletcher, in 1965, that the notice would have to be removed.

'Who's to make me?' said Mrs Fletcher, bristling.

'Well, dear,' said Mrs Pemberton, 'you'll have to do as you think best, but I wouldn't like to see you get had up, and personally I've never found the need in the first place.'

Mrs Fletcher went on at some length about individual liberty and diabolical interferences therein and how you couldn't pass laws to make people think differently to what they always had done. Mrs Pemberton pointed out, smoothly, that all this was true enough but what was clear as day was that you could pass laws until you were blue in the face but there would still be ways and means.

Mrs Fletcher removed the notice and took instructions from Mrs Pemberton as to ways and means. There were seldom, if ever, misunderstandings or unpleasantnesses, and Adelaide Terrace remained much as it had been before. At the far end, where Mrs Pemberton's influence was weakest, there was a certain falling-off. An Indian family took one of the flats and were to be seen on Sundays immaculately dressed, pushing a pram in Adelaide Gardens. Their eldest son, in grey flannel trousers, navy blazer, spotless white shirt and puce turban, cycled down the street to school every day. Avril, watching once from the window, was misguided enough to say that they seemed quite nice people; her mother was unmanageable for a week.

And now, lying there in the dark, she listened to the voice – a little hectoring in tone – as it went on and on. Instructing. Lecturing. 'Remember the Bishop?' it said. 'Now supposing *he* had come to the door . . .'

'I know,' said Avril. 'I said as much to mother at the time.'

The Bishop of somewhere in Africa, he had been, but you couldn't tell that at once from the name. He had come as visiting preacher to St Bartholomew's, one autumn Sunday. They had been invited to the Vicar's after the service, for coffee, because Mrs Pemberton was treasurer, then, of the Mothers' Union. And he had been as black as your hat. Big and black and beaming. Avril had thought, at first, seeing him climb into the pulpit, that her mother wouldn't go to the vicarage. But she had. She had gone, and sat there, and drunk coffee and eaten biscuits. And afterwards she had said that she wouldn't have Mrs Brinton's job, not for the world. Mrs Brinton was the Vicar's wife. And Avril had said what she had said and there had been unpleasantness between them. And now here was the voice, harking back.

'I spoke my mind,' said Avril sulkily.

She had never taken up arms against her mother lightly: the cost was too high. As the years went by, she did so less and less, the instinctive resistance of her youth snuffed out by her mother's more implacable temperament. She ceased to counter Mrs Pemberton's vaunted opinions and preferences, ceased to say, from time to time, 'There are two sides to everything, mother,' and 'Well, personally, I do think . . .' She took to silence.

By and large, she conceded Adelaide Terrace as Mrs Pemberton's territory and guarded jealously the privacy of her life beyond it, what little there was – the voluntary evenings at the Scout and Guide hut, her Red Cross afternoon, and her job at Hackle and Starbuck.

Never, for instance, would she have told Mrs Pemberton about Gloria.

Gloria came to the office as a temp when the senior, and permanent, secretary, had to have several weeks' sick leave after an operation. She was seventeen, fresh from school, an indifferent typist, as noisy as a puppy, and West Indian. Her abundant, frizzy hair was worn in two huge puffs elaborately teased out at either side of her head; she had wide, flat features with large brown eyes, big lips delicately painted; there was a bloom to her skin that entranced Avril. Surreptitiously she kept glancing at Gloria; bewildered, she realised that she found the girl beautiful.

Gloria bounced and giggled her way through the days and played merry hell with the filing system. The office was torn between amusement and irritation; Mr Hackle, who had been as startled as Avril when Gloria appeared from the agency, grumbled at the mangled letters with which Gloria presented him, and enjoyed, like Avril, the throaty laughter that brightened office hours. Gloria teased the office boy, charmed clients, bungled every telephone message, and spent much time in the washroom attending to her appearance. At the typewriter, she moaned and whimpered and, every now and then, leaned back to indulge in a huge luxuriant stretch that made it seem as though her plump rubbery young body might spring apart entirely, like an over-ripe pea-pod.

One day, looking across at Avril, she said, 'Hey, that's nice.'

'What?' said Avril.

'That sweater you got on. It suits you – it's your colour, blue. You look really good today.'

Avril had flushed and muttered something and gone back to the letter she was typing. Later, tidying her hair before she left the office, she stared at herself in the mirror, turning this way and that, adjusting the collar of her jacket.

She had been sorry when Gloria left, and Maureen Davidson returned, with her migraines and her proficiency and her faint odour of Lifebuoy soap.

Guiltily, she dismissed recollections of Gloria and returned to here and now, and to the voice, which seemed to be concluding its homily.

'. . . as quickly as you can, with the normal period of notice to the present tenants.'

As she listened, the corners of Avril's mouth turned up in an incredulous smile.

'*All* black?' she said.

'Every one of them,' said the voice sternly.

There was not a great deal of difficulty with Mr Harris, Sandra Lee and the nursing sister. Since she gave formal notice to all three at once, it was simply assumed that she wished to reclaim the house for her own occupation. Mr Harris, who had been there for nine years, was clearly a little put out, but gave her a large box of chocolates as a parting present and made over to her the tradescantia in the scullery, which he thought might not take kindly to a move. The nursing sister asked if she wasn't going to rattle around rather, all on her own. Sandra Lee vanished, wordless, into the obscurity from which she had come.

The process, allowing for the correct periods of notice, took nearly four months. Not until the last tenant had departed did Avril place her advertisement in the *Gazette*; she had decided to deal with the attic room first, and retained her usual wording, except that she added 'Married couples not objected to.'

There was a flood of responses. Avril, turning away, with her mother's murmured formula of regret – 'So sorry . . . already taken . . . person who called last night' – first a young Irish couple, and then a Scottish nurse and another girl of indeterminate extraction, realised that covertly exercised discrimination is indeed extremely easy.

The Singhs presented themselves at the door on a Tuesday morning. By Friday they were installed in the attic.

On Saturday morning, returning from the shops, Avril was halted, key in the lock, by Mrs Fletcher, springing from her own door at the sound as though released by an elastic. 'I been wanting to have a word with you, dear,' she said. 'I must say I couldn't hardly believe my eyes, seeing them pull up in the taxi like that, with all their stuff. I said to myself what old Mrs P. would say I don't even like to think . . .'

Avril stood there, her foot inside her own door, half-listening, and it came to her with sudden welcome clarity that, in nearly thirty years of enforced congress, she had never really liked Mrs Fletcher. It was as though you might discover that tea, bread, or some other unconsidered object of routine was not really to your taste. She stared at her opening and closing mouth, the tuft of hairs that crowned a surface irregularity on her chin, the cameo brooch that puckered the neck of her blouse, and thought: silly old bag.

'. . . seen some perfectly nice people come to the door, Sunday and Monday, after you put your ad in,' concluded Mrs Fletcher, 'so I don't know what to think, I simply don't.' She stared at Avril. 'And who are they, one would like to know?'

'They're my new tenants,' said Avril coolly (she liked that: *my* new tenants). 'They've taken the attic room.'

There was a silence. In Mrs Fletcher's face, whole volumes of analysis, speculation, and adjustment to circumstances were written, revised, rewritten; granite assumptions crumbled to dust, and were reconstructed in other forms. When she spoke again, it was from twenty miles away, and ten years on. She said, 'That girl's expecting. I daresay you'll not have noticed that.'

Avril, who had not, flushed a little, and went into the house.

The Singhs were quiet tenants; they pattered up and down the stairs like well-behaved children, talking to each other in low tones if at all. Occasionally, radio music, turned low, seeped from beneath their door, and with it, culinary smells.

With complete detachment, Avril considered the smells. She had once taken a meal in an Indian restaurant with two girls from the office and had not, in fact, much cared for it. The smells, at first, raised a whisker of alarm. And then, considering over a day or two, she decided that they were no more, indeed rather less, disagreeable than the bacon (cut-price, she had always suspected) Mr Harris used to do himself for breakfast every day. In fact, they grew on you.

Over the next three weeks she filled the first-floor front and back. The front went within three days to a bescarved and bespectacled student from Nigeria. The back was less straightforward; there was a tussle of wills with a forceful woman who refused to believe that the room had already been taken within an hour of the advertisement (the 'occasional small unpleasantness' that old Mrs Pemberton had grown accustomed to) but Avril held her own, then and for a further day and a half until the arrival of an immensely fat black dental nurse called Brenda.

In the silence and darkness of her room she said, 'All right?' There being no reply, she assumed that her arrangements had met with approval.

The house was no longer so quiet. The Nigerian student turned out to have many friends, some of whom, Avril suspected, were not entirely transitory visitors. Having always respected the privacy of her tenants (unlike her mother, who kept duplicate keys and made forays into their rooms in their absence) she made no comment. He and Brenda struck up a friendship, conducted for the most part rather noisily on the stairs. Both, though, were unfailingly genial; the Nigerian cleared a blocked sink in the kitchen and Brenda, when Avril took to her bed with a throat infection, plied her with hot drinks laced with suspect but delicious substances. She would stand at Avril's bedroom door, entirely filling it, brandishing a thermos and shouting encouragingly, as though to a slightly deaf child; she was a maturer and more strident version of Gloria.

Avril felt a greater affinity with the Singhs, their deprecating smiles and self-effacing comings and goings. Mrs Singh – Kamala, as she whispered once, in a rare moment of intimacy – was indeed swelling week by week, as Avril had now to observe and admit. Nothing was said, until one day Brenda, in raucous progress up the stairs, said casually, 'That Kamala, she goin' to have it any day now', which alarmed Avril but left her better prepared for contingencies. When, a week or so later, she heard Mr Singh come down the stairs with more than usual haste, and then his soft voice on the telephone, asking for the doctor, she was calm and indeed quite excited. Being familiar with the processes of childbirth from her reading of novels (though the kind of novel, admittedly, in which the narrative tended to shift, at the crucial moment, to the role of non-participant characters such as husbands and sisters) she amassed all the kettles and saucepans she could find and set them to boil. Only as they began to hum, did it occur to her that she really did not know for what all this boiling water was required: the novels never went into that. And when she came out into the hall to find Kamala, smiling weakly, coming down the stairs on her husband's arm, suitcase in hand, she was distinctly disappointed. The birth was to take place in hospital, apparently. She went rather glumly back into her room, and forgot the saucepans, which were boiling briskly ten minutes later, when Brenda returned, filling the house with steam and prompting much noisy comment and enquiry. Avril, who suspected that she might have been rumbled, gave some sheepish explanations about sterilising jamjars.

Kamala returned, after what Avril thought a surprisingly short period, with a tiny, fragile baby (a boy, apparently) cocooned in yards of shocking pink blanketing. The Nigerian produced a couple of bottles of wine for the household to drink the baby's health; everybody gathered in the kitchen, the Singhs silent but beaming, Brenda and the Nigerian loudly talkative, Avril, who had seldom in her life touched alcohol, feeling increasingly unstable, but stimulated. It was all rather enjoyable; afterwards, she watched television, a little restlessly, and tried not to pay attention to the curious sounds from the Nigerian's room, where he and Brenda were completing the evening on their own.

Mrs Fletcher, tight-lipped, had complained a number of times about the pitch of Brenda's transistor radio. She spoke seldom to Avril, but was frequently to be seen in the street, in eloquent discourse with one or other of the neighbours. They are talking about me, Avril would think, and found that she did not care at all.

It was curious: she was a person who had always been deeply sensitive to the opinions of others.

At night, in the privacy of her room, she checked with the voice for approval and encouragement, and received it. Her life, in every other respect, continued much as it always had done: she went to the office, on Monday and Tuesday mornings and Thursday and Friday afternoons, to the Scout and Guide hut on Monday evenings, the Red Cross on Thursdays, St Bartholomew's on Sunday for communion and again for evensong. She was not entirely surprised when the Vicar called one day. He was a man easily swayed by others (an opinion she seemed always to have had, though only now did it express itself – tacitly – with ease and conviction) and she heard in his voice the conspiratorial tones of Mrs Fletcher. He sat uneasily on the edge of a chair and asked Avril if she had been keeping well lately; afterwards, the two indentations of his behind remained for some while on the upholstery, prolonging the tension of the visit. When Avril replied, shortly, that she had, he hummed and hawed, reflected on the weather, the new block of flats springing up alongside the churchyard, and his summer holiday plans, before hoping that if she, er, ever felt at all, er, in need of a chat she must remember that she had many good friends in the neighbourhood, many good friends. There was a silence, at the end of which the Vicar made the proposition that some people find living alone a bit of a strain, especially after the sad loss of a dear relative, that sometimes possibly, er, a chat with a sympathetic friend . . .

Avril said that she did not live alone.

The Vicar, with some eagerness, said that yes, quite, and since she'd mentioned it he wondered if . . .

Avril asked what he wondered. And the Vicar's voice had trailed off, and with it the Vicar, till all that was left of him were those two dents in the chair seat.

Avril wondered if the voice had ever addressed the Vicar, in the darkness of *his* nights.

The Singh baby prospered. Mr Harris's tradescantia in the scullery died; the Nigerian presented Avril with a rather violent oil-painting attributed to his brother which she felt obliged to hang on the stairs. She did not like it and indeed had asked the voice for guidance over the matter, and the voice had suggested the darkish corner on the first-floor landing. She frequently asked the voice for guidance, these days, and was frequently given it.

When Brenda, coming in from work one evening, heard her in one of the boxrooms, she peered inquisitively through the door.

'My, you got a lot of stuff in there, Miss Pemberton. You havin' a tidy-up, then?'

'The room's going to be used,' said Avril. 'I have to clear it out.'

'You expectin' a visitor, then?'

Avril, distracted by the problem of a broken table-lamp, replied that she was making room for a further lodger. Brenda did not receive this news with the enthusiasm Avril had expected: she said it was enough hassle getting that Pius to hurry up with the bathroom in the mornings and the shelves in the scullery were cram full as it was. She implied a fit of profiteering on Avril's part. Avril ignored this, with dignity.

She got rid of the first two applicants for the room, who were unsuitable; the third threw her into a quandary. He stood before her on the doorstep, small, slight, brown, and almond-eyed. Avril had little idea from which part of the world he hailed, but knew on which side of the dividing-line her mother would have placed him. She hesitated, showed him the room, and succumbed.

In the night she was woken by the voice (she had been sleeping much better of late). It was displeased.

Avril said defensively, 'Well, mother wouldn't ever have taken him.'

The voice continued, didactic in its assertions as to what was what. Avril, lying there in the dark, felt a twinge of resentment: there was a note, a distinct note, of Mrs Pemberton's hectoring dogmatism. She pointed out, sulkily, that it was too late to do anything about it now, and Mr Lee had looked a good dark brown to her. She did not say that in any case she had rather taken to him, a nice-spoken boy who had stood aside to let her come down the stairs first.

The voice, unmollified, issued further instructions.

'*Both* the boxrooms?' said Avril. And then, thoughtfully, 'Very well, then.'

The Health Visitor sat at the kitchen table and said that she had just thought she would pop in, since she was in the house anyway to see Mrs Singh. She said the baby was coming along nicely. Avril agreed. She said you must miss your mother a lot, I gather it's three or four years since she died. Avril agreed, wondered from whom the gathering had been done, saw Mrs Fletcher pass the window, bundled against the spring wind, and shoot a quick glance sideways. Looking after yourself all right, are you? said the Health Visitor. Avril said she was, and observed the Health Visitor's quick, surreptitious professional examination of the room.

The Health Visitor believed that Avril was thinking of letting another room. Avril neither confirmed nor denied this; with a spurt of indignation she thought, nosey thing. The Health Visitor made some enquiries about toilets, and washbasins, which Avril answered with restraint. The Health Visitor left. Through the window, Avril watched Mrs Fletcher's interception of her, in Adelaide Terrace.

Mr Lee had been installed for a week when she put her second advertisement in the *Gazette*. She had cleared out and prepared the second boxroom during the daytime, in the absence of all the other tenants except Mrs Singh and the baby, who kept themselves to themselves on the top floor. Consequently, the first they knew of her new arrangements was the arrival of the new tenant.

There were comments, amounting to open hostility. The Singhs said nothing, but pattered with a little more assertion in their journeys up and down stairs. The Nigerian grumbled, outside Avril's kitchen door, about the additional strain on the resources of the scullery: he had quite a nasty temper, Avril realised. Brenda said, 'She *stayin'* here, that Chinese girl? You running some kind of United Nations in this house, Miss Pemberton?' A sour expression replaced her normal grin.

The voice, too, had its say.

'I will choose my own tenants,' said Avril, in the darkness of her bedroom. 'I will use my own discrimination.' She lay there, these nights, with the house silent around her, and contemplated the filling of it, and the nature of the filling of it, and her part therein, and experienced the most satisfactory feeling of having created. The house was a kaleidoscope, but the jugglings of its occupancy were no longer random: they had form. She ceased to pay much attention to the voice, which nagged on irritatingly from beside the wardrobe.

The atmosphere of the house was no longer harmonious, but Avril did not notice; she was preoccupied with her own plans.

She transferred her possessions from the second floor to her ground-floor sitting-room by degrees, those that she could handle on her own. The bed, which presented too great a problem, she left where it was, and ordered a new one for herself from the furniture shop in the High Street. It was its delivery that alerted Brenda; she stood, hands on massive hips, at the turn in the stairs and said, 'You not letting *another* room, Miss Pemberton?' This house getting too full by half, you know, that lavatory up here's only working half-cock again, you're going to have the health people after you, you not careful.' Avril went into her room and closed the door, intent upon the phrasing of the advertisement for the *Gazette*.

After she had installed Mr Achimota in what had been her bedroom, she locked herself into her sitting-room, whenever she was in the house. She did not really feel like talking to people, and was dimly aware of unrest around her. People whispered on the stairs, and sometimes did not whisper: on one occasion she heard Brenda's raised voice saying, 'She barmy, I'm telling you, she not right in her head any more.'

The Health Visitor hammered on the door, once. She said. 'I'd like to have a chat with you, dear, just for a few minutes.' Avril ignored her.

At night, she held dialogues with the voice, but nowadays it was she who did much of the talking: the voice had grown feebler and feebler and as it whined on, asserting and instructing, its tones had become more and more like those of Mrs Pemberton, but diminished, and susceptible to counter-arguments in a way that Mrs Pemberton never had been. 'Nobody's right all the time,' said Avril, 'not even You. Not on every subject. Now in my opinion . . .'

Mrs Fletcher had avoided her for months, crossing the street when they happened to coincide in Adelaide Terrace. Now, Avril noticed, other neighbours did the same, or observed her furtively, in shops or from adjacent pews in St Bartholomew's. Hurt, though not greatly so, Avril maintained a lonely dignity. She missed, more, the convivial atmosphere that had prevailed in the house during the early months of its reorganisation. Nowadays, there were arguments on the stairs about the bathroom and the scullery, complaints about the lavatory and the telephone, noise and contention. Moreover, it seemed to her that her tenants did not like her, which distressed her more than anything: they were, after all, her chosen people, each and every one of them. Thus isolated, she was prepared even to relinquish the upper hand and mention this to the voice, to seek, maybe, its advice and guidance as in the old days; the voice, disconcertingly, was silent. She lay alone in her bedroom and brooded on what had come about.

And so, when next she heard the Health Visitor in the hall she opened her door.

The Health Visitor did not mince her words. She said there were too many people in the house, too few lavatories, and a smell of drains from out the back somewhere that must be investigated forthwith. She was brisk, but not unpleasant. Avril, less disposed to hostility than on the previous occasion, promised to summon a plumber. The Health Visitor, studying her intently across the table, said, 'And another thing, dear, it's neither here nor there but you do seem to go in for coloured people as tenants, don't you? You've got some of your neighbours properly upset, I can tell you, though as I say that's neither here nor there.'

And so it came about that Avril, because she never had anyone to talk to these days, and because the Health Visitor seemed really quite a nice little body after all, began to tell her about the voice. And as she talked, the Health Visitor, who had been gathering her belongings and indeed had got up from the chair to go, sat down again, and let her bag slither to the floor, and listened with an expression that grew more and more alert and more and more unfathomable. She said, 'Yes?' and 'I see, dear' and nodded and smiled her nice professional smile; it was quite impossible to know what she thought. 'So you see,' Avril concluded, 'it wasn't altogether my choice, though I'm not saying I wasn't perfectly willing to go along with it, more than willing.' And the Health Visitor said yes, she quite understood that, and then she patted Avril on the hand and said she'd look in again, quite soon, in a few days' time maybe.

The conversation, Avril found, had been a release. She'd been keeping herself to herself too much, she realised, no wonder people had been behaving as though she were a bit peculiar or something. And, thinking things over, and remembering the Health Visitor's sympathetic, encouraging interest, it came to her that her experience had been a singular one and, as such, should be shared, not kept from others. And the one person, she reflected (though with slight regret, for she had never really cared much for the man), with whom it should be shared, whose professional concern, after all, it was, was the Vicar. She telephoned the vicarage, and made an appointment to call that evening.

Later, she mulled over her disappointment in the privacy of her room. She had not, before her visit, speculated much if at all about what kind of response she would get: she had expected professional interest, that was all there was to it. And what she had met with had been something quite different.

It could most nearly be described, she thought with anger, as embarrassment. He had sat there, that rather colourless man (even her mother, she now recalled, used to describe him as wishy-washy), and avoided her eye and leapt with alacrity to the phone when it rang and eventually, it seemed to her, cut short the visit and bundled her from the house. There had been a look on his face of alarm, no less. He had said not one thing that had been in any way appropriate. And, Avril thought with bitterness, which, if any, of his parishioners can ever before have come to him and told him, in cold blood and in all humility, what I told him?

She went about her affairs, but in a state of some cynicism. The voice remained silent, though she made tentative overtures, in the privacy of her nights.

The Health Visitor returned, bringing with her another woman, described as Mrs Hamilton who would like a little chat with you, dear. Mrs Hamilton had the same quality of attentive, sympathetic and yet non-committal interest as the Health Visitor. She wondered if Avril would like to tell her about this voice she sometimes heard and Avril, with the bitter taste of the Vicar's inadequacy still in her mouth, was glad to do so. Mrs Hamilton asked if she still had conversations with the voice and Avril explained that a coolness had arisen, but she hoped in time to put that right. She might possibly, she realised now, have been a bit assertive with it, a bit forceful; she would make amends for that. I like, Avril said, talking to it, even if it was, to begin with, on the bullying side, inclined to order people around, if you see what I mean. I don't mind telling you, she went on confidingly, it reminded me of my mother, there was quite a resemblance there.

Mrs Hamilton listened and nodded and smiled. She asked Avril some questions, questions that were maybe a bit personal, Avril thought, and that did not have anything to do with what they had been talking about, or not in any way that she could see. But she seemed a nice enough person, and Avril did not really mind; nor did she mind, though she was surprised, when Mrs Hamilton asked if she would come and have a chat (everybody seemed to want to chat . . .) with a colleague of hers, a Doctor someone, at a place where Mrs Hamilton worked, called the Clinic.

It was nice to have people taking so much interest in you.

And at the Clinic they took even more interest. They nodded and listened and from time to time jotted down a few words on a little white notepad. They seemed to have nothing to do but listen, these people. Avril began, at their suggestion, to pay regular visits to the Clinic; the visits became part of the cycle of her week, like the Red Cross, and the Scout and Guide hut, and evensong. And as the visits went on the voice was heard once more, in the solitude of the nights. And Avril, pleased to have something more substantial and up-to-date for her new friends reported everything it said, though what it had to say was sometimes embarrassing. For it evidently distrusted these people. Don't, it said. Don't go there. Don't talk to them. Don't talk to them about me.

They won't understand, it said. It spoke sulkily. It knew what it was talking about, it said. It had come across all this before. If you knew what I know, it said darkly, if you'd seen what I've seen. They're what we're up against, it said, people like that.

Avril answered conciliatingly. She placated. She tried to conceal her visits to the Clinic.

The voice, of course, knew.

She thought the voice a little uncompromising; the people at the Clinic, after all, displayed no such unswerving prejudice, where the voice was concerned. They were interested, not hostile.

The situation in the house deteriorated; the drains flooded again, Brenda and the Chinese girl, at loggerheads, had a scrap on the stairs in which blood was shed.

At the Clinic, they wondered, in their quiet friendly voices, if Avril would like to come in for a few weeks. For a rest, they said, for treatment. They used the expression in-patient, which startled Avril. She had not realised how things were, until it was put like that, and now it seemed too late to turn back.

But it's not that I . . . she wanted to say, there's no question of . . . But there, now, were the little white notebooks, and the filing cabinets and her name on a pink form, and it seemed so much easier to go along with them, be obliging, and in any case it was not all that disagreeable a place, the Clinic, and the problems of the house, its drains and its plumbing and its tenantry, hung round her neck like so many albatrosses.

She did not tell the voice. She packed her small case that very afternoon and left. Neither did she tell the tenants. With sudden detachment, she thought, well, they will have to sort things out for themselves, I have played my part, I have arranged the house, as I was told, now they must take care of themselves. I have myself to think of.

And in a different bed, that night, she waited for the voice. And presently, in the populated gloom of the ward, it manifested itself. Now look where you have got us, it complained, now look where you have landed us.

Listen, it said, craftily, listen and do as I tell you. Tell them that this is what I said to you . . . Tell them that this is what I told you to do . . .

It lectured on, with renewed confidence, so loudly that she thought it impossible that she alone could hear.

FROM PACK OF CARDS

First response

- Where do you think the voice came from?

- Was Avril Pemberton mad?

- What is your impression of her street, her neighbours and of Mrs Fletcher in particular?

- How would you explain the Vicar's behaviour?

- What do you think the atmosphere was like in Avril's house before the voice and then later, when the house was full? Why did things begin to go wrong?

- Do you think that Avril will respond to treatment? Will the voice disappear? What will happen to her tenants?

Looking closely

Talk

Working in a small group, consider very carefully what Avril did and try to explain whether you think she was right. What do you think the voice that she hears is? Should she have listened to the voices of her neighbours instead? If you had been her neighbour what would your advice to Avril have been at the various stages of the story?

Role play

Working in a pair, choose an important moment from the story then try to improvise one of Avril's conversations with the voice.

Working in a small group, prepare and try out one of the following situations in which each person takes a role:

1. Mrs Fletcher, the Vicar and some other neighbours meet at the church and discuss Avril's household. (Choose a specific point in the story.)

2. Avril has just gone into hospital and Brenda calls a tenants' meeting to discuss what they are going to do; the health visitor could also be there.

3. Work out a case conference in which various 'professional people' meet to discuss Avril's case; you could include the health visitor, the Vicar, the Doctor and others e.g. a social worker, psychiatrist, local council officer with responsibility for rented housing etc.

Write

1. Write a detailed study of Avril Pemberton's character and of her relationships with others. Points to consider are: what we know of her past and her relationship with her dominating mother; her feelings towards Mrs Fletcher; how her attitudes to people differ from those of Mrs Fletcher and of her mother; her social habits and her job; the fact that she did not notice that Mrs Singh was pregnant; her feelings towards Gloria; your views on the source of the voice; the way she 'organised' her house for her new tenants; how her behaviour changes, especially towards the end of the story.

2. Write one of the following letters:

• a personal letter from Mrs Fletcher to a friend who holds similar views about people but who lives out in the country. The letter would mainly be about Avril's house and tenants;

• a formal letter from the Vicar to the psychiatrist who has asked the Vicar to give his views on Avril's behaviour;

• a personal letter from Brenda to a friend (also a nurse) whom she used to work with. Choose a precise moment in the story for Brenda to describe;

• an official letter from the health visitor to the local council about Avril's house and tenants.

3. Imagine that Avril's house becomes something of a local scandal with some people praising what she did and others criticising her, and that a local journalist gets hold of the story. Write up a local newspaper article, including comments from some of the characters, or a script for a local radio station's programme.

4. Imagine that you are the psychiatrist assigned to the case. You have been asked to write a report on Avril, including information from other sources, and a recommendation of what should happen to her. You might include written information or records of interviews from various characters. Think carefully about the formal language the psychiatrist would use in such a report.

5. 'The Homecoming' – continue the story after Avril's treatment is over and she returns home. What does she decide to do? Who is there to greet her? What does the future hold for her? What are the reactions of Mrs Fletcher, the Vicar and so on?

This next extract comes from a novel which tells the story of two men, one a policeman – Mr Justice – and one a criminal – Mr Love. It tells how their lives and personalities are shaped by their environment and their professions and has a great deal to say about the similarities between them. It is set in London and descriptions of the city play an important part in the novel.

Mr Love and Justice

Stepney, in the early morning, has a macabre, poetic beauty. It is one of those areas of London that is thoroughly confused about itself, being in transition from various ancient states of being to new ones it is still busy searching for. The City, which still preserves its Roman quality of ending very abruptly at its ancient gates, towers beyond Aldgate pump, then stops: so that gruesome Venetian financial palaces abut on to semi-slums. From the dowdy baroque of Liverpool street station, smoke and thunder fall on Spitalfields market with its vigorous dawn life and odour of veg, fruit, and flowers – like blended essences of the citizens' duties, delights, and fantasies. Below the windowless brick warehouses of the Port of London Authority, the road life of Wentworth street – almost unknown elsewhere in London where roads are considered means by which you move from place to place, not places in themselves – bubbles, overspills, and sways in argument and shrill persuasion, to the offstage squawks of thousands of slaughtered chickens. Old Montague street with its doorless shops that open outward in the narrow thoroughfare, and its discreet, secretive synagogues, has still the flavour of a semi-voluntary ghetto. Farther south, in Commercial road, are the nocturnal vice caffs that members of parliament and of Royal Commissions are wont to visit, invariably accompanied by a detective-inspector to ensure that their expedition will reveal nothing characteristic of the area; and which, when suppressed, pop up again immediately elsewhere, or under different names with different men of straw at the identical old address. In Cable street, below, the castaways from Africa and the Caribbean perform a perpetual, melancholy, wryly humorous ballet of which they are themselves the only audience. Amid incredible slums – which, one may imagine, with the huge new blocks replacing them, are preserved there by authority to demonstrate the contrast of before-and-after – are pieces of railway architecture of grimly sombre grandeur. Then come the docks with masts and funnels strangely emerging above chimney-tops, and house-locked basins, the entry to which by narrow canals and swinging bridges seems, to the landsman, an impossibility, were it not for the cargo boats nestling snugly between the derelict tenements. Suddenly, beyond this, you come upon the river:

which this far down, lined with wharves and cranes and bearing great ocean-loving steamers, is no longer the pretty, grubby, playground of the higher reaches but already, by now, the sea.

A great charm of the area is that only here, in one sense, is London really a capital city at all. For what, elsewhere in the world, distinguishes capitals from their bleak provincial brethren is that they're open for business all night, and for seven days in the week. Thanks to the markets, seamen, and Commonwealth minorities, in Stepney you can eat and drink, as well as other things, at any hour you choose to; and thanks to the alternation of the Jewish sabbath with the Gentile, the shops and markets never close. All that remains astonishing, since this is England, about this delightful state of affairs, is that no one has yet managed to suppress it.

COLIN MACINNES

Talk

Pair work
Look over the passage carefully and sum up together what impression you gain of Stepney from the passage. Who actually lives in the area and what do the people there do? Would you describe Stepney as a multicultural area? Does your impression from the story tie in with your impression from the photographs on the following page?

Group work
What do you think the writer meant by his last sentence? Do you consider that too much of life in England is subject to controls or even suppression?

Write

Choose an area that you know well and write a description of it that would help a stranger to gain a sense of what life is like there. Think about the general atmosphere, the different sorts of people, the buildings and streets and so on. Have another look at the passage to see the sort of vocabulary that Macinnes uses.

Talk

Pair work
Are there any similarities between what is happening to Stepney and the way in which Avril's area is changing?

Long Distance

Though my mother was already two years dead
Dad kept her slippers warming by the gas,
put hot water bottles her side of the bed
and still went to renew her transport pass.

You couldn't just drop in. You had to phone.
He'd put you off an hour to give him time
to clear away her things and look alone
as though his still raw love were such a crime.

He couldn't risk my blight of disbelief
though sure that very soon he'd hear her key
scrape in the rusted lock and end his grief.
He *knew* she'd just popped out to get the tea.

I believe life ends with death, and that is all.
You haven't both gone shopping; just the same,
in my new black leather phone book there's your name
and the disconnected number I still call.

TONY HARRISON
FROM SELECTED POEMS

- Why do you think the poem is called 'Long Distance'?

- Why has the poet kept his parents' telephone number?

Talk

How does the poet's father behave even though his wife is dead? What kind of relationship do you think his mother and father must have had? Do you feel that the son writing the poem is annoyed with his father's behaviour?

Write

1. The poet states quite clearly "I believe life ends with death, and that is all"; do you feel the same? What is your attitude toward religion? These are such big questions that they may seem impossible to answer. Do not treat this as a formal piece of writing, simply jot down your feelings and ideas and see if they make sense to you. You might then discuss them with others who have tried to express their beliefs.

2. Poetry can be one of the best forms for expressing powerful feelings, especially if you have a sense of loss about

someone or something. Tony Harrison manages to keep his
words and his rhymes very simple and the tone of his poem
very personal; try a poem of your own.

Links with story	Compare the feelings between Avril and her mother and between the poet's father and his wife. Both individuals clearly leave a kind of influence behind them; what is it like?

The Irish Jokes

They spread alarmingly, ethnic caricatures
Featuring Irishmen as thick Micks with huge hands.
They are the club comic's cheap laugh, swelling his sad
Repertoire of in-law, wife, Jew, and blue funnies.
Daily they creep up and jab your shoulder, as now:
How can you spot an Irishman in the car wash?
   He's the one on the bicycle!
Germ-like they pass from mouth to mouth, a verbal 'flu
Which children quickly catch and bring home loud from school.

Perhaps it's the notion of being green as a Treen
Or living on a leaky raft in the Atlantic
Or sheer despair at the chain-reaction killings:
Humour as rank as marsh-gas when all solutions
Founder against nailed sheets of corrugated iron.
One can but listen and smile as the jokes hit home,
   Bullets of fun leaving you weak
At the knee-caps. They will continue to trouble,
Like laughter heard in bars where bombs burst just last year.

**WES MAGEE
FROM STANDPOINTS**

- Do you like Irish jokes?

- Do you think that jokes about people's race and/or colour are offensive?

- How does this writer feel about them? Pick out one line that you think gives a clear idea of his views.

"Do you know the one about the Englishman, Irishman and Scotsman . . . "

Talk

Group work

Is this a good poem or is it just a speech in lines? Work through the poem together and work out first how you think it should be read aloud. What kind of voice and feeling should be used? Look through the poem again for evidence of what makes this a 'poetic' piece rather than just a speech. If it were set out differently would it lose anything?

Pair work

"They spread alarmingly, ethnic caricatures". Do you agree with this statement? What kinds of caricatures have you heard? Do you think that most people use them consciously or unconsciously? Does it matter to you if you use them?

Write

Wes Magee clearly feels very strongly that 'Irish Jokes' are in fact dangerous and, in a sense, tragic. Perhaps you feel strongly about a subject that many other people do not take seriously? If so use the poet's example to help you express your views, try to concentrate some of the anger and frustration into a compact poem.

Links with story

In pairs talk about what evidence we have of the prejudice shown by Avril's neighbours and others from her community. Is there any similarity between it and the subject of 'The Irish Jokes'? Make brief notes on what you decide so that you can discuss them later with the rest of the class.

Mrs Silly

WILLIAM TREVOR

Michael couldn't remember a time when his father had been there. There'd always been the flat where he and his mother lived, poky and cluttered even though his mother tried so. Every Saturday his father came to collect him. He remembered a blue car and then a greenish one. The latest one was white, an Alfa-Romeo.

Saturday with his father was the highlight of the week. Unlike his mother's flat, his father's house was spacious and nicely carpeted. There was Gillian, his father's wife, who never seemed in a hurry, who smiled and didn't waste time. Her smile was cool, which matched the way she dressed. Her voice was quiet and reliable: Michael couldn't imagine it ever becoming shrill or weepy or furious, or in any other way getting out of control. It was a nice voice, as nice as Gillian herself.

His father and Gillian had two little girls, twins of six, two years younger than Michael. They lived hear Haslemere, in a half-timbered house in pretty wooded countryside. On Saturday mornings the drive from London took over an hour, but Michael never minded and on the way back he usually fell asleep. There was a room in the house that his father and Gillian had made his own, which the twins weren't allowed to enter in his absence. He had his Triang train circuit there, on a table that had been specially built into the wall for it.

It was in this house, one Saturday afternoon, that Michael's father brought up the subject of Elton Grange. 'You're nearly nine, you know,' his father said. 'It's high time, really, old chap.'

Elton Grange was a preparatory school in Wiltshire, which Michael's father had gone to himself. He'd mentioned it many times before and so had Michael's mother, but in Michael's mind it was a place that belonged to the distant future – with Radley, where his father had gone, also. He certainly knew that he wasn't going to stay at the primary school in Hammersmith for ever, and had always taken it for granted that he would move away from it when the rest of his class moved, at eleven. He felt, without actually being able to recall the relevant conversation, that his mother had quite definitely implied this. But it didn't work out like that. 'You should go in September,' his father said, and that was that.

'Oh, darling,' his mother murmured when the arrangements had all been made. 'Oh, Michael, I'll miss you.'

His father would pay the fees and his father would in future give him pocket money, over and above what his mother gave him. He'd like it at Elton Grange, his father promised. 'Oh yes, you'll like it,' his mother said too.

She was a woman of medium height, five foot four, with a round, plump face and plump arms and legs. There was a soft prettiness about her, about her light-blue eyes and her wide, simple mouth and her fair, rather fluffy hair. Her hands were always warm, as if expressing the warmth of her nature. She wept easily and often said she was silly to weep so. She talked a lot, getting carried away when she didn't watch herself: for this failing, too, she regularly said she was silly. 'Mrs Silly', she used to say when Michael was younger, condemning herself playfully for the two small follies she found it hard to control.

She worked as a secretary for an Indian, a Mr Ashaf, who had an office-stationery business. There was the shop – more of a warehouse, really – with stacks of swivel chairs and filing-cabinets on top of one another and green metal desks, and cartons containing continuation paper and top-copy foolscap and flimsy, and printed invoices. There were other cartons full of envelopes, and packets of paper-clips, drawing-pins and staples. The carbon-paper supplies were kept in the office behind the shop, where Michael's mother sat in front of a typewriter, typing invoices mainly. Mr Ashaf, a small wiry man, was always on his feet, moving between the shop and the office, keeping an eye on Michael's mother and on Dolores Welsh who looked after the retail side. Before she'd married, Michael's mother had been a secretary in the Wedgwood Centre, but returning to work at the time of her divorce she'd found it more convenient to work for Mr Ashaf since his premises were only five minutes away from where she and Michael lived. Mr Ashaf was happy to employ her on the kind of part-time basis that meant she could be at home every afternoon by the time Michael got in from school. During the holidays Mr Ashaf permitted her to take the typewriter to her flat, to come in every morning to collect what work there was and hand over what she'd done the day before. When this arrangement wasn't convenient, due to the nature of the work, Michael accompanied her to Mr Ashaf's premises and sat in the office with her or with Dolores Welsh in the shop. Mr Ashaf used occasionally to give him a sweet.

'Perhaps I'll change my job,' Michael's mother said brightly, a week before he was due to become a boarder at Elton Grange. 'I could may-be go back to the West End. Nice to have a few more pennies.' She was cheering herself up – he could tell by the way she looked at him. She packed his belongings carefully, giving him many instructions about looking after himself, about keeping himself warm and changing any clothes that got wet. 'Oh, darling,' she said at Paddington on the afternoon of his departure. 'Oh, darling, I'll miss you so!'

He would miss her, too. Although his father and Gillian were in every way more fun than his mother, it was his mother he loved. Although she fussed and was a nuisance sometimes, there was always the warmth, the cosiness of climbing into her bed on Sunday mornings or watching Magic Roundabout together. He was too big for Magic Roundabout now, or so he considered, and he rather thought he was too big to go on climbing into her bed. But the memories of all this cosiness had become part of his relationship with her.

She wept as they stood together on the platform. She held him close to her, pressing his head against her breast. 'Oh, darling!' she said. 'Oh, my darling.'

Her tears damped his face. She sniffed and sobbed, whispering that she didn't know what she'd do. 'Poor thing!' someone passing said. She blew her nose. She apologized to Michael, trying to smile. 'Remember where your envelopes are,' she said. She'd addressed and stamped a dozen envelopes for him so that he could write to her. She wanted him to write at once, just to say he'd arrived safely.

'And don't be homesick now,' she said, her own voice trembling again. 'Big boy, Michael.'

The train left her behind. He waved from the corridor window, and she gestured at him, indicating that he shouldn't lean out. But because of the distances between them he couldn't understand what the gesture meant. When the train stopped at Reading he found his writing-paper and envelopes in his overnight bag and began to write to her.

At Elton Grange he was in the lowest form, Miss Brooks's form. Miss Brooks, grey-haired at sixty, was the only woman on the teaching staff. She did not share the men's common-room but sat instead in the matrons' room, where she smoked Senior Service cigarettes between lessons. There was pale tobacco-tinged hair on her face and on Tuesday and Friday afternoons she wore jodhpurs, being in charge of the school's riding. Brookie she was known as.

The other women at Elton Grange were Sister, and the undermatron Miss Trenchard, the headmaster's wife Mrs Lyng, the lady cook Miss Arland, and the maids. Mrs Lyng was a stout woman, known among the boys as Outsize Dorothy, and Sister was thin and brisk. Miss Trenchard and Miss Arland were both under twenty-three, Miss Arland was pretty and Miss Trenchard wasn't. Miss Arland went about a lot with the history and geography master, Cocky Marshall, and Miss Trenchard was occasionally seen with the P.T. instructor, a Welshman, who was also in charge of the carpentry shop. Among the older boys Miss Trenchard was sometimes known as Tampax.

Twice a week Michael wrote to his mother, and on Sundays he wrote to his father as well. He told them that the headmaster was known to everyone as A.J.L. and he told them about the rules, how no boy in the three lower forms was permitted to be seen with his hands in his pockets and how no boy was permitted to run through A.J.L.'s garden. He said the food was awful because that was what everyone else said, although he quite liked it really.

At half-term his father and Gillian came. They stayed in the Grand, and Michael had lunch and tea there on the Saturday and on the Sunday, and just lunch on the Monday because they had to leave in the afternoon. He told them about his friends, Carson and Tichbourne, and his father suggested that next half-term Carson and Tichbourne might like to have lunch or tea at the Grand. 'Or maybe Swagger Thompson,' Michael said. Thompson's people lived in Kenya and his grandmother, with whom he spent the holidays, wasn't able to come at half-term. 'Hard up,' Michael said.

Tichbourne and Carson were in Michael's dormitory, and one other boy, called Andrews: they were all aged eight. At night, after lights out, they talked about most things: about their families and the houses they lived in and the other schools they'd been at. Carson told about the time he'd put stink-bombs under the chair-legs when people were coming to play bridge, and Andrews about the time he'd been caught, by a policeman, stealing strawberries.

'What's it like?' Andrews asked in the dormitory one night. 'What's it like, a divorce?'

'D'you see your mother?' Tichbourne asked, and Michael explained that it was his mother he lived with, not his father.

'Often wondered what it's like for the kids,' Andrews said. 'There's a woman in our village who's divorced. She ran off with another bloke, only the next thing was he ran off with someone else.'

'Who'd your mum run off with?' Carson asked.

'No one.'

'Your dad run off then?'

'Yes.'

His mother had told him that his father left her because they didn't get on any more. He hadn't left her because he knew Gillian. He hadn't met Gillian for years after that.

'D'you like her?' Andrews asked. 'Gillian?'

'She's all right. They've got twins now, my dad and Gillian. Girls.'

'I'd hate it if my mum and dad got divorced,' Tichbourne said.

'Mine quarrelled all last holidays,' Carson said, 'about having a room decorated.'

'Can't stand it when they quarrel,' Andrews said.

Intrigued by a situation that was strange to them, the other boys often asked after that about the divorce. How badly did people have to quarrel before they decided on one? Was Gillian different from Michael's mother? Did Michael's mother hate her? Did she hate his father?

'They never see one another,' Michael said. 'She's not like Gillian at all.'

At the end of the term the staff put on a show called Staff Laughs. Cocky Marshall was incarcerated all during one sketch in a wooden container that was meant to be a steam bath. Something had gone wrong with it. The steam was too hot and the catch had become jammed. Cocky Marshall was red in the face and nobody knew if he was putting it on or not until the end of the sketch, when he stepped out of the container in his underclothes. Mr Waydelin had to wear a kilt in another sketch and Miss Arland and Miss Trenchard were dressed up in rugby togs, with Cocky Marshall's and Mr Brine's scrum caps. The Reverend Green – mathematics and divinity – was enthusiastically applauded in his Mrs Wagstaffe sketch. A.J.L. did his magic, and as a grand finale the whole staff, including Miss Brooks, sang together, arm-in-arm, on the small stage. 'We're going home,' they sang. 'We're going home. We're on the way that leads to home. We've seen the good things and the bad and now we're absolutely mad. We're g-o-i-n-g home.' All the boys joined in the chorus, and that night in Michael's dormitory they ate Crunchie, Galaxy and Mars Bars and didn't wash their teeth afterwards. At half-past twelve the next day Michael's mother was waiting for him at Paddington.

At home, nothing was different. On Saturdays his father came and drove him away to the house near Haslemere. His mother talked about Dolores Welsh and Mr Ashaf. She hadn't returned to work in the West End. It was quite nice really, she said, at Mr Ashaf's.

Christmas came and went. His father gave him a new Triang locomotive and Gillian gave him a pogo-stick and the twins a magnet and a set of felt-pens. His mother decorated the flat and put fairy-lights on a small Christmas tree. She filled his stocking on Christmas Eve when he was asleep and the next day, after they'd had their Christmas dinner, she gave him a football and a glove puppet and a jigsaw of Windsor Castle. He gave her a brooch he'd bought in Woolworth's. On 14 January he returned to Elton Grange.

Nothing was different at Elton Grange either, except that Cocky Marshall had left. Nobody had known he was going to leave, and some boys said he had been sacked. But others denied that, claiming that he'd gone of his own accord, without giving the required term's notice. They said A.J.L. was livid.

Three weeks passed and then one morning Michael received a letter from his father saying that neither he nor Gillian would be able to come at half-term because he had to go to Tunisia on business and wanted to take Gillian with him. He sent some money to make up for the disappointment.

In a letter to his mother, not knowing what to say because nothing much was happening, Michael revealed that his father wouldn't be there at half-term. *Then I shall come*, his mother wrote back.

She stayed, not in the Grand, but in a boarding-house called Sans Souci, which had coloured gnomes fishing in a pond in the front garden, and a black gate with one hinge broken. They weren't able to have lunch there on the Saturday because the woman who ran it, Mrs Malone, didn't do lunches. They had lunch in the Copper Kettle, and since Mrs Malone didn't do teas either they had tea in the Copper Kettle as well. They walked around the town between lunch and tea, and after tea they sat together in his mother's bedroom until it was time to catch the bus back to school.

The next day she said she'd like to see over the school, so he brought her into the chapel, which once had been the gate-lodge, and into the classrooms and the gymnasium and the art-room and the changing-rooms. In the carpentry shop the P.T. instructor was making a cupboard. 'Who's that boy?' his mother whispered, unfortunately just loud enough for the P.T. instructor to hear. He smiled. Swagger Thompson, who was standing about doing nothing, giggled.

'But how could he be a boy?' Michael asked dismally, leading the way on the cinder path that ran around the cricket pitch. 'Boys at Elton only go up to thirteen and a half.'

'Oh dear, of course,' his mother said. She began to talk of other things. She spoke quickly. Dolores Welsh, she thought, was going to get married, Mr Ashaf had wrenched his arm. She'd spoken to the landlord about the damp that kept coming in the bathroom, but the landlord had said that to cure it would mean a major upheaval for them.

All the time she was speaking, while they walked slowly on the cinder path, he kept thinking about the P.T. instructor, unable to understand how his mother could ever have mistaken him for a boy. It was a cold morning and rather damp, not raining heavily, not even drizzling, but misty in a particularly wetting kind of way. He wondered where they were going to go for lunch, since the woman in the Copper Kettle had said yesterday that the café didn't open on Sundays.

'Perhaps we could go and look at the dormitories?' his mother suggested when they came to the end of the cinder path.

He didn't want to, but for some reason he felt shy about saying so. If he said he didn't want to show her the dormitories, she'd ask him why and he wouldn't know what to say because he didn't know himself.

'All right,' he said.

They walked through the dank mist, back to the school buildings, which were mostly of red brick, some with a straggle of Virginia creeper on them. The new classrooms, presented a year ago by the father of a boy who had left, were of pinker brick than the rest. The old classrooms had been nicer, Michael's father said: they'd once been the stables.

There were several entrances to the house itself. The main one, approached from the cricket pitch by crossing A.J.L.'s lawns and then crossing a large, almost circular gravel expanse, was grandiose in the early Victorian style. Stone pillars supported a wide gothic arch through which, in a sizeable vestibule, further pillars framed a heavy oak front door. There were croquet mallets and hoops in a wooden box in this vestibule, and deck-chairs and two coloured golfing umbrellas. There was an elaborate wrought-iron scraper and a revolving brush for taking the mud from shoes and boots. On either side of the large hall-door there was a round window, composed of circular, lead-encased panes. 'Well, at least they haven't got rid of those,' Michael's father had said, for these circular windows were a feature that boys who had been to Elton Grange often recalled with affection.

The other entrances to the house were at the back and it was through one of these, leading her in from the quadrangle and the squat new classrooms, past the kitchens and the staff lavatory, that Michael directed his mother on their way to the dormitories. All the other places they'd visited had been outside the house itself – the gymnasium and the changing-rooms were converted outbuildings, the carpentry shop was a wooden shed tucked neatly out of the way beside the garages, the art-room was an old conservatory, and the classroom block stood on its own, forming two sides of the quadrangle.

'What a nice smell!' Michael's mother whispered as they passed the kitchens, as Michael pressed himself against the wall to let Miss Brooks, in her jodhpurs, go by. Miss Brooks was carrying a riding stick and had a cigarette going. She didn't smile at Michael, nor at Michael's mother.

They went up the back stairs and Michael hoped they wouldn't meet anyone else. All the boys, except the ones like Swagger Thompson whose people lived abroad, were out with their parents and usually the staff went away at half-term, if they possibly could. But A.J.L. and Outsize Dorothy never went away, nor did Sister, and Miss Trenchard had been there at prayers.

'How ever do you find your way through all these passages?' his mother whispered as he led her expertly towards his dormitory. He explained, in a low voice also, that you got used to the passages.

'Here it is,' he said, relieved to find that neither Sister nor Miss Trenchard was laying out clean towels. He closed the door behind them. 'That's my bed there,' he said.

He stood against the door with his ear cocked while she went to the bed and looked at it. She turned and smiled at him, her head a little on one side. She opened a locker and looked inside, but he explained that the locker she was looking in was Carson's. 'Where'd that nice rug come from?' she asked, and he said that he'd written to Gillian to say he'd been cold once or twice at night, and she'd sent him the rug immediately. 'Oh,' his mother said dispiritedly. 'Well, that was nice of Gillian,' she added.

She crossed to one of the windows and looked down over A.J.L.'s lawns to the chestnut trees that surrounded the playing-fields. It really was a beautiful place, she said.

She smiled at him again and he thought, what he'd never thought before, that her clothes were cheap-looking. Gillian's clothes were clothes you somehow didn't notice: it didn't occur to you to think they were cheap-looking or expensive. The women of Elton Grange all dressed differently, Outsize Dorothy in woollen things, Miss Brooks in suits, with a tie, and Sister and Miss Trenchard and Miss Arland always had white coats. The maids wore blue overalls most of the time but sometimes you saw them going home in the evenings in their ordinary clothes, which you never really thought about and certainly you never thought were cheap-looking.

'Really beautiful,' she said, still smiling, still at the window. She was wearing a headscarf and a maroon coat and another scarf at her neck. Her handbag was maroon also, but it was old, with something broken on one of the buckles: it was the handbag, he said to himself, that made you think she was cheaply dressed.

He left the door and went to her, taking her arm. He felt ashamed that he'd thought her clothes were cheap-looking. She'd been upset when he'd told her that the rug had been sent by Gillian. She'd been upset and he hadn't bothered.

'Oh, Mummy,' he said.

She hugged him to her, and when he looked up into her face he saw the mark of a tear on one of her cheeks. Her fluffy hair was sticking out a bit beneath the headscarf, her round, plump face was forcing itself to smile.

'I'm sorry,' he said.

'Sorry? Darling, there's no need.'

'I'm sorry you're left all alone there, Mummy.'

'Oh, but I'm not at all. I've got the office every day, and one of these days I really will see about going back to the West End. We've been awfully busy at the office, actually, masses to do.'

The sympathy he'd showed caused her to talk. Up to now – ever since they'd met the day before – she'd quite deliberately held herself back in this respect, knowing that to chatter on wouldn't be the thing at all. Yesterday she'd waited until she'd returned to Sans Souci before relaxing. She'd had a nice long chat with Mrs Malone on the landing, which unfortunately had been spoiled by a man in one of Mrs Malone's upper rooms poking his head out and asking for a bit of peace. 'Sorry about that,' she'd heard Mrs Malone saying to him later. 'Couldn't really stop her.' – a statement that had spoiled things even more. 'I'm ever so sorry,' she'd said quietly to Mrs Malone at breakfast.

'Let's go down now,' Michael said.

But his mother didn't hear this remark, engaged as she was upon making a series of remarks herself. She was no longer discreetly whispering, but chattering on with more abandon than she had even displayed on Mrs Malone's stairs the night before. A flush had spread over her cheeks and around her mouth and on the portion of her neck which could be seen above her scarf. Michael could see she was happy.

'We'll have to go to Dolores' wedding,' she said. 'On the eighth. The eighth of May, a Thursday I think it is. They're coming round actually, Dolores and her young chap, Brian Haskins he's called. Mr Ashaf says he wouldn't trust him, but actually Dolores is no fool.'

'Let's go down now, Mum.'

She said she'd like to see the other dormitories. She'd like to see the senior dormitories, into one of which Michael would eventually be moving. She began to talk about Dolores Welsh and Brian Haskins again and then about Mrs Malone, and then about a woman Michael had never heard of before, a person called Peggy Urch.

He pointed out that the dormitories were called after imperial heroes. His was Drake, others were Raleigh, Nelson, Wellington, Marlborough and Clive. 'I think I'll be moving to Nelson,' Michael said. 'Or Marlborough. Depends.' But he knew she wasn't listening, he knew she hadn't taken in the fact that the dormitories were named like that. She was talking about Peggy Urch when he led her into Marlborough.

Outsize Dorothy was there with Miss Trenchard, taking stuff out of Verschoyle's locker because Verschoyle had just gone to the sanatorium.

'Very nice person,' Michael's mother was saying. 'She's taken on the Redmans' flat – the one above us, you know.'

It seemed to Michael that his mother didn't see Outsize Dorothy and Miss Trenchard. It seemed to him for a moment that his mother didn't quite know where she was.

'Looking for me?' Outsize Dorothy said. She smiled and waddled towards them. She looked at Michael, waiting for him to explain who this visitor was. Miss Trenchard looked, too.

'It's my mother,' he said, aware that these words were inept and inelegant.

'I'm Mrs Lyng,' Outsize Dorothy said. She held out her hand and Michael's mother took it.

'The Matron,' she said. 'I've heard of you, Mrs Lyng.'

'Well actually,' Outsize Dorothy contradicted with a laugh, 'I'm the headmaster's wife.' All the flesh on her body wobbled when she laughed. Tichbourne said he knew for a fact she was twenty stone.

'What a lovely place you have, Mrs Lyng. I was just saying to Michael. What a view from the windows!'

Outsize Dorothy told Miss Trenchard to go on getting Verschoyle's things together, in a voice that implied that Miss Trenchard wasn't paid to stand about doing nothing in the dormitories. All the women staff – the maids and Sister and Miss Arland and Miss Trenchard – hated Outsize Dorothy because she'd expect them, even Sister, to go on rooting in a locker while she talked to a parent. She wouldn't in a million years say: 'This is Miss Trenchard, the undermatron.'

'Oh, I'm afraid we don't have much time for views at Elton,' Outsize Dorothy said. She was looking puzzled, and Michael imagined she was thinking that his mother was surely another woman, a thinner, smarter, quieter person. But then Outsize Dorothy wasn't clever, as she often light-heartedly said herself, and was probably saying to herself that she must be confusing one boy's mother with another.

'Dorothy!' a voice called out, a voice which Michael instantly and to his horror recognized as A.J.L.'s.

'We had such a view at home!' Michael's mother said. 'Such a gorgeous view!' She was referring to her own home, a rectory in Somerset somewhere. She'd often told Michael about the rectory and the view, and her parents, both dead now. Her father had received the call to the Church late in life: he'd been in the Customs and Excise before that.

'Here, dear,' Outsize Dorothy called out. 'In Marlborough.'

Michael knew he'd gone red in the face. His stomach felt hot also, the palms of his hands were clammy. He could hear the clatter of the headmaster's footsteps on the uncarpeted back stairs. He began to pray, asking for something to happen, anything at all, anything God could think of.

His mother was more animated than before. More fluffy hair had slipped out from beneath her headscarf, the flush had spread over a greater area of her face. She was talking about the lack of view from the flat where she and Michael lived in Hammersmith, and about Peggy Urch who'd come to live in the flat directly above them and whose view was better because she could see over the poplars.

'Hullo,' A.J.L. said, a stringy, sandy man, the opposite of Outsize Dorothy and in many ways the perfect complement. Tichbourne said he often imagined them naked in bed, A.J.L. winding his stringiness around her explosive bulk.

Hands were shaken again. 'Having a look round?' A.J.L. said. 'Staying at the Grand?'

Michael's mother said she wasn't staying at the Grand but at Sans Souci, did he know it? They'd been talking about views, she said, it was lovely to have a room with a view, she hoped Michael wasn't giving trouble, her husband of course – well, ex-husband now – had been to this school in his time, before going on to Radley. Michael would probably go to Radley too.

'Well, we hope so,' A.J.L. said, seizing the back of Michael's neck. 'Shown her the new classrooms, eh?'

'Yes, sir.'

'Shown her where we're going to have our swimming-pool?'

'Not yet, sir.'

'Well, then.'

His mother spoke of various diseases Michael had had, measles and whooping cough and chicken-pox, and of diseases he hadn't had, mumps in particular. Miss Trenchard was like a ghost, all in white, still sorting out the junk in Verschoyle's locker, not daring to say a word. She was crouched there, with her head inside the locker, listening to everything.

'Well, we mustn't keep you,' A.J.L. said, shaking hands again with Michael's mother. 'Always feel free to come.'

There was such finality about these statements, more in the headmaster's tone than in the words themselves, that Michael's mother was immediately silent. The statements had a physical effect on her, as though quite violently they had struck her across the face. When she spoke again it was in the whisper she had earlier employed.

'I'm sorry,' she said. 'I'm ever so sorry for going on so.'

A.J.L. and Outsize Dorothy laughed, pretending not to understand what she meant. Miss Trenchard would tell Miss Arland. Sister would hear and so would Brookie, and the P.T. Instructor would say that this same woman had imagined him to be one of the boys. Mr Waydelin would hear, and Square-jaw Simpson – Cocky Marshall's successor – and Mr Brine and the Reverend Green.

'I have enjoyed it,' Michael's mother whispered. 'So nice to meet you.'

He went before her down the back stairs. His face was still red. They passed by the staff lavatory and the kitchens, out on to the concrete quadrangle. It was still misty and cold.

'I bought things for lunch,' she said, and for an awful moment he thought that she'd want to eat them somewhere in the school or in the grounds – in the art-room or the cricket pavilion. 'We could have a picnic in my room,' she said.

They walked down the short drive, past the chapel that once had been the gate-lodge. They caught a bus after a wait of half an hour, during which she began to talk again, telling him more about Peggy Urch, who reminded her of another friend she'd had once, a Margy Bassett. In her room in Sans Souci she went on talking, spreading out on the bed triangles of cheese and tomatoes and rolls and biscuits and oranges. They sat in her room when they'd finished, eating Rollo. At six o'clock they caught a bus back to Elton Grange. She wept a little when she said goodbye.

Michael's mother did not, as it happened, ever arrive at Elton Grange at half-term again. There was no need for her to do so because his father and Gillian were always able to come themselves. For several terms he felt embarrassed in the presence of A.J.L. and Outsize Dorothy and Miss Trenchard, but no one at school mentioned the unfortunate visit, not even Swagger Thompson, who had so delightedly overheard her assuming the P.T. Instructor to be one of the boys. School continued as before and so did the holidays, Saturdays in Haslemere and the rest of the week in Hammersmith, news of Mr Ashaf and Dolores Welsh, now Dolores Haskins. Peggy Urch, the woman in the flat upstairs, often came down for a chat.

Often, too, Michael and his mother would sit together in the evenings on the sofa in front of the electric fire. She'd tell him about the rectory in Somerset and her father who had received the call to the Church late in his life, who'd been in the Customs and Excise. She'd tell him about her own childhood, and even about the early days of her marriage. Sometimes she wept a little, hardly at all, and he would take her arm on the sofa and she would smile and laugh. When they sat together on the sofa or went out together, to the cinema, or for a walk by the river or to the teashop called the Maids of Honour near Kew Gardens, Michael felt that he would never want to marry because he'd prefer to be with his mother. Even when she chatted on to some stranger in the Maids of Honour he felt he loved her: everything was different from the time she'd come to Elton Grange because away from Elton Grange things didn't matter in the same way.

Then something unpleasant threatened. During his last term at Elton Grange Michael was to be confirmed. 'Oh, but of course I must come,' his mother said.

It promised to be worse than the previous occasion. After the service you were meant to bring your parents in to tea in the Great Hall and see that they had a cup of tea and sandwiches and cakes. You had to introduce them to the Bishop of Bath and Wells. Michael imagined all that. In bed at night he imagined his father and Gillian looking very smart, his father chatting easily to Mr Brine, Gillian smiling at Outsize Dorothy, and his mother's hair fluffing out from beneath her headscarf. He imagined his mother and his father and Gillian having to sit together in a pew in chapel, as naturally they'd be expected to, being members of the same party.

'There's no need to,' he said in the flat in Hammersmith. 'There's really no need to, Mum.'

She didn't mention his father and Gillian, although he'd repeatedly said that they'd be there. It was as if she didn't want to think about them, as if she was deliberately pretending that they'd decided not to attend. She'd stay in Sans Souci again, she said. They'd have a picnic in her room, since the newly confirmed were to be excused school tea on the evening of the service. 'Dinner at the Grand, old chap,' his father said. 'Bring Tichbourne if you want to.'

Michael returned to Elton Grange at the end of the Easter holidays, leaving his mother in a state of high excitement at Paddington Station because she'd be seeing him again within five weeks. He thought he might invent an illness a day or two before the confirmation, or say at the last moment that he had doubts. In fact, he did hint to the Reverend Green that he wasn't certain about being quite ready for the occasion, but the Reverend Green sharply told him not to be silly. Every time he went down on his knees at the end of a session with the Reverend Green he prayed that God might come to his rescue. But God did not, and all during the night before the confirmation service he lay awake. It wasn't just because she was weepy and embarrassing, he thought: it was because she dressed in that cheap way, it was because she was common, with a common voice that wasn't at all like Gillian's or Mrs Tichbourne's or Mrs Carson's or even Outsize Dorothy's. He couldn't prevent these thoughts from occurring. Why couldn't she do something about her fluffy hair? Why did she have to gabble like that? 'I think I have a temperature,' he said in the morning, but when Sister took it it was only 98.

Before the service the other candidates waited outside the chapel to greet their parents and godparents, but Michael went into the chapel early and took up a devout position. Through his fingers he saw the Reverend Green lighting the candles and preparing the altar. Occasionally, the Reverend Green glanced at Michael, somewhat suspiciously.

'Defend, O Lord, this Thy child,' said the Bishop of Bath and Wells, and when Michael walked back to his seat he kept his head down, not wanting to see his parents and Gillian. They sang Hymn 459. 'My God, accept,' sang Michael, 'my heart this day.'

He walked with Swagger Thompson down the aisle, still with his eyes down. 'Fantastic,' said Swagger Thompson outside the chapel, for want of anything better to say. 'Bloody fantastic.' They waited for the congregation to come out.

Michael had godparents, but his father had said that they wouldn't be able to attend. His godmother had sent him a prayer-book.

'Well done,' his father said. 'Well done, Mike.'

'What lovely singing!' Gillian murmured. She was wearing a white dress with a collar that was slightly turned up, and a white wide-rimmed hat. On the gravel outside the chapel she put on dark glasses against the afternoon sun.

'You mother's here somewhere,' his father said. 'You'd better see to her, Mike.' He spoke quietly, with a hand resting for a moment on Michael's shoulder. 'We'll be all right,' he added.

Michael turned. She was standing alone, as he knew she would be. Unable to prevent himself, he wished she wouldn't always wear head-scarves. 'Oh, darling,' she said.

She took his hands and pulled him towards her. She kissed him, apologizing for the embrace but saying that it was a special occasion. She wished her father were alive, she said.

'Tea in the Great Hall,' A.J.L. was booming, and Outsize Dorothy was waddling about in flowered yellow, smiling at the faces of parents and godparents. 'Do come and have tea,' she gushed.

'Oh, I'd love a cup of tea,' Michael's mother whispered.

The crowd was moving through the sunshine, suited men, the Reverend Green in his cassock, the Bishop in crimson, women in their garden-party finery. They walked up the short drive from the chapel. They passed through the wide gothic arch that heralded the front door, through the vestibule where the croquet set was tidily in place and the deck-chairs neat against a wall. They entered what A.J.L. had years ago christened the Great Hall, where buttered buns and sandwiches and cakes and sausage-rolls were laid out on trestle tables. Miss Trenchard and Miss Arland were in charge of two silver-plated tea-urns.

'I'll get you something to eat,' Michael said to his mother, leaving her although he knew she didn't want to be left. 'Seems no time since I was getting done myself,' he heard his father saying to A.J.L.

Miss Arland poured a cup of tea for his mother and told him to offer her something to eat. He close a plate of sausage-rolls. She smiled at him. 'Don't go away again,' she whispered.

But he had to go away again because he couldn't stand there holding the sausage-rolls. He darted back to the table and left the plate there, taking one for himself. When he returned to his mother she'd been joined by the Reverend Green and the Bishop.

The Bishop shook Michael's hand and said it had been a very great pleasure to confirm him.

'My father was in the Church,' Michael's mother said, and Michael knew that she wasn't going to stop now. He watched her struggling to hold the words back, crumbling the pastry of her sausage-roll beneath her fingers. The flush had come into her cheeks, there was a brightness in her eyes. The Bishop's face was kind: she couldn't help herself, when kindness like that was there.

'We really must be moving,' the Reverend Green said, but the Bishop only smiled, and on and on she went about her father and the call he'd received so late in life. 'I'm sure you knew him, my lord,' was one suggestion she made, and the Bishop kindly agreed that he probably had.

'Mrs Grainer would like to meet the Bishop,' Outsize Dorothy murmured to the Reverend Green. She looked at Michael's mother and Michael could see her remembering her and not caring for her.

'Well, if you'll excuse us,' the Reverend Green said, seizing the Bishop's arm.

'Oh Michael dear, isn't that a coincidence!'

There was happiness all over her face, bursting from her eyes, in her smile and her flushed cheeks and her fluffy hair. She turned to Mr and Mrs Tichbourne, who were talking to Mrs Carson, and said the Bishop had known her father, apparently quite well. She hadn't even been aware that it was to be this particular bishop today, it hadn't even occurred to her while she'd been at the confirmation service that such a coincidence could be possible. Her father had passed away fifteen years ago, he'd have been a contemporary of the Bishop's. 'He was in the Customs and Excise,' she said, 'before he received the call.'

They didn't turn away from her. They listened, putting in a word or two, about coincidences and the niceness of the Bishop. Tichbourne and Carson stood eating sandwiches, offering them to one another. Michael's face felt like a bonfire.

'We'll probably see you later,' Mr Tichbourne said, eventually edging his wife away. 'We're staying at the Grand.'

'Oh no, I'm at Sans Souci. Couldn't ever afford the Grand!' She laughed.

'Don't think we know the Sans Souci,' Mrs Tichbourne said.

'Darling, I'd love another cup of tea,' his mother said to Michael, and he went away to get her one, leaving her with Mrs Carson. When he returned she was referring to Peggy Urch.

It was then, while talking to Mrs Carson, that Michael's mother fell. Afterwards she said that she'd felt something slimy under one of her heels and had moved to rid herself of it. The next thing she knew she was lying on her back on the floor, soaked in tea.

Mrs Carson helped her to her feet. A.J.L. hovered solicitously. Outsize Dorothy picked up the cup and saucer.

'I'm quite all right,' Michael's mother kept repeating. 'There was something slippy on the floor, I'm quite all right.'

She was led to a chair by A.J.L. 'I think we'd best call on Sister,' he said. 'Just to be sure.'

But she insisted that she was all right, that there was no need to go bothering Sister. She was as white as a sheet.

Michael's father and Gillian came up to her and said they were sorry. Michael could see Tichbourne and Carson nudging one another, giggling. For a moment he thought of running away, hiding in the attics or something. Half a buttered bun had got stuck to the sleeve of his mother's maroon coat when she'd fallen. Her left leg was saturated with tea.

'We'll drive you into town,' his father said. 'Horrible thing to happen.'

'It's just my elbow,' his mother whispered. 'I came down on my elbow.'

Carson and Tichbourne would imitate it because Carson and Tichbourne imitated everything. They'd stand there, pretending to be holding a cup of tea, and suddenly they'd be lying flat on their backs. 'I think we'd best call on Sister,' Carson would say, imitating A.J.L.

His father and Gillian said goodbye to Outsize Dorothy and to A.J.L. His mother, reduced to humble silence again, seemed only to want to get away. In the car she didn't say anything at all and when they reached Sans Souci she didn't seem to expect Michael to go in with her. She left the car, whispering her thanks, a little colour gathering in her face again.

That evening Michael had dinner with Gillian and his father in the

Grand. Tichbourne was there also, and Carson, and several other boys, all with their parents. 'I can drive a few of them back,' his father said, 'save everyone getting a car out.' He crossed the dining-room floor and spoke to Mr Tichbourne and Mr Carson and the father of a boy called Mallabedeely. Michael ate minestrone soup and chicken with peas and roast potatoes. Gillian told him what the twins had been up to and said his father was going to have a swimming-pool put in. His father returned to the table and announced that he'd arranged to drive everyone back at nine o'clock.

Eating his chicken, he imagined his mother at Sans Souci, sitting on the edge of the bed, probably having a cry. He imagined her bringing back to London the stuff she'd bought for a picnic in her room. She'd never refer to any of that, she'd never upbraid him for going to the Grand for dinner when she'd wanted him to be with her. She'd consider it just that she should be punished.

As they got into the car, his father said he'd drive round by Sans Souci so that Michael could run in for a minute. 'We're meant to be back by a quarter past,' Michael said quickly. 'I've said goodbye to her,' he added, which wasn't quite true.

It would perhaps have been different if Tichbourne and Carson hadn't been in the car. He'd have gone in and paused with her for a minute because he felt pity for her. But the unattractive façade of Sans Souci, the broken gate of the small front garden and the fishermen gnomes would have caused further nudging and giggling in his father's white Alfa-Romeo.

'You're sure now?' his father said. 'I'll get you there by a quarter past.'

'No, it's all right.'

She wouldn't be expecting him. She wouldn't even have unpacked the picnic she'd brought.

'Hey, was that your godmother?' Tichbourne asked in the dormitory. 'The one who copped it on the floor?'

He began to shake his head and then he paused and went on shaking it. An aunt, he said, some kind of aunt, he wasn't sure what the relationship was. He hadn't thought of saying that before, yet it seemed so simple, and so right and so natural, that a distant aunt should come to a confirmation service and not stay, like everyone else, in the Grand. 'God, it was funny,' Carson said, and Tichbourne did his imitation, and Michael laughed with his friends. He was grateful to them for assuming that such a person could not be his mother. A.J.L. and Outsize Dorothy and Miss Trenchard knew she was his mother, and so did the Reverend Green, but for the remainder of his time at Elton Grange none of these people would have cause to refer to the fact in public. And if by chance A.J.L. did happen to say in class tomorrow that he hoped his mother was all right after her fall, Michael would say afterwards that A.J.L. had got it all wrong.

In the dark, he whispered to her in his mind. He said he was sorry, he said he loved her better than anyone.

First response

- Why does Michael "whisper to her in his mind"? Why is he so sorry?

- Does Michael always feel embarrassed about his mother? What happens to him whilst he is at Elton Grange?

- How do you feel towards his father and Gillian?

- Do you think you would have found Michael's mother embarrassing?

- Do you think that Mrs Silly is a fair nickname for her?

Talk

Group work

1. Who do you feel is to blame for Michael's embarrassment about his mother? Is it simply the fact that he is growing up and becoming self-conscious? Is it the nature of Elton Grange and of the boys who go there? Is it his mother's character and behaviour? Is it mainly to do with the contrast between Michael's home with his mother and the spacious house and smart car belonging to his father and Gillian?

2. Michael goes away to school at a very early age. Do you think that Elton Grange (or somewhere similar) would have suited you at the same age? How do you feel about children going to boarding school? What are the advantages and disadvantages of such a system for children and their parents?

Pair work

From your knowledge of the story, what do you think were the likely causes of Michael's parents' divorce? You could begin by jotting down what Michael actually says about the matter and then by trying to agree on how far this is the truth.

Role play	**1.** What would Michael say if he did get asked by AJL in class what happened to his mother? First improvise that conversation and then a later one between Michael and one of his friends.

2. When Michael next goes home, what will he say to his mother when they talk about the confirmation? Improvise their conversation about school generally and the confirmation in particular.

Write	**1.** Write several letters, at least one by Michael and one by his mother, that show their characters and feelings about each other, about school and so on.

2. Write a close study of Michael's character. What sort of person is he? What kind of relationships does he have with his mother, his father and with other boys his age? How does he grow up and change during the course of the story? What factors influence the way he grows up and, in particular, the way he begins to understand his mother?

3. Continue the story and describe the next few days. How does Michael cope with the questions and jokes that he has to suffer?

Her People was published in 1982 when Kathleen Dayus was 79. It is an account of her childhood years, spent in the slums of Birmingham, and is particularly vivid in its descriptions of family and neighbourhood life in Edwardian England.

Her People

They were dirty old houses; everyone had vermin or insects of some description. There were fleas, bugs, rats, mice and cockroaches – you name it, we had it. But I'll still say this for our mum; although we were as poor as the rest, she always kept us clean. Many times we had to stay in bed while she took the clothes from us to wash and dry in front of the fire so that we could go to school the next day looking clean.

Our mum was also very cruel and spiteful towards us, especially to me, and I could never make out why until I was old enough to be told. I can picture her now as I write. She was a large, handsome woman, except in her ugly moods. She weighed about sixteen stone and always wore a black alpaca frock, green with age, which reached down to her ankles, and a black apron on top. On her feet she wore button-up boots, size eight, which it was my job to clean and fasten with a steel button hook that hung by the fireplace. Mum always pretended she couldn't bend when she wanted her boots buttoned. She had long, black hair which she was always brushing and combing. She twisted it round her hand and swung it into a bun on top of her head. Then she'd look in the mirror and plunge a long hatpin through the bun. She called this hatpin her 'weapon'. Sometimes when she went out she'd put Dad's cap on top which made her look taller. She was always on the go, one way or another. I felt sorry for her at times and I tried my best to love her but we all lived in fear when she started to shout. When she did start you knew it. You had to move quickly, for it was no sooner the word than the blow!

Many a time we felt the flat of her hand, Liza, Frankie and me. We never knew what for at times, but down would come the cane from its place on the wall. If we tried to run away then we really had it. Neither our parents nor the neighbours had any time to give us any love or affection and they didn't listen to our troubles. We were little drudges and always in the way. You may ask who was to blame for us growing up like this in squalor, poverty and ignorance. We were too young to understand why then, and I don't think I understand yet, but there it was, we had to make the best of it. My dad would listen to us sometimes but only when Mum wasn't about, or if he'd had an extra drop of beer. It was at these times that I liked him best because sometimes, not always, he was jolly. This wasn't very often because he was out of work, and had only Mum or his pals to rely on to buy him a drink. He had to do an odd job or two before Mum gave him his beer money. Sometimes he did odd jobs for other people on the sly, before the relief officer made his visit.

Our dad never hit us. He would tell us off and show us the strap but he left the correcting to Mum, and she did enough for both. So we young ones tried very hard to behave ourselves when Dad was out and he was more times out than in. He always said he couldn't stand her 'tantrums' but my brother Jack took over when Dad was out, pushing us this way then that and giving us the occasional back-hander if we didn't do what he told us.

We saw very little of my brother Charlie; he only came home to sleep. Mother's tantrums got on his nerves also.

Frankie and I were the best of pals. He always tried to get me out of trouble, but he often got me into some. But I still loved him.

My sister Liza was very spiteful to me as well as being artful and although I tried to love her she pushed me away and pinched me on the sly when she had the chance. I couldn't do much about this because she was bigger than I was and very fat besides. When she did give me a sly dig I just had to grin and bear it and keep out of her and Mum's way. I still had to sleep with Liza and if she didn't pinch me she'd kick me out of bed. It was no good complaining, because Liza was always telling lies and Mum would believe her: she couldn't do wrong in Mum's eyes.

I remember one night very clearly. It was about one o'clock in the morning. I woke very thirsty so I crept quietly out of bed so as not to wake Liza or Frankie and went downstairs to get a drink of water. There wasn't any in the house, only a drop of warm water in the kettle. After satisfying my thirst I tiptoed back upstairs but when I got halfway up I heard Mum say, 'No! You can put it away! I've already had a baker's dozen. I'm 'avin' no mower so yow can get to sleep!'

I was always a very inquisitive child so I sat on the stairs to listen for more but I only heard the bed creak, so off up to the attic I went. I was feeling cold in my torn and threadbare chemise, one of Mary's cutdowns. I lay awake that night trying to puzzle out what my mum meant. I thought maybe she had eaten too much and wasn't feeling well so next morning when I came downstairs I said, 'Don't you feel well, Mum . . . have you eaten too much?'

At once she glared down at me and shouted, 'What do yer mean . . . 'ave I eaten too much?'

'Well, I heard you say to Dad you'd already had a baker's dozen,' I answered, trembling a little.

Mum went red in the face and cried out, 'And where did yer 'ear that?'

Then timidly I explained how I came down the stairs for a drink of water but before I could finish she slapped me across the face and shouted, 'That'll teach yer ter sit listenin' on the stairs!'

I moved back quickly as she lifted her hand once again so I was quite surprised when she seemed to have second thoughts.

'I'll get yer dad ter settle with yow.'

Whether she told him or not I never found out but I was determined to find out one way or another what was meant by a baker's dozen. So that same night I waited for Mary to come up to bed and after Liza and Frankie fell asleep I crept over to her bed.

'Are you awake, Mary?' I whispered in the dark.

'Yes. What do yer want?' she snapped. She didn't usually snap at me, but I could see why she didn't want to be bothered at that time of night. I began to tiptoe back to bed when she lit the candle and called me.

'Come on, Katie. What is it you want?' she asked more pleasantly.

Just then Mum shouted up the attic stairs. 'Let's 'ave less noise up theea!'

Mary smiled as she put her finger to her lips. 'Hush,' she whispered. 'Come and get into bed beside me and get warm then you can tell me all about it.'

I snuggled up close and felt very comforted. I could have gone straight off to sleep, but Mary wanted to know what was troubling me.

'Can you tell me what a baker's dozen is, Mary?' I managed to ask between yawns.

'Why? Where did you hear that?' She sat up in bed looking at me quizzically, and as I told her a broad smile spread across her face.

'You were lucky to get away with only your face slapped.' I was wide awake by now.

'Well, what does it mean?'

'It means Mum didn't want Dad to love her and to have any more babies. She's already had thirteen which is what's called a "baker's dozen" and you being the thirteenth, Mum calls you the "scraping of the pot".'

I could still see her smiling in the candlelight as she whispered to herself, 'I must tell Albert about this when we meet.'

'But if I'm the last, what became of the others in between?'

'They all died before you were ever thought of,' she answered sadly. 'Now lie down and go to sleep.'

We both snuggled up to keep warm after she blew out the candle. Although I was warm and comfortable I couldn't help but think about those other seven who had died. Maybe they were happier in the other world, I thought. There wouldn't have been room for them here, and Mum and Dad wouldn't have been able to feed us all. And with all these thoughts in my mind I eventually dropped off to sleep.

KATHLEEN DAYUS

- In pairs, look through the passage to see what we learn about the life of the family. Jot down the facts that you discover and then add your impression of what life was like in that household.

- What shows that the narrator was young and innocent at the time of these incidents?

Talk

In groups, talk about what impression you gain from the passage of Kathleen's childhood. Do you feel that her family were a happy group? Do you think that large families have any advantages over smaller ones?

Write

This is a piece of autobiographical writing mainly centred on Kathleen's overhearing her mother's rejection of her father's advances one night; an event that causes great amusement in the family.

Try writing a piece about your own family which centres on a particular incident or event and which shows different characters and attitudes. This need not be a funny event, just something in which the whole family became involved.

Links with story	Compare the relationship between Michael and his mother and Kathleen with hers. Their respective families are clearly different but does this mean that their relationships are also?

This extract is from a short story about two boys at a rather shabby private school in Ireland who, though quite different characters, become companions for a while. Cummins' parents own a small general shop and send him a regular parcel to supplement the food he is given at school. They are a small and very loving family who have to struggle to send their son to this school and they are very proud to do so. Denis' parents are separated and his mother is always complaining that his father does not give her enough money so she has to send him to a poor school. For most of the story Denis feels pity and some contempt for Cummins and his family because he thinks that they are rather naive in liking the school; this feeling gives him a sense of superiority. Towards the end of the story he starts to receive parcels himself and he takes this at first as a sign that his mother truly loves him, something that in his heart he doubts.

Pity

At the same time it left unexplained something about Francis himself. Denis knew that if he was an only child with a mother and father like that, he would not allow them to remain in ignorance for long. He would soon get away from the filthy dormitory and the brutal society. At first he thought that Francis probably thought it a fine place too, and in a frenzy of altruism decided that it was his duty to talk to Mrs Cummins and tell her the whole truth about it, but then he realised that Francis could not possibly have been taken in in the same way as his parents. He was a weakling and a prig, but he had a sort of country cuteness which enabled him to see through fellows. No, Francis was probably putting up with it because he felt it was his duty, or for the sake of his vocation, because he thought that life was like that, a vale of tears, and whenever he was homesick or when fellows jeered at him, he probably went to the chapel and offered it up. It seemed very queer to Denis because when he was homesick or mad he waited till lights were out and then started to bawl in complete silence for fear his neighbours would hear.

He made a point of impressing on his mother the lavishness of the Cumminses, and told her all about the accordion and the pistol and the weekly parcels with a vague hope of creating larger standards of generosity in her, but she only said that Irish shopkeepers were rotten with money and didn't know how to spend it, and that if only Denis's father would give her what she was entitled to he might go to the best college in Ireland where he would meet only the children of professional people.

All the same, when he went back to school there was a change. A parcel arrived for him, and when he opened it there were all the things he had mentioned to her. For a while he felt a little ashamed. It was probably true that his father did not give her all the money she needed, and that she could only send him parcels by stinting herself; but still, it was a relief to be able to show off in front of the others whose parents were less generous.

That evening he ran into Cummins who smiled at him in his pudding-faced way.

'Do you want anything, Denis?' he asked. 'I have a parcel if you do.'

'I have a parcel of my own today,' Denis said cockily. 'Would you like peaches? I have peaches.'

'Don't be eating it all now,' Cummins said with a comic wail. 'You won't have anything left tomorrow if you do.'

'Ah, what difference does it make?' said Denis with a shrug, and with reckless abandonment he rewarded his friends and conciliated his foes with the contents of his parcel. Next evening he was almost as bad as ever.

'Jay, Denis,' Cummins said with amused resignation, 'you're a blooming fright. I told you what was going to happen. How are you going to live when you grow up if you can never keep anything?'

'Ah, boy,' Denis said, in his embarrassment doing the big shot, 'you wait till I am grown up and you'll see.'

'I know what I'll see all right,' Cummins said, shaking his head sadly. 'Better men than you went to the wall. 'Tis the habits we learn at this age that decide what we're going to be later on. And anyway, how are you going to get a job? Sure, you won't learn anything. If you'd even learn the piano I could teach you.'

Cummins was a born preacher, and Denis saw that there was something in what he said, but no amount of preaching could change him. That was the sort he was. Come day, go day, God send Sunday – and anyway it didn't really make much difference because Cummins with his thrifty habits usually had enough to keep him going till the next parcel came.

Then, about a month later as Denis was opening his weekly parcel under the eyes of his gang, Anthony Harty stood by, gaping with the rest. Harty was a mean, miserable creature from Clare who never got anything, and was consumed with jealousy of everyone who did.

'How well you didn't get any parcels last year, and now you're getting them all the time, Halligan,' he said suspiciously.

'That's only because my mother didn't know about the grub in this place,' Denis declared confidently.

'A wonder she wouldn't address them herself, so,' sneered Harty.

'What do you mean, Harty?' Denis asked, going up to him with his fists clenched. 'Are you looking for a puck in the gob?'

'I'm only saying that's not the writing on your letters,' replied Harty, pointing at the label.

'And why would it be?' shouted Denis. 'I suppose it could be the shopkeepers'.'

'That looks to me like the same writing as on Cummins's parcels,' said Harty.

'And what's wrong with that?' Denis asked, feeling a pang of terror. 'I suppose she could order them there, couldn't she?'

'I'm not saying she couldn't,' said Harty in his sulky, sneering tone, 'I'm only telling you what I think.'

Denis could not believe it, but at the same time he could get no further pleasure from the parcel. He put it back in his locker and went out by himself and skulked away among the trees. It was a dull, misty February day. He took out his wallet in which there was a picture of his mother and Martha, and two letters he had received from his mother. He read the letters through, but there was no reference to any parcel that she was sending. He still could not believe but that there was some simple explanation, and that she had intended the parcels as a surprise, but the very thought of the alternative made his heart turn over. It was something he could talk to nobody about, and after lights out, he twisted and turned madly, groaning at the violence of his own restlessness, and the more he turned, the clearer he saw that the parcels had come from the Cumminses and not from his mother.

He had never before felt so humiliated. Though he had not realised it he had been buoyed up less by the parcels than by the thought that his mother cared so much for him; he had been filled with a new love of her, and now all the love was turning back on him and he realised that he hated her. But he hated the Cumminses worse. He saw that he had pitied and patronised Francis Cummins because he was weak and priggish and because his parents were only poor, ignorant country shopkeepers who did not know a good school from a bad one, while they all the time had been pitying him because he had no one to care for him as the Cumminses cared for Francis. He could clearly imagine the three Cumminses discussing him, his mother and his father exactly as his mother and he had discussed them. The only difference was that however ignorant they might be they had been right. It was he and not Francis who deserved pity.

'What ails you, Halligan?' the chap in the next bed asked – the beds were ranked so close together that one couldn't even sob in peace.

'Nothing ails me,' Denis said between his teeth.

Next day he bundled up what remained of the parcel and took it to Cummins's dormitory. He had intended just to leave it and walk out but Cummins was there himself, sitting on his bed with a book, and Denis had to say something.

'That's yours, Cummins,' he said. 'And if you ever do a thing like that again, I'll kill you.'

'What did I do, Denis?' Cummins wailed, getting up from his bed.

'You got your mother to send me that parcel.'

'I didn't. She did it herself.'

'But you told her to. Who asked you to interfere in my business, you dirty spy?'

'I'm not a spy,' Cummins said, growing agitated. 'You needed it and I didn't – what harm is there in that?'

'There is harm. Pretending my mother isn't as good as yours – a dirty old shopkeeper.'

'I wasn't, Denis,' Cummins said excitedly. 'Honest, I wasn't. I never said a word against your mother.'

'What did he do to you, Halligan?' one of the fellows asked, affecting to take Cummins's part.

'He got his people to send me parcels, as if I couldn't get them myself if I wanted them,' Denis shouted, losing control of himself. 'I don't want his old parcels.'

'Well, that's nothing to cry about.'

'Who's crying?' shouted Denis. 'I'm not crying. I'll fight him and you and the best man in the dormitory.'

He waited a moment for someone to take up his challenge, but they only looked at him curiously, and he rushed out because he knew that in spite of himself he was crying. He went straight to the lavatory and had his cry out there on the seat. It was the only place they had to cry, the only one where there was some sort of privacy. He cried because he had thought he was keeping his secret so well and that no one but himself knew how little toughness and insubordination there was in him till Cummins had come and pried it out.

After that he could never be friendly with Cummins again. It wasn't as Cummins thought that he bore a grudge. It was merely that for him it would have been like living naked.

FRANK O'CONNOR
FROM STORIES OF FRANK O'CONNOR

- Who was the parcel from?

- Why is Denis so upset at the end?

- What makes him feel as if "it would have been like living naked" to be friendly with Cummins again?

Talk
What do you make of these two very different characters? In pairs, jot down what you feel you have learned about them and their relationship. Would you advise Denis to try and make friends with Cummins and to overcome his awkwardness?

Role play

Pair work
Imagine that Denis and Cummins meet by chance a few weeks later. Improvise their conversation.

Write
1.   Write a letter home for each of the two boys using a combination of the extract and your imagination. How far would each boy mention what happened and how would each one explain it.

2.   Continue the story. How do the other boys treat Denis now they know about the parcels? How will Denis and Cummins behave towards each other?

Links with story
Compare Michael's feelings and situation with those of Denis. Think about the relation of each one to his mother and also the way they both try to hide something from the other boys at school.

The Frank O'Connor story is called simply 'Pity'. What single emotion would you choose as an alternative title for 'Mrs Silly'?

Jesus and his Mother

My only son, more God's than mine,
Stay in this garden ripe with pears.
The yielding of their substance wears
A modest and contented shine:
And when they weep with age, not brine
But lazy syrup are their tears.
'I am my own and not my own.'

He seemed much like another man,
That silent foreigner who trod
Outside my door with lily rod:
How could I know what I began
Meeting the eyes more furious than
The eyes of Joseph, those of God?
I was my own and not my own.

And who are these twelve labouring men?
I do not understand your words:
I taught you speech, we named the birds,
You marked their big migrations then
Like any child. So turn again
To silence from the place of crowds.
'I am my own and not my own.'

Why are you sullen when I speak?
Here are your tools, the saw and knife
And hammer on your bench. Your life
Is measured here in week and week
Planned as the furniture you make,
And I will teach you like a wife
To be my own and all my own.

Who like an arrogant wind blown
Where he may please, needs no content?
Yet I remember how you went
To speak with scholars in furred gown.
I hear an outcry in the town;
Who carried that dark instrument?
'One all his own and not his own.'

Treading the green and nimble sward
I stare at a strange shadow thrown.
Are you the boy I bore alone,
No doctor near to cut the cord?
I cannot reach to call you Lord,
Answer me as my only son.
'I am my own and not my own.'

THOMAS GUNN
FROM THE SENSE OF MOVEMENT

- Why is it that Mary cannot call Jesus "Lord"?

- What do you think she would like him to do?

- What do you think is the "strange shadow thrown" that Mary seems to fear?

Talk

Pair work

Prepare a joint reading of the poem that you can either perform for the class or a small group. Pay particular attention to the last line of each verse. Each line is almost the same. What kinds of difference should you bring out in your reading?

Group work

What kind of relationship is the poet suggesting must have existed between Mary and Jesus? In the poem, how does she feel towards her son. Does she want him to be famous and admired? What sense do you gain of his feelings towards her?

Write

Thom Gunn has written a story in rhyme. It is a particularly famous story that everyone can recognise; he has simply told it from one point of view. Try writing your own story in rhyme in a similar way. You could for example write about Joseph's feelings or you might take one of the disciples for your subject. You might prefer to retell a story from another religion in this simple format.

Links with story

Are there any similarities between the relationship of Jesus and Mary and of Michael and his mother? How much influence do they have over the future lives of their respective sons?

John Aubrey wrote hundreds of "lives", that is, descriptions of people which he thought worth recording. His lives can be as short as two words or as long as twenty three thousand! He did not try to be a systematic historian and so simply wrote down what he knew and what he had heard; often this was no more than gossip.

Edward de Vere, Earl of Oxford

This Earle of Oxford, making of his low obeisance to Queen Elizabeth, happened to let a Fart, at which he was so abashed and ashamed that he went to Travell, 7 yeares. On his returne the Queen welcomed him home, and sayd, My Lord, I had forgott the Fart.

JOHN AUBREY
FROM AUBREY'S BRIEF LIVES

<table>
<tr><td>Talk</td><td>

Group work

Can each member of the group be brave enough to tell a story about something that happened that was really embarrassing? If everyone manages to tell a story, see if you can choose the one that would make the funniest short story to write.

</td></tr>
<tr><td>Write</td><td>

1.   Write a story about an embarrassing moment; you do not have to include the Queen!

2.   Even famous and dignified people do it! Write a story of a day in the life of someone famous in which you show how ordinary they really are.

</td></tr>
</table>

Next Term, We'll Mash You

Inside the car it was quiet, the noise of the engine even and subdued, the air just the right temperature, the windows tight-fitting. The boy sat on the back seat, a box of chocolates, unopened, beside him, and a comic, folded. The trim Sussex landscape flowed past the windows: cows, white-fenced fields, highly-priced period houses. The sunlight was glassy, remote as a coloured photograph. The backs of the two heads in front of him swayed with the motion of the car.

His mother half-turned to speak to him. 'Nearly there now, darling.'

The father glanced downwards at his wife's wrist. 'Are we all right for time?'

'Just right. Nearly twelve.'

'I could do with a drink. Hope they lay something on.'

'I'm sure they will. The Wilcoxes say they're awfully nice people. Not really the schoolmaster-type at all, Sally says.'

The man said, 'He's an Oxford chap.'

'Is he? You didn't say.'

'Mmn.'

'Of course, the fees are that much higher than the Seaford place.'

'Fifty quid or so. We'll have to see.'

The car turned right, between white gates and high, dark, tight-clipped hedges. The whisper of the road under the tyres changed to the crunch of gravel. The child, staring sideways, read black lettering on a white board: 'St Edward's Preparatory School. Please Drive Slowly'. He shifted on the seat, and the leather sucked at the bare skin under his knees, stinging.

The mother said, 'It's a lovely place. Those must be the playing-fields. Look, darling, there are some of the boys.' She clicked open her handbag, and the sun caught her mirror and flashed in the child's eyes; the comb went through her hair and he saw the grooves it left, neat as distant ploughing.

'Come on, then, Charles, out you get.'

The building was red brick, early nineteenth century, spreading out long arms in which windows glittered blackly. Flowers, trapped in neat beds, were alternate red and white. They went up the steps, the man, the woman, and the child two paces behind.

The woman, the mother, smoothing down a skirt that would be ridged from sitting, thought: I like the way they've got the maid all done up properly. The little white apron and all that. She's foreign, I suppose. Au pair. Very nice. If he comes here there'll be Speech Days and that kind of thing. Sally Wilcox says it's quite dressy – she got that cream linen coat for coming down here. You can see why it costs a bomb. Great big grounds and only an hour and a half from London.

They went into a room looking out into a terrace. Beyond, dappled lawns, gently shifting trees, black and white cows grazing behind iron railings. Books, leather chairs, a table with magazines – *Country Life, The Field, The Economist.* 'Please, if you would wait here. The Headmaster won't be long.'

Alone, they sat, inspected. 'I like the atmosphere, don't you, John?'

'Very pleasant, yes.' Four hundred a term, near enough. You can tell it's a cut above the Seaford place, though, or the one at St Albans. Bob Wilcox says quite a few City people send their boys here. One or two of the merchant bankers, those kind of people. It's the sort of contact that would do no harm at all. You meet someone, get talking at a cricket match or what have you . . . Not at all a bad thing.

'All right, Charles? You didn't get sick in the car, did you?'

The child had black hair, slicked down smooth to his head. His ears, too large, jutted out, transparent in the light from the window, laced with tiny, delicate veins. His clothes had the shine and crease of newness. He looked at the books, the dark brown pictures, his parents, said nothing.

'Come here, let me tidy your hair.'

The door opened. The child hesitated, stood up, sat, then rose again with his father.

'Mr and Mrs Manders? How very nice to meet you — I'm Margaret Spokes, and will you please forgive my husband who is tied up with some wretch who broke the cricket pavilion window and will be just a few more minutes. We try to be organised but a schoolmaster's day is always just that bit unpredictable. Do please sit down and what will you have to revive you after that beastly drive? You live in Finchley, is that right?'

'Hampstead, really,' said the mother. 'Sherry would be lovely.' She worked over the headmaster's wife from shoes to hairstyle, pricing and assessing. Shoes old but expensive – Russell and Bromley. Good skirt. Blouse could be Marks and Sparks – not sure. Real pearls. Super Victorian ring. She's not gone to any particular trouble – that's just what she'd wear anyway. You can be confident, with a voice like that, of course. Sally Wilcox says she knows all sorts of people.

The headmaster's wife said, 'I don't know how much you know about us. Prospectuses don't tell you a thing, do they? We'll look round everything in a minute, when you've had a chat with my husband. I gather you're friends of the Wilcoxes, by the way. I'm awfully fond of Simon – he's down for Winchester, of course, but I expect you know that.'

The mother smiled over her sherry. Oh, I know that all right. Sally Wilcox doesn't let you forget that.

'And this is Charles? My dear, we've been forgetting all about you! In a minute I'm going to borrow Charles and take him off to meet some of the boys because after all you're choosing a school for him, aren't you, and not for you, so he ought to know what he might be letting himself in for and it shows we've got nothing to hide.'

The parents laughed. The father, sherry warming his guts, thought that this was an amusing woman. Not attractive, of course, a bit homespun, but impressive all the same. Partly the voice, of course; it takes a bloody expensive education to produce a voice like that. And other things, of course. Background and all that stuff.

'I think I can hear the thud of the Fourth Form coming in from games, which means my husband is on the way, and then I shall leave you with him while I take Charles off to the common-room.'

For a moment the three adults centred on the child, looking, judging. The mother said, 'He looks so hideously pale, compared to those boys we saw outside.'

'My dear, that's London, isn't it? You just have to get them out, to get some colour into them. Ah, here's James. James – Mr and Mrs Manders. You remember, Bob Wilcox was mentioning at Sports Day . . .'

The headmaster reflected his wife's style, like paired cards in Happy Families. His clothes were mature rather than old, his skin well-scrubbed, his shoes clean, his geniality untainted by the least condescension. He was genuinely sorry to have kept them waiting, but in this business one lurches from one minor crisis to the next . . . And this is Charles? Hello, there, Charles. His large hand rested for a moment on the child's head, quite extinguishing the thin, dark hair. It was as though he had but to clench his fingers to crush the skull. But he took his hand away and moved the parents to the window, to observe the mutilated cricket pavilion, with indulgent laughter.

And the child is borne away by the headmaster's wife. She never touches him or tells him to come, but simply bears him away like some relentless tide, down corridors and through swinging glass doors, towing him like a frail craft, not bothering to look back to see if he is following, confident in the strength of magnetism, or obedience.

And delivers him to a room where boys are scattered among inky tables and rungless chairs and sprawled on a mangy carpet. There is a scampering, and a rising, and a silence falling, as she opens the door.

'Now this is the Lower Third, Charles, who you'd be with if you come to us in September. Boys, this is Charles Manders, and I want you to tell him all about things and answer any questions he wants to ask. You can believe about half of what they say, Charles, and they will tell you the most fearful lies about the food, which is excellent.'

The boys laugh and groan; amiable, exaggerated groans. They must like the headmaster's wife: there is licensed repartee. They look at her with bright eyes in open, eager faces. Someone leaps to hold the door for her, and close it behind her. She is gone.

The child stands in the centre of the room, and it draws in around him. The circle of children contracts, faces are only a yard or so from him; strange faces, looking, assessing.

Asking questions. They help themselves to his name, his age, his school. Over their heads he sees beyond the window an inaccessible world of shivering trees and high racing clouds and his voice which has floated like a feather in the dusty schoolroom air dies altogether and he becomes mute, and he stands in the middle of them with shoulders humped, staring down at feet: grubby plimsolls and kicked brown sandals. There is a noise in his ears like rushing water, a torrential din out of which voices boom, blotting each other out so that he cannot always hear the words. Do you? they say, and Have you? and What's your? and the faces, if he looks up, swing into one another in kaleidoscopic patterns and the floor under his feet is unsteady, lifting and falling.

And out of the noises comes one voice that is complete, that he can hear. 'Next term, we'll mash you,' it says. 'We always mash new boys.'

And a bell goes, somewhere beyond doors and down corridors, and suddenly the children are all gone, clattering away and leaving him there with the heaving floor and the walls that shift and swing, and the headmaster's wife comes back and tows him away, and he is with his parents again, and they are getting into the car, and the high hedges skim past the car windows once more, in the other direction, and the gravel under the tyres changes to black tarmac.

'Well?'

'I liked it, didn't you?' The mother adjusted the car around her, closing windows, shrugging into her seat.

'Very pleasant, really. Nice chap.'

'I liked him. Not quite so sure about her.'

'It's pricey, of course.'

'All the same . . .'

'Money well spent, though. One way and another.'

'Shall we settle it, then?'

'I think so. I'll drop him a line.'

The mother pitched her voice a notch higher to speak to the child in the back of the car. 'Would you like to go there, Charles? Like Simon Wilcox. Did you see that lovely gym, and the swimming-pool? And did the other boys tell you all about it?'

The child does not answer. He looks straight ahead of him, at the road coiling beneath the bonnet of the car. His face is haggard with anticipation.

PENELOPE LIVELY
FROM PACK OF CARDS

- Why is Charles "haggard with anticipation" at the end of the story?

- Do you think that he is suited to this school?

- What do you think are his parents' main reasons for wanting to send him there?

Talk   What kind of family do the Manders seem to you? Look through the story for details of their attitudes and behaviour. Choose three details that seem to you especially important.

Role play   What will the Head and his wife say about these prospective parents; improvise their conversation later that day.

Write   1. Continue the story and describe Charles' first few days at the school.

2. Imagine that Charles has been at the school for several weeks, write a page of his diary and a page from a letter to his parents; how similar or different would they be?

Links with story   Compare Michael's family with Charles'; what are their different reasons for sending their respective sons to a private boarding school, and what kinds of relationships exist in the two families? Do you think that the two writers have similar views about boarding schools?

Weekend

FAY WELDON

By seven-thirty they were ready to go. Martha had everything packed into the car and the three children appropriately dressed and in the back seat, complete with educational games and wholewheat biscuits. When everything was ready in the car Martin would switch off the television, come downstairs, lock up the house, front and back, and take the wheel.

Weekend! Only two hours' drive down to the cottage on Friday evenings; three hours' drive back on Sunday nights. The pleasures of greenery and guests in between. They reckoned themselves fortunate, how fortunate!

On Fridays Martha would get home on the bus at six-twelve and prepare tea and sandwiches for the family: then she would strip four beds and put the sheets and quilt covers in the washing machine for Monday: take the country bedding from the airing basket, plus the books and the games, plus the weekend food – acquired at intervals throughout the week, to lessen the load – plus her own folder of work from the office, plus Martin's drawing materials (she was a market researcher in an advertising agency, he a freelance designer) plus hairbrushes, jeans, spare T-shirts, Jolyon's antibiotics (he suffered from sore throats), Jenny's recorder, Jasper's cassette player and so on – ah, the so on! – and would pack them all, skilfully and quickly, into the boot. Very little could be left in the cottage during the week. ('An open invitation to burglars': Martin) Then Martha would run round the house tidying and wiping, doing this and that, finding the cat at one neighbour's and delivering it to another, while the others ate their tea; and would usually, proudly, have everything finished by the time they had eaten their fill. Martin would just catch the BBC2 news, while Martha cleared away the tea table, and the children tossed up for the best positions in the car. 'Martha,' said Martin, tonight, 'you ought to get Mrs Hodder to do more. She takes advantage of you.'

Mrs Hodder came in twice a week to clean. She was over seventy. She charged two pounds an hour. Martha paid her out of her own wages: well, the running of the house was Martha's concern. If Martha chose to go out to work – as was her perfect right, Martin allowed, even though it wasn't the best thing for the children, but that must be Martha's moral responsibility – Martha must surely pay her domestic stand-in. An evident truth, heard loud and clear and frequent in Martin's mouth and Martha's heart.

'I expect you're right,' said Martha. She did not want to argue. Martin had had a long hard week, and now had to drive. Martha couldn't. Martha's licence had been suspended four months back for drunken driving. Everyone agreed that the suspension was unfair: Martha seldom drank to excess: she was for one thing usually too busy pouring drinks for other people or washing other people's glasses to get much inside herself. But Martin had taken her out to dinner on her birthday, as was his custom, and exhaustion and excitement mixed had made her imprudent, and before she knew where she was, why there she was, in the dock, with a distorted lamp-post to pay for and a new bonnet for the car and six months' suspension.

So now Martin had to drive her car down to the cottage, and he was always tired on Fridays, and hot and sleepy on Sundays, and every rattle and clank and bump in the engine she felt to be somehow her fault.

Martin had a little sports car for London and work: it could nip in and out of the traffic nicely: Martha's was an old estate car, with room for the children, picnic baskets, bedding, food, games, plants, drink, portable television and all the things required by the middle classes for weekends in the country. It lumbered rather than zipped and made Martin angry. He seldom spoke a harsh word, but Martha, after the fashion of wives, could detect his mood from what he did not say rather than what he did, and from the tilt of his head, and the way his crinkly, merry eyes seemed crinklier and merrier still – and of course from the way he addressed Martha's car.

'Come along, you old banger you! Can't you do better than that? You're too old, that's your trouble. Stop complaining. Always complaining, it's only a hill. You're too wide about the hips. You'll never get through there.'

Martha worried about her age, her tendency to complain, and the width of her hips. She took the remarks personally. Was she right to do so? The children noticed nothing: it was just funny lively laughing Daddy being witty about Mummy's car. Mummy, done for drunken driving. Mummy, with the roots of melancholy somewhere deep beneath the bustling, busy, everyday self. Busy: ah so busy!

Martin would only laugh if she said anything about the way he spoke to her car and warn her against paranoia. 'Don't get like your mother, darling.' Martha's mother had, towards the end, thought that people were plotting against her. Martha's mother had led a secluded, suspicious life, and made Martha's childhood a chilly and a lonely time. Life now, by comparison, was wonderful for Martha. People, children, houses, conversations, food, drink, theatres – even, now, a career. Martin standing between her and the hostility of the world – popular, easy, funny Martin, beckoning the rest of the world into earshot.

Ah, she was grateful: little earnest Martha, with her shy ways and her penchant for passing boring exams – how her life had blossomed out! Three children too – Jasper, Jenny and Jolyon – all with Martin's broad brow and open looks, and the confidence born of her love and care, and the work she had put into them since the dawning of their days.

Martin drives. Martha, for once, drowses.

The right food, the right words, the right play. Doctors for the tonsils: dentists for the molars. Confiscate guns: censor television: encourage creativity. Paints and paper to hand: books on the shelves: meetings with teachers. Music teachers. Dancing lessons. Parties. Friends to tea. School plays. Open days. Junior orchestra.

Martha is jolted awake. Traffic lights. Martin doesn't like Martha to sleep while he drives.

Clothes. Oh, clothes! Can't wear this: must wear that. Dress shops. Piles of clothes in corners: duly washed, but waiting to be ironed, waiting to be put away.

Get the piles off the floor, into the laundry baskets. Martin doesn't like a mess.

Creativity arises out of order, not chaos. Five years off work while the children were small: back to work with seniority lost. What, did you think something was for nothing? If you have children, mother, that is your reward. It lies not in the world.

Have you taken enough food? Always hard to judge.

Food. Oh, food! Shop in the lunch-hour. Lug it all home. Cook for the freezer on Wednesday evenings while Martin is at his car-maintenance evening class, and isn't there to notice you being unrestful. Martin likes you to sit down in the evenings. Fruit, meat, vegetables, flour for home-made bread. Well, shop bread is full of pollutants. Frozen food, even your own, loses flavour. Martin often remarks on it. Condiments. Everyone loves mango chutney. But the expense!

London Airport to the left. Look, look, children! Concorde? No, idiot, of course it isn't Concorde.

Ah, to be all things to all people: children, husband, employer, friends! It can be done: yes, it can: super woman.

Drink. Home-made wine. Why not? Elderberries grown thick and rich in London: and at least you know what's in it. Store it in high cupboards: lots of room: up and down the step-ladder. Careful! Don't slip. Don't break anything.

No such thing as an accident. Accidents are Freudian slips: they are wilful, bad-tempered things.

Martin can't bear bad temper. Martin likes slim ladies. Diet. Martin rather likes his secretary. Diet. Martin admires slim legs and big bosoms. How to achieve them both? Impossible. But try, oh try, to be what you ought to be, not what you are. Inside and out.

Martin brings back flowers and chocolates: whisks Martha off for holiday weekends. Wonderful! The best husband in the world: look into his crinkly, merry, gentle eyes; see it there. So the mouth slopes away into something of a pout. Never mind. Gaze into the eyes. Love. It must be love. You married him. *You*. Surely *you* deserve true love?

Salisbury Plain. Stonehenge. Look, children, look! Mother, we've seen Stonehenge a hundred times. Go back to sleep.

Cook! Ah cook. People love to come to Martin and Martha's dinners. Work it out in your head in the lunch-hour. If you get in at six-twelve, you can seal the meat while you beat the egg white while you feed the cat while you lay the table while you string the beans while you set out the cheese, goat's cheese, Martin loves goat's cheese, Martha tries to like goat's cheese – oh, bed, sleep, peace, quiet.

Sex! Ah sex. Orgasm, please. Martin requires it. Well, so do you. And you don't want his secretary providing a passion you neglected to develop. Do you? Quick, quick, the cosmic bond. Love. Married love.

Secretary! Probably a vulgar suspicion: nothing more. Probably a fit of paranoics, à la mother, now dead and gone.
At peace.
R.I.P.
Chilly, lonely mother, following her suspicions where they led.

Nearly there, children. Nearly in paradise, nearly at the cottage. Have another biscuit.

Real roses round the door.

Roses. Prune, weed, spray, feed, pick. Avoid thorns. One of Martin's few harsh words.

'Martha, you can't not want roses! What kind of person am I married to? An anti-rose personality?'

Green grass. Oh, God, grass. Grass must be mown. Restful lawns, daisies bobbing, buttercups glowing. Roses and grass and books. Books.

Please, Martin, do we have to have the two hundred books, mostly twenties' first editions, bought at Christie's book sale on one of your afternoons off? Books need dusting.

Roars of laughter from Martin, Jasper, Jenny and Jolyon. Mummy says we shouldn't have the books: books need dusting!

Roses, green grass, books and peace.

Martha woke up with a start when they got to the cottage, and gave a little shriek which made them all laugh. Mummy's waking shriek, they called it.

Then there was the car to unpack and the beds to make up, and the electricity to connect, and the supper to make, and the cobwebs to remove, while Martin made the fire. Then supper – pork chops in sweet and sour sauce ('Pork is such a *dull* meat if you don't cook it properly': Martin), green salad from the garden, or such green salad as the rabbits had left. ('Martha, did you really net them properly? Be honest, now!': Martin) and sauté potatoes. Mash is so stodgy and ordinary, and instant mash unthinkable. The children studied the night sky with the aid of their star map. Wonderful, rewarding children!

Then clear up the supper: set the dough to prove for the bread: Martin already in bed: exhausted by the drive and lighting the fire. ('Martha, we really ought to get the logs stacked properly. Get the children to do it, will you?': Martin) Sweep and tidy: get the TV aerial right. Turn up Jasper's jeans where he has trodden the hem undone. ('He can't go around like *that*, Martha. Not even Jasper': Martin)

Midnight. Good night. Weekend guests arriving in the morning. Seven for lunch and dinner on Saturday. Seven for Sunday breakfast, nine for Sunday lunch. ('Don't fuss, darling. You always make such a fuss': Martin) Oh, God, forgotten the garlic squeezer. That means ten minutes with the back of a spoon and salt. Well, who wants *lumps* of garlic? No one. Not Martin's guests. Martin said so. Sleep.

Colin and Katie. Colin is Martin's oldest friend. Katie is his new young wife. Janet, Colin's other, earlier wife, was Martha's friend. Janet was rather like Martha, quieter and duller than her husband. A nag and a drag, Martin rather thought, and said, and of course she'd let herself go, everyone agreed. No one exactly excused Colin for walking out, but you could see the temptation.

Katie versus Janet.

Katie was languid, beautiful and elegant. She drawled when she spoke. Her hands were expressive: her feet were little and female. She had no children.

Janet plodded round on very flat, rather large feet. There was something wrong with them. They turned out slightly when she walked. She had two children. She was, frankly, boring. But Martha liked her: when Janet came down to the cottage she would wash up. Not in the way that most guests washed up – washing dutifully and setting everything out on the draining board, but actually drying and putting away too. And Janet would wash the bath and get the children all sat down, with chairs for everyone, even the littlest, and keep them quiet and satisfied so the grown-ups – well, the men – could get on with their conversation and their jokes and their love of country weekends, while Janet stared into space, as if grateful for the rest, quite happy.

Janet would garden, too. Weed the strawberries, while the men went for their walk; her great feet standing firm and square and sometimes crushing a plant or so, but never mind, oh never mind. Lovely Janet; who understood.

Now Janet was gone and here was Katie.

Katie talked with the men and went for walks with the men, and moved her ashtray rather impatiently when Martha tried to clear the drinks round it.

Dishes were boring, Katie implied by her manner, and domesticity was boring, and anyone who bothered with that kind of thing was a fool. Like Martha. Ash should be allowed to stay where it was, even if it was in the butter, and conversations should never be interrupted.

Knock, knock. Katie and Colin arrived at one-fifteen on Saturday morning, just after Martha had got to bed. 'You don't mind? It was the moonlight. We couldn't resist it. You should have seen Stonehenge! We didn't disturb you? Such early birds!'

Martha rustled up a quick meal of omelettes. Saturday nights' eggs. ('Martha makes a lovely omelette': Martin) ('Honey, make one of your mushroom omelettes: cook the mushrooms separately, remember, with lemon. Otherwise the water from the mushrooms gets into the egg, and spoils everything.') Sunday supper mushrooms. But ungracious to say anything.

Martin had revived wonderfully at the sight of Colin and Katie. He brought out the whisky bottle. Glasses. Ice. Jug for water. Wait. Wash up another sinkful, when they're finished. 2 a.m.

'Don't do it tonight, darling.'
'It'll only take a sec.' Bright smile, not a hint of self-pity.
Self-pity can spoil everyone's weekend.
Martha knows that if breakfast for seven is to be manageable the sink must be cleared of dishes. A tricky meal, breakfast. Especially if bacon, eggs, and tomatoes must all be cooked in separate pans. ('Separate pans mean separate flavours!': Martin)

She is running around in her nightie. Now if that had been Katie – but there's something so *practical* about Martha. Reassuring, mind; but the skimpy nightie and the broad rump and the thirty-eight years are all rather embarrassing. Martha can see it in Colin and Katie's eyes. Martin's too. Martha wishes she did not see so much in other people's eyes. Her mother did, too. Dear, dead mother. Did I misjudge you?

This was the second weekend Katie had been down with Colin but without Janet. Colin was a photographer: Katie had been his accessoriser. First Colin and Janet: then Colin, Janet and Katie: now Colin and Katie!

Katie weeded with rubber gloves on and pulled out pansies in mistake for weeds and laughed and laughed along with everyone when her mistake was pointed out to her, but the pansies died. Well, Colin had become with the years fairly rich and fairly famous, and what does a fairly rich and famous man want with a wife like Janet when Katie is at hand?

On the first of the Colin/Janet/Katie weekends Katie had appeared out of the bathroom. 'I say,' said Katie, holding out a damp towel with evident distaste, 'I can only find this. No hope of a dry one?' And Martha had run to fetch a dry towel and amazingly found one, and handed it to Katie who flashed her a brilliant smile and said, 'I can't bear damp towels. Anything in the world but damp towels,' as if speaking to a servant in a time of shortage of staff, and took all the water so there was none left for Martha to wash up.

The trouble, of course, was drying anything at all in the cottage. There were no facilities for doing so, and Martin had a horror of clothes lines which might spoil the view. He toiled and moiled all week in the city simply to get a country view at the weekend. Ridiculous to spoil it by draping it with wet towels! But now Martha had brought more towels, so perhaps everyone could be satisfied. She would take nine damp towels back on Sunday evenings in a plastic bag and see to them in London.

On this Saturday morning, straight after breakfast, Katie went out to the car – she and Colin had a new Lamborghini, hard to imagine Katie in anything duller – and came back waving a new Yves St Laurent towel. 'See! I brought my own, darlings.'

They'd brought nothing else. No fruit, no meat, no vegetables, not even bread, certainly not a box of chocolates. They'd gone off to bed with alacrity, the night before, and the spare room rocked and heaved: well, who'd want to do washing-up when you could do that, but what about the children? Would they get confused? First Colin and Janet, now Colin and Katie?

Martha murmured something of her thoughts to Martin, who looked quite shocked. 'Colin's my best friend. I don't expect him to bring anything,' and Martha felt mean. 'And good heavens, you can't protect the kids from sex for ever; don't be so prudish,' so that Martha felt stupid as well. Mean, complaining, and stupid.

Janet had rung Martha during the week. The house had been sold over her head, and she and the children had been moved into a small flat. Katie was trying to persuade Colin to cut down on her allowance, Janet said.

'It does one no good to be materialistic,' Katie confided. 'I have nothing. No home, no family, no ties, no possessions. Look at me! Only me and a suitcase of clothes.' But Katie seemed highly satisfied with the me, and the clothes were stupendous. Katie drank a great deal and became funny. Everyone laughed, including Martha. Katie had been married twice. Martha marvelled at how someone could arrive in their mid-thirties with nothing at all to their name, neither husband, nor children, nor property and not mind.

Mind you, Martha could see the power of such helplessness. If Colin was all Katie had in the world, how could Colin abandon her? And to what? Where would she go? How would she live? Oh, clever Katie.

'My teacup's dirty,' said Katie, and Martha ran to clean it, apologising, and Martin raised his eyebrows, at Martha, not Katie.

'I wish *you'd* wear scent,' said Martin to Martha, reproachfully. Katie wore lots. Martha never seemed to have time to put any on, though Martin bought her bottle after bottle. Martha leapt out of bed each morning to meet some emergency – miaowing cat, coughing child, faulty alarm clock, postman's knock – when was Martha to put on scent? It annoyed Martin all the same. She ought to do more to charm him.

Colin looked handsome and harrowed and younger than Martin, though they were much the same age. 'Youth's catching,' said Martin in bed that night. 'It's since he found Katie.' Found, like some treasure. Discovered; something exciting and wonderful, in the dreary world of established spouses.

On Saturday morning Jasper trod on a piece of wood ('Martha, why isn't he wearing shoes? It's too bad': Martin) and Martha took him into the hospital to have a nasty splinter removed. She left the cottage at ten and arrived back at one, and they were still sitting in the sun, drinking, empty bottles glinting in the long grass. The grass hadn't been cut. Don't forget the bottles. Broken glass means more mornings at the hospital. Oh, don't fuss. Enjoy yourself. Like other people. Try.

But no potatoes peeled, no breakfast cleared, nothing. Cigarette ends still amongst old toast, bacon rind and marmalade. 'You could have done the potatoes,' Martha burst out. Oh, bad temper! Prime sin. They looked at her in amazement and dislike. Martin too.

'Goodness,' said Katie. 'Are we doing the whole Sunday lunch bit on Saturday? Potatoes? Ages since I've eaten potatoes. Wonderful!'

'The children expect it,' said Martha.

So they did. Saturday and Sunday lunch shone like reassuring beacons in their lives. Saturday lunch: family lunch: fish and chips. ('So much better cooked at home than bought': Martin) Sunday. Usually roast beef, potatoes, peas, apple pie. Oh, of course. Yorkshire pudding. Always a problem with oven temperatures. When the beef's going slowly, the Yorkshire should be going fast. How to achieve that? Like big bosom and little hips.

'Just relax,' said Martin. 'I'll cook dinner, all in good time. Splinters always work their own way out: no need to have taken him to hospital. Let life drift over you, my love. Flow with the waves, that's the way.'

And Martin flashed Martha a distant, spiritual smile. His hand lay on Katie's slim brown arm, with its many gold bands.

'Anyway, you do too much for the children,' said Martin. 'It isn't good for them. Have a drink.'

So Martha perched uneasily on the step and had a glass of cider, and wondered how, if lunch was going to be late, she would get cleared up and the meat out of the marinade for the rather formal dinner that would be expected that evening. The marinaded lamb ought to cook for at least four hours in a low oven; and the cottage oven was very small, and you couldn't use that and the grill at the same time and Martin liked his fish grilled, not fried. Less cholesterol.

She didn't say as much. Domestic details like this were very boring, and any mild complaint was registered by Martin as a scene. And to make a scene was so ungrateful.

This was the life. Well, wasn't it? Smart friends in large cars and country living and drinks before lunch and roses and bird song – 'Don't drink *too* much,' said Martin, and told them about Martha's suspended driving licence.

The children were hungry so Martha opened them a can of beans and sausages and heated that up. ('Martha, do they have to eat that crap? Can't they wait?': Martin)

Katie was hungry: she said so, to keep the children in face. She was lovely with children – most children. She did not particularly like Colin and Janet's children. She said so, and he accepted it. He only saw them once a month now, not once a week.

'Let me make lunch,' Katie said to Martha. 'You do so much, poor thing!'

And she pulled out of the fridge all the things Martha had put away for the next day's picnic lunch party – Camembert cheese and salad and salami and made a wonderful tomato salad in two minutes and opened the white wine – 'not very cold, darling. Shouldn't it be chilling?' – and had it all on the table in five amazing competent minutes. 'That's all we need, darling,' said Martin. 'You are funny with your fish-and-chip Saturdays! What could be nicer than this? Or simpler?'

Nothing, except there was Sunday's buffet lunch for nine gone, in place of Saturday's fish for six, and would the fish stretch? No. Katie had had quite a lot to drink. She pecked Martha on the forehead. 'Funny little Martha,' she said. 'She reminds me of Janet. I really do like Janet.' Colin did not want to be reminded of Janet, and said so. 'Darling, Janet's a fact of life,' said Katie. 'If you'd only think about her more, you might manage to pay her less.' And she yawned and stretched her lean, childless body and smiled at Colin with her inviting, naughty little girl eyes, and Martin watched her in admiration.

Martha got up and left them and took a paint pot and put a coat of white gloss on the bathroom wall. The white surface pleased her. She was good at painting. She produced a smooth, even surface. Her legs throbbed. She feared she might be getting varicose veins.

Outside in the garden the children played badminton. They were bad-tempered, but relieved to be able to look up and see their mother working, as usual: making their lives for ever better and nicer: organising, planning, thinking ahead, side-stepping disaster, making preparations, like a mother hen, fussing and irritating: part of the natural boring scenery of the world.

On Saturday night Katie went to bed early: she rose from her chair and stretched and yawned and poked her head into the kitchen where Martha was washing saucepans. Colin had cleared the table and Katie had folded the napkins into pretty creases, while Martin blew at the fire, to make it bright. 'Good night,' said Katie.

Katie appeared three minutes later, reproachfully holding out her Yves St Laurent towel, sopping wet. 'Oh dear,' cried Martha. 'Jenny must have washed her hair!' And Martha was obliged to rout Jenny out of bed to rebuke her, publicly, if only to demonstrate that she knew what was right and proper. That meant Jenny would sulk all weekend, and that meant a treat or an outing mid-week, or else by the following week she'd be having an asthma attack. 'You fuss the children too much,' said Martin. 'That's why Jenny has asthma.' Jenny was pleasant enough to look at, but not stunning. Perhaps she was a disappointment to her father? Martin would never say so, but Martha feared he thought so.

An egg and an orange each child, each day. Then nothing too bad would go wrong. And it hadn't. The asthma was very mild. A calm, tranquil environment, the doctor said. Ah, smile, Martha smile. Domestic happiness depends on you. 21×52 oranges a year. Each one to be purchased, carried, peeled and washed up after. And what about potatoes. 12×52 pounds a year? Martin liked his potatoes carefully peeled. He couldn't bear to find little cores of black in the mouthful. ('Well, it isn't very nice, is it?': Martin)

Martha dreamt she was eating coal, by handfuls, and liking it.

Saturday night. Martin made love to Martha three times. Three times? How virile he was, and clearly turned on by the sounds from the spare room. Martin said he loved her. Martin always did. He was a courteous lover; he knew the importance of foreplay. So did Martha. Three times.

Ah, sleep. Jolyon had a nightmare. Jenny was woken by a moth. Martin slept through everything. Martha pottered about the house in the night.

There was a moon. She sat at the window and stared out into the summer night for five minutes, and was at peace, and then went back to bed because she ought to be fresh for the morning.

But she wasn't. She slept late. The others went out for a walk. They'd left a note, a considerate note: 'Didn't wake you. You looked tired. Had a cold breakfast so as not to make too much mess. Leave everything 'til we get back.' But it was ten o'clock, and guests were coming at noon, so she cleared away the bread, the butter, the crumbs, the smears, the jam, the spoons, the spilt sugar, the cereal, the milk (sour by now) and the dirty plates, and swept the floors, and tidied up quickly, and grabbed a cup of coffee, and prepared to make a rice and fish dish, and a chocolate mousse and sat down in the middle to eat a lot of bread and jam herself. Broad hips. She remembered the office work in her file and knew she wouldn't be able to do it. Martin anyway thought it was ridiculous for her to bring work back at the weekends. 'It's your holiday,' he'd say. 'Why should they impose?' Martha loved her work. She didn't have to smile at it. She just did it.

Katie came back upset and crying. She sat in the kitchen while Martha worked and drank glass after glass of gin and bitter lemon. Katie liked ice and lemon in gin. Martha paid for all the drink out of her wages. It was part of the deal between her and Martin – the contract by which she went out to work. All things to cheer the spirit, otherwise depressed by a working wife and mother, were to be paid for by Martha. Drink, holidays, petrol, outings, puddings, electricity, heating: it was quite a joke between them. It didn't really make any difference: it was their joint money, after all. Amazing how Martha's wages were creeping up, almost to the level of Martin's. One day they would overtake. Then what?

Work, honestly, was a piece of cake.

Anyway, poor Katie was crying. Colin, she'd discovered, kept a photograph of Janet and the children in his wallet. 'He's not free of her. He pretends he is, but he isn't. She has him by a stranglehold. It's the kids. His bloody kids. Moaning Mary and that little creep Joanna. It's all he thinks about. I'm nobody.'

But Katie didn't believe it. She knew she was somebody all right. Colin came in, in a fury. He took out the photograph and set fire to it, bitterly, with a match. Up in smoke they went. Mary and Joanna and Janet. The ashes fell on the floor. (Martha swept them up when Colin and Katie had gone. It hardly seemed polite to do so when they were still there.) 'Go back to her,' Katie said. 'Go back to her. I don't care. Honestly, I'd rather be on my own. You're a nice old-fashioned thing. Run along then. Do your thing, I'll do mine. Who cares?'

'Christ, Katie, the fuss! She only just happens to be in the photograph. She's not there on purpose to annoy. And I do feel bad about her. She's been having a hard time.'

'And haven't you, Colin? She twists a pretty knife, I can tell you. Don't you have rights too? Not to mention me. Is a little loyalty too much to expect?'

They were reconciled before lunch, up in the spare room. Harry and Beryl Elder arrived at twelve-thirty. Harry didn't like to hurry on Sundays; Beryl was flustered with apologies for their lateness. They'd brought artichokes from their garden. 'Wonderful,' cried Martin. 'Fruits of the earth? Let's have a wonderful soup! Don't fret, Martha. I'll do it.'

'Don't fret.' Martha clearly hadn't been smiling enough. She was in danger, Martin implied, of ruining everyone's weekend. There was an emergency in the garden very shortly – an elm tree which had probably got Dutch elm disease – and Martha finished the artichokes. The lid flew off the blender and there was artichoke purée everywhere. 'Let's have lunch outside,' said Colin. 'Less work for Martha.'

Martin frowned at Martha: he thought the appearance of martyrdom in the face of guests to be an unforgivable offence.

Everyone happily joined in taking the furniture out, but it was Martha's experience that nobody ever helped to bring it in again. Jolyon was stung by a wasp. Jasper sneezed and sneezed from hay fever and couldn't find the tissues and he wouldn't use loo paper. ('Surely you remembered the tissues, darling?': Martin)

Beryl Elder was nice. 'Wonderful to eat out,' she said, fetching the cream for her pudding, while Martha fished a fly from the liquefying Brie ('You shouldn't have bought it so ripe, Martha': Martin) – 'except it's just some other woman has to do it. But at least it isn't *me*.' Beryl worked too, as a secretary, to send the boys to boarding school, where she'd rather they weren't. But her husband was from a rather grand family, and she'd been only a typist when he married her, so her life was a mass of amends, one way or another. Harry had lately opted out of the stockbroking rat race and become an artist, choosing integrity rather than money, but that choice was his alone and couldn't of course be inflicted on the boys.

Katie found the fish and rice dish rather strange, toyed at it with her fork, and talked about Italian restaurants she knew. Martin lay back soaking in the sun: crying, 'Oh, this is the life.' He made coffee, nobly, and the lid flew off the grinder and there were coffee beans all over the kitchen especially in amongst the row of cookery books which Martin gave Martha Christmas by Christmas. At least they didn't have to be brought back every weekend. ('The burglars won't have the sense to steal those': Martin)

Beryl fell asleep and Katie watched her, quizzically. Beryl's mouth was open and she had a lot of fillings, and her ankles were thick and her waist was going, and she didn't look after herself. 'I love women,' sighed Katie. 'They look so wonderful asleep. I wish I could be an earth mother.'

Beryl woke with a start and nagged her husband into going home, which he clearly didn't want to do, so didn't. Beryl thought she had to get back because his mother was coming round later. Nonsense! Then Beryl tried to stop Harry drinking more home-made wine and was laughed at by everyone. He was driving, Beryl couldn't, and he did have a nasty scar on his temple from a previous road accident. Never mind.

'She does come on strong, poor soul,' laughed Katie when they'd finally gone. 'I'm never going to get married,' – and Colin looked at her yearningly because he wanted to marry her more than anything in the world, and Martha cleared the coffee cups.

'Oh don't *do* that,' said Katie, 'do just sit *down*, Martha, you make us all feel bad,' and Martin glared at Martha who sat down and Jenny called out for her and Martha went upstairs and Jenny had started her first period and Martha cried and cried and knew she must stop because this must be a joyous occasion for Jenny or her whole future would be blighted, but for once, Martha couldn't.

Her daughter Jenny: wife, mother, friend.

First response

- What makes Martha cry at the end of the story?

- What are your feelings about Martha and Martin? What sort of people are they?

- Do you think that Colin and Katie are good friends for Martha and Martin?

- People are always telling Martha to relax and do less work, do you think they are right? Why does she ignore their advice?

- Why do you think Martha finds her job so easy?

- If you knew Martha and she asked your advice about her marriage what would you say to her?

> **Talk**

Pair work
Look through the story and discuss the character of Martha in detail. Jot down what you feel are the main points of her character. Once you have your notes compare them with another pair; what picture of Martha emerges?

Group work
The story has a very simple title *Weekend*. Decide as a group what you feel the story is about and choose a title that describes its theme and ideas.

> **Role play**

A Sunday magazine is running a series about families with more than one home. The reporter arranges to come and interview Martin, Martha and their children about the advantages of having two homes. Work in a small group and take on some or all of the roles for this interview.

> **Write**

1. Imagine that the same characters assemble at the cottage in a few months time. Write about that weekend.

2. Write about the weekend featured in the story but tell it from the point of view of one or more different characters e.g. Martin, Colin, Katie etc.

3. Write a study of Martha's character and of her relationships with others. What do you think Fay Weldon wants us to feel towards her?

4.   Imagine that Janet telephones Martha and they talk about the weekend. Write their conversation and also their thoughts, perhaps, in the form of a script with thoughts in brackets. Think about the awkwardness of the situation for Martha and for Janet and how well they knew each other once.

How would Janet feel about Katie, and how much of Katie's conversation about Janet would Martha wish to relate?

Maiden Name

Marrying left your maiden name disused.
Its five light sounds no longer mean your face,
Your voice, and all your variants of grace;
For since you were so thankfully confused
By law with someone else, you cannot be
Semantically the same as that young beauty:
It was of her that these two words were used.

Now it's a phrase applicable to no one,
Lying just where you left it, scattered through
Old lists, old programmes, a school prize or two,
Packets of letters tied with tartan ribbon –
Then is it scentless, weightless, strengthless, wholly
Untruthful? Try whispering it slowly.
No, it means you. Or, since you're past and gone,

It means what we feel now about you then:
How beautiful you were, and near, and young,
So vivid, you might still be there among
Those first few days, unfingermarked again.
So your old name shelters our faithfulness,
Instead of losing shape and meaning less
With your depreciating luggage laden.

PHILIP LARKIN
FROM THE COLLECTED POEMS

- What do you think the poet wants us to feel about the maiden name of the woman in the poem?

- Is this a sad or celebratory poem?

- The poet takes great care with sound in this poem. Are there any lines that you especially like the sound of?

Talk   Should either partner change name on marrying?
Does it matter whether a woman is called Ms or Mrs?

Write   Imagine that in a few years' time a female friend of yours
writes to tell you that she is getting married and feels
uncertain about whether to keep her own name. Write back
with your advice.

Old Woman

So much she caused she cannot now account for
As she stands watching day return, the cool
Walls of the house moving towards the sun.
She puts some flowers in a vase and thinks
    "There is not much I can arrange
In here and now, but flowers are suppliant

As children never were. And love is now
A flicker of memory, my body is
My own entirely. When I lie at night
I gather nothing now into my arms,
    No child or man, and where I live
Is what remains when men and children go."

Yet she owns more than residue of lives
That she has marked and altered. See how she
Warns time from too much touching her possessions
By keeping flowers fed, by polishing
    Her fine old silver. Gratefully
She sees her own glance printed on grandchildren.

Drawing the curtains back and opening windows
Every morning now, she feels her years
Grow less and less. Time puts no burden on
Her now she does not need to measure it.
    It is acceptance she arranges
And her own life she places in the vase.

ELIZABETH JENNINGS
FROM THE COLLECTED POEMS

Talk

Pair work

- Look at the last line again. Why is it "her own life" that she can now arrange?

- What seems to be the main mood of this old woman as she looks back over her life?

- Do you think that she feels lonely?

Group work

Does getting married mean giving up your independence?
Do men and women give up different things when they marry?
Do men and women have different expectations of marriage?
Compare the ideas of marriage presented in the poem, in the story and in this picture. Which do you think is the most accurate?

Write

What makes a good relationship? Write down, just for yourself, what you think your partner would need to be like for you both to be happy?

Talk

Study the cartoon on the next page very carefully and then:-

1. Write a caption to go under each particular image.

2. Jot down what you think is the main message of the cartoon.

Compare your ideas for 1. and 2. then see if you can agree on common captions and message.

Could you draw or describe a series of images like these to accompany key moments in the story 'Weekend'; a kind of cartoon strip version?

A Super Woman's Day

This next extract is from a section of *Sons and Lovers* called 'The Early Married Life of the Morels'. Mr Morel is a miner; he is physically a strong man but no real match for the moral strength of his wife. He has spent the day drinking with a friend while Mrs Morel has been working at home as usual, looking after their children; at this point she is pregnant with another child.

Sons and Lovers

Mrs Morel, listening to their mournful singing, went indoors. Nine o'clock passed, and ten, and still 'the pair' had not returned. On a doorstep somewhere a man was singing loudly, in a drawl, 'Lead, kindly Light'. Mrs Morel was always indignant with the drunken men that they must sing that hymn when they got maudlin.

'As if "Genevieve" weren't good enough,' she said.

The kitchen was full of the scent of boiled herbs and hops. On the hob a large black saucepan steamed slowly. Mrs Morel took a panchion, a great bowl of thick red earth, streamed a heap of white sugar into the bottom, and then, straining herself to the weight, was pouring in the liquor.

Just then Morel came in. He had been very jolly in the Nelson, but coming home had grown irritable. He had not quite got over the feeling of irritability and pain, after having slept on the ground when he was so hot; and a bad conscience afflicted him as he neared the house. He did not know he was angry. But when the garden-gate resisted his attempts to open it, he kicked it and broke the latch. He entered just as Mrs Morel was pouring the infusion of herbs out of the saucepan. Swaying slightly, he lurched against the table. The boiling liquor pitched. Mrs Morel started back.

'Good gracious,' she cried, 'coming home in his drunkenness!'

'Comin' home in his what?' he snarled, his hat over his eye.

Suddenly her blood rose in a jet.

'Say you're *not* drunk!' she flashed.

She had put down her saucepan, and was stirring the sugar into the beer. He dropped his two hands heavily on the table, and thrust his face forward at her.

' "Say you're not drunk," ' he repeated. 'Why, nobody but a nasty little bitch like you 'ud 'ave such a thought.'

He thrust his face forward at her.

'There's money to bezzle with, if there's money for nothing else.'

'I've not spent a two-shillin' bit this day,' he said.

'You don't get as drunk as a lord on nothing,' she replied. 'And,' she cried, flashing into sudden fury, 'if you've been sponging on your beloved Jerry, why, let him look after his children, for they need it.'

'It's a lie, it's a lie. Shut your face, woman.'

They were now at battle-pitch. Each forgot everything save the hatred of the other and the battle between them. She was fiery and furious as he. They went on till he called her a liar.

'No,' she cried, starting up, scarce able to breathe. 'Don't call me that – you, the most despicable liar that ever walked in shoe-leather.' She forced the last words out of suffocated lungs.

'You're a liar!' he yelled, banging the table with his fist. 'You're a liar, you're a liar.'

She stiffened herself with clenched fists.

'The house is filthy with you,' she cried.

'Then get out on it – it's mine. Get out on it!' he shouted. 'It's me as brings th' money whoam, not thee. It's my house, not thine. Then get out on't – get out on't!'

'And I would,' she cried, suddenly shaken into tears of impotence. 'Ah, wouldn't I, wouldn't I have gone long ago, but for those children. Ay, haven't I repented not going years ago, when I'd only the one' – suddenly drying into rage. 'Do you think it's for *you* I stop – do you think I'd stop one minute for *you*?'

'Go, then,' he shouted, beside himself. 'Go!'

'No!' she faced round. 'No,' she cried loudly, 'you shan't have it *all* your own way; you shan't do *all* you like. I've got those children to see to. My word,' she laughed, 'I should look well to leave them to you.'

'Go,' he cried thickly, lifting his fist. He was afraid of her. 'Go!'

'I should be only too glad. I should laugh, laugh, my lord, if I could get away from you,' she replied.

He came up to her, his red face, with its bloodshot eyes, thrust forward, and gripped her arms. She cried in fear of him, struggled to be free. Coming slightly to himself, panting, he pushed her roughly to the outer door, and thrust her forth, slotting the bolt behind her with a bang. Then he went back into the kitchen, dropped into his armchair, his head, bursting full of blood, sinking between his knees. Thus he dipped gradually into a stupor, from exhaustion and intoxication.

The moon was high and magnificent in the August night. Mrs Morel, seared with passion, shivered to find herself out there in a great white light, that fell cold on her, and gave a shock to her inflamed soul. She stood for a few moments helplessly staring at the glistening great rhubarb leaves near the door. Then she got the air into her breast. She walked down the garden path, trembling in every limb, while the child boiled within her. For a while she could not control her consciousness; mechanically she went over the last scene, then over it again, certain phrases, certain moments coming each time like a brand red-hot down on her soul; and each time she enacted again the past hour, each time the brand came down at the same points, till the mark was burnt in, and the pain burnt out, and at last she came to herself. She must have been half an hour in this delirious condition. Then the presence of the night came again to her. She glanced round in fear. She had wandered to the side garden, where she was walking up and down the path beside the currant bushes under the long wall. The garden was a narrow strip, bounded from the road, that cut transversely between the blocks, by a thick thorn hedge.

She hurried out of the side garden to the front, where she could stand as if in an immense gulf of white light, the moon streaming high in face of her, the moonlight standing up from the hills in front, and filling the valley where the Bottoms crouched, almost blindingly. There panting and half weeping in reaction from the stress, she murmured to herself over and over again: 'The nuisance! the nuisance!'

She became aware of something about her. With an effort she roused herself to see what it was that penetrated her consciousness. The tall white lilies were reeling in the moonlight, and the air was charged with their perfume, as with a presence. Mrs Morel gasped slightly in fear. She touched the big, pallid flowers on their petals, then shivered. They seemed to be stretching in the moonlight. She put her hand into one white bin: the gold scarcely showed on her fingers by moonlight. She bent down to look at the binful of yellow pollen; but it only appeared dusky. Then she drank a deep draught of the scent. It almost made her dizzy.

Mrs Morel leaned on the garden gate, looking out, and she lost herself awhile. She did not know what she thought. Except for a slight feeling of sickness, and her consciousness in the child, herself melted out like scent into the shiny, pale air. After a time the child, too, melted with her in the mixing-pot of moonlight, and she rested with the hills and lilies and houses, all swum together in a kind of swoon.

When she came to herself she was tired for sleep. Languidly she looked about her; the clumps of white phlox seemed like bushes spread with linen; a moth ricocheted over them, and right across the garden. Following it with her eye roused her. A few whiffs of the raw, strong scent of phlox invigorated her. She passed along the path, hesitating at the white rosebush. It smelled sweet and simple. She touched the white ruffles of the roses. Their fresh scent and cool, soft leaves reminded her of the morning-time and sunshine. She was very fond of them. But she was tired, and wanted to sleep. In the mysterious out-of-doors she felt forlorn.

There was no noise anywhere. Evidently the children had not been wakened, or had gone to sleep again. A train, three miles away, roared across the valley. The night was very large, and very strange, stretching its hoary distances infinitely. And out of the silver-grey fog of darkness came sounds vague and hoarse: a corncrake not far off, sound of a train like a sigh, and distant shouts of men.

Her quietened heart beginning to beat quickly again, she hurried down the side garden to the back of the house. Softly she lifted the latch; the door was still bolted, shut hard against her. She rapped gently, waited, then rapped again. She must not rouse the children, nor the neighbours. He must be asleep, and he would not wake easily. Her heart began to burn to be indoors. She clung to the door-handle. Now it was cold; she would take a chill, and in her present condition!

Putting her apron over her head and her arms, she hurried again to the side garden, to the window of the kitchen. Leaning on the sill, she could just see, under the blind, her husband's arms spread out on the table, and his black head on the board. He was sleeping with his face lying on the table. Something in his attitude made her feel tired of things. The lamp was burning smokily; she could tell by the copper colour of the light. She tapped at the window more and more noisily. Almost it seemed as if the glass would break. Still he did not wake up.

After vain efforts, she began to shiver, partly from contact with the stone, and from exhaustion. Fearful always for the unborn child, she wondered what she could do for warmth. She went down to the coal-house, where was an old hearthrug she had carried out for the rag-man the day before. This she wrapped over her shoulders. It was warm, if grimy. Then she walked up and down the garden path, peeping every now and then under the blind, knocking, and telling herself that in the end the very strain of his position must wake him.

At last, after about an hour, she rapped long and low at the window. Gradually the sound penetrated to him. When, in despair, she had ceased to tap, she saw him stir, then lift his face blindly. The labouring of his heart hurt him into consciousness. She rapped imperatively at the window. He started awake. Instantly she saw his fists set and his eyes glare. He had not a grain of physical fear. If it had been twenty burglars, he would have gone blindly for them. He glared round, bewildered, but prepared to fight.

'Open the door, Walter,' she said coldly.

His hands relaxed. It dawned on him what he had done. His head dropped, sullen and dogged. She saw him hurry to the door, heard the bolt chock. He tried the latch. It opened – and there stood the silver-grey night, fearful to him, after the tawny light of the lamp. He hurried back.

When Mrs Morel entered, she saw him almost running through the door to the stairs. He had ripped his collar off his neck in his haste to be gone ere she came in, and there it lay with bursten button-holes. It made her angry.

She warmed and soothed herself. In her weariness forgetting everything, she moved about at the little tasks that remained to be done, set his breakfast, rinsed his pit-bottle, put his pit-clothes on the hearth to warm, set his pit-boots beside them, put him out a clean scarf and snap-bag and two apples, raked the fire, and went to bed. He was already dead asleep. His narrow black eyebrows were drawn up in a sort of peevish misery into his forehead, while his cheeks' downstrokes, and his sulky mouth, seemed to be saying: 'I don't care who you are or what you are, I *shall* have my own way.'

Mrs Morel knew him too well to look at him. As she unfastened her brooch at the mirror, she smiled faintly to see her face all smeared with the yellow dust of lilies. She brushed it off, and at last lay down. For some time her mind continued snapping and jetting sparks, but she was asleep before her husband awoke from the first sleep of his drunkenness.

D H LAWRENCE

Talk

Group work

Look over the passage together. What makes this argument such a fierce and passionate one? Do you think they often have arguments?

Pair work

Take one character each and jot down what you learn about them from the passage. Then compare your ideas and try to agree on what kind of relationship you think they have.

Are there any similarities between this passage and *Weekend*? Think about the relationships between Martin and Martha and Mr and Mrs Morel. Are there any points of comparison?

Individual work

The passage is very atmospheric, full first of anger and passion and then of moonlight and flowers; what does it make you think about in your own life?

Sonnet: Mother Love

Women are always fond of growing things.
They like gardening; snipping, watering, pruning,
bringing on the backward, aware of the forward;
planting – not for nothing do they talk of 'nurseries'.
Roses are like children, a source of pride,
tulips are cosseted, primulas are pets.
These are almost as loved as the usual surrogates –
the dogs and cats that stand for families.

Conservation, preservation; it's a lovable aspect
of maternalism (one reason why we're here).
Better than that, this severe matriarchy
is established over *plants*; the bossiness, thank God.
that puts you there (delphiniums), you there
   (wallflowers),
is harmlessly deflected well away from us.

GAVIN EWART
FROM POETRY DIMENSION ANNUAL 3:
THE BEST OF THE POETRY YEAR

- What does the poem make you feel about the role of women?

- What kind of metaphor is Ewart using to describe mother love?

- What is your response to the last line, who is "us"?

- Do you agree with the main idea of the poem?

- Do you have a common reaction to the poem?

Write

Try writing your own poem about a role, perhaps you might write your own version of 'Mother Love'; you could consider writing about a modern woman or girl, or about fatherhood and so on.

Links with story

To what extent do you feel that Martha is like the women described in the poem?

Acknowledgements

The authors and publishers wish to thank the following who have kindly given permission for the use of copyright material.

W. H. Allen & Co. PLC for an extract from *Mr Love and Justice* by Colin Macinnes, Allison and Busby; The Bodley Head for an extract from *Sumitra's Story* by Rukshana Smith; Century Hutchinson Publishing Group Ltd. for 'Sonnet: Mother Love' from *The Collected Ewart 1933–1980* by Gavin Ewart; Collins: Publishers for material from *The Impending Gleam* by Glen Baxter; The English Centre for 'A Country Full of Huts' by Jovita Pereira from *Say What You Think*; Faber and Faber Ltd. For 'Jesus and his Mother' from *The Sense of Movement* by Thom Gunn; Christine Green Ltd. on behalf of the author for 'Kings Cross' from *Victoria Line* by Maeve Binchy, Coronet Books; Hamish Hamilton Ltd. for an extract from 'Pity' by Frank O'Connor from *Stories of Frank O'Connor*; David Higham Associates Ltd. on behalf of the author for 'Old Woman' from *Collected Poems* by Elizabeth Jennings, Carcanet; Lemon Unna & Durbridge Ltd. on behalf of the author for 'Hardly Ever' from *On The Yankee Station* by William Boyd, Hamish Hamilton. Copyright © 1981 by William Boyd; Macmillan, London and Basingstoke, for 'The China Set' from *East End at Your Feet* by Farrukh Dhondy; Wes Magee for 'The Irish Jokes. Copyright © Wes Magee; Methuen, London, for an extract from *Closing* by Zoe Fairbairns; Murray Pollinger on behalf of the author for 'The Voice of God in Adelaide Terrace' and 'Next Term We'll Mash You' from *Corruption* by Penelope Lively, William Heinemann Ltd. and Penguin Books Ltd.; Hodder & Stoughton Ltd. for 'Weekend' from *Watching Me, Watching You* by Fay Weldon; Peters Fraser and Dunlop Group Ltd. on behalf of the authors for 'A Super Woman's Day' from *Very Posy* by Posy Simmonds; 'Long Distance' from *Selected Poems* by Tony Harrison; and 'Mrs Silly' from *The Stories of William Trevor* by William Trevor, *Woman's Realm*; Polygon for 'Poem for My Sister' from *Dreaming Frankenstein* and *Collected Poems* by Liz Lochhead; Unwin Hyman Ltd. for 'Schoolboy' from *Little Johnny's Confession* by Brian Patten; Virago Press Ltd for extracts from *Bitter Sweet Dreams* by Ann-Marie Jebbett, 1987. Copyright © Ann-Marie Jebbett; and *Her People* by Kathleen Dayus, 1982. Copyright © Kathleen Dayus 1982.

For photographic sources: Barnabys Picture Library pages 33 left, 82, 110; J. Allen Cash page 27 bottom; FAO page 82 top; Popperfoto page 33 right.

Every effort has been made to trace all copyright holders, but if any have been inadvertently overlooked the publishers will be pleased to make the necessary arrangement at the first opportunity.